MW00813004

Battle of the Casbah

Based on a true story

DAVID LEE CORLEY

DAVID LEE CORLEY

"War is cruelty. There is no use trying to reform it. The crueler it is, the sooner it will be over."

— William Tecumseh Sherman

"Under the clouds of war, it is humanity hanging on a cross of iron."

— Dwight D. Eisenhower

PROLOGUE

In 1954, the people of Algeria revolted against their colonial master - France. It was the beginning of a long and bloody war.

The French saw Algeria not as a colony but as part of France, an extension of the mainland across the Mediterranean Sea. Millions of Europeans visited each year to enjoy the sundrenched beaches, sidewalk cafés and modern boutiques of Algiers and the coastal cities. There were also one million Pieds-Noirs – European settlers that had been offered inexpensive farmland by the French government in exchange for immigrating to Algeria. France had owned Algeria for almost one hundred and fifty years, and the French weren't about to give it up.

The Algerian resistance was made up of several underground organizations. Most had consolidated with the largest organization – the National Liberation Front known as the FLN. The Algerian National Movement, known as the MNA, was the only holdout of any significance. The FLN and the MNA fought bitterly for control of the revolution.

The War for Algerian Independence had been raging for over two years when France suddenly shifted gears and sent twenty thousand elite paratroopers and soldiers to Egypt to fight in the Suez Crisis. Although the Egyptian conflict only lasted seven days, the pause in fighting gave the Algerian rebels time to regroup and organize.

The French paratroopers had returned to find they must fight a very different kind of war when our story begins.

1

ONE

September 9, 1956 – Countryside, Algeria

It was night. A truck's engine growled as it approached the top of a hill. The glow of a distant city broke the dark horizon. At the bottom of the hill was a French army roadblock. The Algerian driver and passenger exchanged a concerned look. "I thought you said this way was clear?" said the driver.

"It was as of this morning. This is new," said the passenger. "Should we try and make a run for it?"

"In this heap? No. They'll just run us down. Just stay calm and act like everything is normal. We'll be alright," said the driver proceeding down the hill toward the roadblock.

Flagged down by a French soldier, the truck rolled to a stop. Two soldiers approached the driver's side, and a third moved to the passenger side. There were two more soldiers handling a light machine gun set up on the side of the road and surrounded with sandbags. The driver rolled down his window. A French corporal, the commander of the unit, asked for their papers while the two other soldiers moved toward the back of the truck.

The two soldiers flipped up the canvas covering the back of the truck's cargo area. There was a wall of boxes filled with floor tiles stacked to the roof of the truck. Neither of the soldiers looked too excited about lifting the heavy boxes to inspect the back properly. They were just about ready to close the canvas when one of the soldiers heard something moving from behind the boxes. "Did you hear that?" said the soldier.

"Hear what?" said the other.

"I don't know. I'm going to check it out," said the soldier. He stepped on to the back of the truck and began unloading the heavy boxes.

Inside the cab, the passenger carefully reached down under the seat and picked up a grenade, which he set in his lap to hide it from view. He rolled down his window and lit a cigarette.

As the soldier unloading the back of the truck lifted a box, he saw the end of a double-barreled shotgun emerge from the darkness. It fired, blowing his head off. His headless body fell backward off the truck and landed next to the other soldier. He was shocked for a moment, then reached for the rifle slung over his shoulder. He wasn't fast enough, and the second barrel of the shogun fired, hitting him in the chest. He fell to the ground gasping for breath.

Inside the cab, the driver raised a pistol and shot the French corporal in the face. He fell dead. The passenger pulled the pin on the grenade and tossed it next to the machine gunner as he began to fire at the truck raking the passenger side. The passenger tried to duck behind the door, but it was no use. The machinegun bullets punched holes in the passenger-side door and riddled the passenger in the chest and stomach.

Outside the truck, the grenade exploded, and the machinegun fell silent. Shrapnel had shredded both the gunner and the loader.

The driver checked on the passenger and realized there was nothing to be done for him. He would be dead in a few moments. The driver stepped from the truck, walked over to the machine-gunner and loader, and fired his pistol into them multiple times until he was sure they were dead.

The man in the back of the truck climbed out from behind the boxes, revealing a compartment filled with a variety of military weapons. He reloaded his shotgun and fired both barrels into the face of the French soldier with the chest wound. There wasn't much left.

The driver examined the exterior of the passenger side of the truck. There were a dozen bullet holes in the sheet metal, and the passenger window was shattered. It was obvious they had been in a gunfight. "Shit," said the driver as the man from the back walked up beside him. "We'll never get past another roadblock. We'll have to find another way to smuggle the weapons into Algiers."

"How's Ghazi?" said the man from the back.

"Ghazi's dead."

"Damn."

"I told him he should use his pistol instead of the grenade. He didn't listen. Damn near got me killed too."

"Ah well, he's in heaven now. God is great."

"Yes. God is great. Let's see if that machinegun is still operational. We could use it."

They moved off to check the French machinegun. They would take all the weapons and ammunition from the dead French soldiers and add them to the shipment they were carrying. The rebels were in great need of weapons. If it could kill Frenchmen, it had value.

Soummam Valley, Algeria

It was just past eleven o'clock at night when Abane Ramdane, a slightly overweight Algerian in his mid-thirties, rode a well-worn motorcycle into the Soummam Valley in Central Algeria. It was rough terrain, like much of Algeria's countryside. The dirt road was carpeted with knee-deep potholes and dried mud ruts, making it difficult to maneuver.

Approaching the top of a hill, he turned off his motorcycle's headlamp, cut the engine, and rolled to a stop. He looked down at a village. It was quiet. Most of the residents were asleep. The moon shone on a slow-moving river bordering the town. There were a few lights still shining in the windows, and he could hear a distant conversation.

He wanted a cigarette after the long ride, but he knew better. It would give away his position. He wouldn't take that kind of risk until he was sure he had not been betrayed. He waited and watched. He wasn't sure what to look for but knew he would recognize the signs of an ambush if he saw them.

He had served in the French Army during World War II and had graduated college, which was rare for a native Algerian, most of whom could not read or write. He was a confident man. Some said too confident. There was little doubt he thought highly of his fighting skills and mind for strategy.

After several minutes, he was satisfied that there were no French soldiers in the village waiting to arrest him. He started the motorcycle's engine, turned on the headlamp, and rode down into the village.

He rolled to a stop and parked his motorbike in front of the only coffee house. He glanced through the window as a last-minute precaution. He saw eight men sitting around a table with one empty chair. Those eight plus Ramdane were founders of the FLN, the underground organization fighting for Algeria's independence from the French.

Krim Belkacem, Benyoucef Benkhedda, and Saad Dahlab were all Algerian exiles that had come from Cairo. Their job was to finance the revolution, buy weapons, and garner international support while under the protection of Nasser, Egypt's president.

Mourad Didouche, Rabah Bit, and Ben Boulaïd were FLN commanders stationed throughout Algeria. They primarily carried out terrorist-type attacks on the French soldiers and the Pied-Noir settlers.

Larbi Ben M'hidi, known as Si Larbi, was the youngest in the group and the commander of all Mujahideen forces throughout Algeria. He was brave beyond reason and cunning beyond his years. His men respected his fighting ability and were loyal to his commands. It was unusual for one so young to lead so many.

Yacef Saadi had traveled from Paris, where he was stationed and carried out his terrorist attacks. He was a bomb maker and the architect of the Café Wars. He used his personally-trained sirens - young Algerian women dressed like Europeans - to place his bombs and assassinate prominent French officials and soldiers. He was considered one of the most effective operatives in the entire FLN organization.

Ramdane was in charge of all military operations in Algeria. He lived and operated in secret out of the Casbah in Algiers. He was the most powerful of the

6

group, having taken the place of Ben Bella when he was captured earlier in the year.

While Ramdane respected the dedication of his fellow compatriots, he didn't like them much, and he knew the feeling was mutual. They had all come from different organizations with different political views and approaches to independence. Their former organizations had consolidated under the FLN when it became clear that they were stronger together than separate. They needed all the help they could get to fight the French, who vastly outnumbered them. It was not an easy task uniting under one banner. Even the executive council to which all these men belonged was a compromise created to prevent any one leader from gaining too much control. It was not a very efficient way to fight a war, especially a guerilla war. They did their best not to get in each other's way, but it was often not possible. Guns had been drawn more than once at executive council meetings. These were violent, capable men. It took a great deal of constraint not to kill each other.

Ramdane entered. He had chosen this coffee house because the villagers were staunch FLN supporters, and he knew he and his fellow leaders could talk freely without fear of the French hearing about their meeting.

"You're late," said Dahlab.

"Somebody had to be," said Ramdane.

"Yes, but why is it always you?"

"The French have created more checkpoints in and out of Algiers. My face is known. I have to be cautious."

"Be cautious by leaving an hour earlier next time."

"In the spirit of cooperation... of course."

"Sit, my friend," said Belkacem pouring a cup from a silver pot already on the table. "Have some tea."

"Thank you. I hope it's hot."

"It was an hour ago," said Dahlab with a sarcastic smile.

"So tell us about Algiers," said Benkhedda. "How goes the struggle?"

"It's progressing... slowly. The French are bringing in more and more troops each day."

"More targets for your bombs," said Benkhedda.

"That is true, but these are targets with guns."

"We have guns," said Si Larbi.

"That is also true, but they outnumber us twenty to one."

"We didn't come here for excuses," said Dahlab.

"I'm not making excuses. We will win. It is Allah's will, and therefore, inevitable. But it will take time and caution. We do not want to lose the ground we have gained. There is little value in spilling blood twice for the same sand."

"That sounds like an excuse," said Dahlab.

"Like I said... it's not an excuse. It's just smart."

"Are you accusing us of being ignorant?" said Dahlab.

Ramdane bit his tongue and said, "I see little value in arguing. We have a war to plan."

"I agree," said Saadi. "We are all on the same side, and there is much that needs to be discussed. Let's stop our bickering."

The others mumbled their approval. "I have a proposal I would like to make," said Ramdane.

"We're listening," said Benkhedda.

"Our Mujahideen forces have been fighting in the countryside for almost two years, and we have gained

8

little. The French paratroopers, with their helicopters and planes, hunt us down like wolves. We cannot put more than a platoon together without drawing unwanted attention and an attack that reduces our numbers even further. Our forces are scattered throughout the mountains and forests."

"We are aware of the situation. What is your point?" said Belkacem.

"We need to change the game. We need to change our strategy."

"In what way?" said Dahlab, genuinely curious.

"We need to admit that we cannot beat the French militarily. But we don't need to either, not to win. We simply need to destroy France's ability to govern effectively. The French people don't care about Algeria. They have proven this time and time again. It's their breadbasket and a nice place to get a tan. That is all. They're losing their stomach for war as they did in Indochina."

"Then why don't they give it up?" said Dahlab.

"Pride, mostly. As they lose their empire, they also lose their influence in the international community. Algeria is the last great jewel in their imperial crown. But if Algeria becomes too much of a burden and costs them more credibility in the eyes of the world, they will abandon it and go back across the Mediterranean. We just need to ensure that that happens. We need to make one final push that shoves them over the edge."

"And how do we do that?" said Benkhedda.

"We concentrate our forces in the capital and make Algiers ungovernable."

"Just pick up and move all our men and resources to Algiers?" said Si Larbi.

"Essentially, yes. The French are distracted by their war in Egypt. It is the perfect time to regroup and reorganize. If we do it right, Algiers can be our Dien Bien Phu."

The members of the council exchanged glances. "It's not such a bad idea," admitted Si Larbi. "Our forces could mix with the Arab population and hide in plain sight."

"And if the French army decides to assault the citizens of Algiers?" said Belkacem.

"All the better. The world will be outraged at their attacks on civilians and turn against the French. That's exactly what we need," said Dahlab jumping in before Ramdane could answer.

"The stronger the French overreact to our invasion, the sooner the people will turn against them. Our tens of thousands will become millions, and the odds will turn against the French," said Ramdane.

"You are not as stupid as you look, my friend," said Dahlab.

Ramdane once again checked his anger at Dahlab's backhanded compliment and simply smiled. It was not the time or place for revenge... that would come later.

Hills of Northern Algeria

The forest was thick with oak trees with shafts of sunlight shining through the canopy of moss-covered branches and green leaves. French paratroopers leapfrogged from tree to tree hunting for the Mujahideen – Islamic rebel fighters. So far, they had found nothing except an abandoned rebel camp in a narrow valley.

Their commander, Colonel Roger Trinquier, was unhappy but not deterred. During an interrogation of a young Algerian woman, his intelligence unit had discovered the location of the band of Mujahideen he had been chasing for weeks. They were responsible for the ambush of several weapon convoys. French soldiers had died. That was unacceptable.

As their search continued with no results, Trinquier began to wonder if this was a trap. It had happened before. A young Algerian willing to sacrifice his or her life in exchange for the lives of French troops. If the girl was lying and he lost even one man, he would ensure that she suffered for many days before dying. Trinquier had a strong sense of justice.

A scout returned and reported, "Colonel, we found something. I think you should have a look."

"Alright," said Trinquier, following the scout through the trees.

After a quarter of a mile, the scout stopped at the top of a hill and handed the colonel his binoculars. Trinquier looked through the binoculars at the valley below and saw a Spanish villa. Behind the villa was a sawmill with a lumber yard stacked with oak planks. "What the hell?" said Trinquier.

He ordered his men to take up defensive positions around the villa and sawmill. He walked down off the hill with his executive officer, Major Royer, and three paratroopers as guards. In front of the villa, Abraham Toledano was waiting, flanked by two of his sons, one armed with the latest submachinegun and the other carrying a hunting rifle with a large scope.

The Toledano family were Sephardic Jews. Their ancestors had come to Algeria from the Iberian

Peninsula in 1492 after they were exiled from Spain and Portugal. When the French occupied Algeria, the Sephardic Jews were considered colonists, even though they had already lived in the area for hundreds of years. Unlike their Arab neighbors, the Sephardic Jews were awarded French citizenship by the 1870 Crémieux Decree and were allowed to buy land at reduced prices. The Toledano family had taken full advantage of these privileges and purchased thousands of acres of forest on which they now lived and operated a lucrative sawmill. Their lumber was prized by furniture makers and wood craftsmen all over the world.

"Welcome, Colonel. We have refreshments and a light lunch waiting for you and your men on the veranda. Not all your men, of course. Just the officers, if you please?" said Toledano.

"Who the hell are you?" said Trinquier.

"Abraham Toledano, and these are two of my sons, Victor and Petros. We own the land on which you are standing."

"You're Jews?"

"Sephardic Jews, yes. Does that make a difference concerning my invitation to lunch?"

"Of course not."

"Good. It will be much more pleasant to talk over food and drink."

"My officers will stay where they are."

"Very well. I hope you are hungry. The women have outdone themselves."

Trinquier followed Toledano to a veranda where lunch was served. "Your sons won't be joining us?" said Trinquier.

"I fear not. They are very protective of their home and business. Like watchdogs, you might say. The

Mujahideen have been very active lately. They mostly leave us alone. They know we are well armed."

"So, you know where they are hiding?"

"In the forest, I would imagine. It is a good place to hide, wouldn't you agree?"

"I am not playing games. They've highjacked several of our weapon convoys. They're arming themselves."

"As do we."

"How have you survived so long living among the Arabs?"

"We do our best to stay out of their way and live among our kind. We also trade with them. Their fruits and vegetables in exchange for wood scraps and charcoal for their cooking fires. One does not want to go to war with their trading partners."

"Your sons, they know the forest, I would imagine?"

"Of course, every foot and tree."

"We need scouts, with your permission, of course."

"I am afraid I must decline."

"Why? You're no friend to the Mujahideen."

"No. We are not. But there is an existing balance, and these are dangerous times."

"You are cowards."

"Perhaps. But we are also survivors."

Trinquier rose in a huff and said, "Thank you for lunch. It was enlightening."

Trinquier was escorted off the estate and back to his men. "How did it go?" said his executive officer.

"Did the engineers bring incendiary grenades?" said Trinquier.

"Of course. Why?"

"Burn it to the ground."

"Burn what?"

"The forest."

"All of it?"

"Every last foot and tree. The Mujahideen cannot hide in it if it does not exist."

"What about the villa and sawmill?"

"That's the Jew's problem," said Trinquier walking off.

The French engineers had little trouble starting the fire across a vast stretch of forest. The winter rains came late in Algeria. The trees and leaves were dry, and there was a hot wind off the Sahara Desert. The incendiary grenades with their white phosphorous burned hot and fast. Within twenty minutes of Trinquier's command, the forest was ablaze.

Trinquier watched from the hillside as the Toledano family, and their workers formed a bucket brigade from the fountain. They dosed the villas' tile roof and the sawmill's wooden sides and support beams with water. It would be a long night as the fire swept over their estate and their livelihood – the forest – burned.

Before the end of the war, the French army would burn two-thirds of the forests in Algeria. They would succeed in depriving the Mujahideen of a hiding place. But it would not have the effect the French desired. Not by a long shot...

Paris, France

Tom Coyle, wearing an American flight jacket, sat across from Colonel Volclain, a French Air Force commander in charge of transportation, as he read through Coyle's file. He didn't look happy.

"You crashed one of our C-119s in the Sinai," said Volclain.

"Technically, it wasn't yours. You sold it to a Spanish company. And I crashed it because I was shot down by an Israeli jet," said Coyle.

"We are still out one expensive plane. You have a bad habit of destroying aircraft, Monsieur Coyle."

"Planes tend to get shot down in war zones."

"Yes, but the enemy seems to like shooting at you more than others."

"I'm not flying the safest routes."

Volclain grunted and went back to reading the file. His mood did not improve. Coyle was getting impatient with the Frenchman. "So, why don't we just save ourselves some time and cut to the chase."

"Cut to the chase?" said Volclain, confused by the American idiom.

"Do you want to hire me or not?"

"You are in luck, Monsieur Coyle. I have just been instructed to prepare transportation for a large number of reserves and their equipment to serve in Algeria. You are one of the few pilots that can fly a C-119, and I need its lift capacity."

"Really?" said Coyle surprised.

"Really," said Volclain, disgusted that he had to stoop so low. "But if you wreck one more of our planes, you are gone for good."

"That sounds fair. When do I start?"

"This afternoon."

"Oh, well… I sort of promised my girlfriend I would take her to dinner. It's her last day before she starts work again."

"Ah, well, it's your girlfriend. We must make allowances. The French Air Force wouldn't dream of inconveniencing your romantic affairs," said Volclain sarcastically. "The job starts this afternoon. Take it or leave it."

"I'll take it."

Algiers, Algeria

Achiary & Company was an import and export business. Its warehouses were in all the major ports along the Algerian coastline. The company imported many of the foodstuffs required by the restaurants and hotels that served the European tourists. Its main export products were wood, wheat, dates, and fish – fresh to France and dried to Italy and Spain. Its warehouses were usually filled to capacity most days. Algeria was a very productive country.

The owner, André Achiary, stayed away from petroleum products. Those were the realm of large corporations with huge budgets that could swallow his family's company whole. He was happy with the niche he and his family had built over the years. He found no burning desire for more. He just wanted things to stay as they were.

Achiary often reminisced about playing soldiers with his brothers and cousins in their grandfather's warehouse when he was a boy. It was perfect, like a giant fortress with plenty of places to hide in ambush. It all ended when his younger brother knocked over a box filled with expensive champagne. One of the bottles broke, and the boys were banned from the warehouse until they were old enough to work.

He was the boss of the warehouse now. As the boss, he understood why his grandfather did what he did. Children continued to be banned from the warehouse. It was a place of business, not a playground.

Achiary's father had been a buyer for the business. He traveled around Algeria for weeks at a time, purchasing entire inventories from farms, lumber mills, and seafood companies. The export side of the business was hungry for product.

Achiary was twelve when he discovered that his father had a second family with an Algerian woman. He saw a photo of her that his father kept hidden deep in his wallet. His father had little time as it was to spend with Achiary and his brothers. Now that time was split even more.

His father died protecting the woman and their children when a band of Mujahideen passing through the village discovered she was sleeping with a Pied-Noir. His father, the woman and their children were hacked to death by Nimchas – Moroccan swords with slightly curved blades. Achiary hated the Mujahideen and the Algerian woman that took his father away from him. It was a long time ago, but his anger still burned strong.

Achiary was sitting in his office overlooking the warehouse. The Algiers warehouse was the company's largest and busiest. It was one of the largest buildings in the entire country, not including football stadiums. He was going over his financial ledger when his warehouse manager entered unannounced. "Boss, we need you on the floor," said the manager with a sense of urgency.

Achiary followed the manager to one of the shipping docks. There he was shown a wooden crate that had fallen and split open. Inside, packed with wooden shavings, was an electric saw for cutting prepared meats such as Italian salami and Spanish Iberico ham. "So, what? Was it damaged?" said Achiary, annoyed at being disturbed for such a minor incident.

The manager brushed aside some of the shavings to reveal a long metal tube that was not part of the saw. It was a German mortar. Achiary and the manager exchanged concerned looks. "You want me to call the police?" said the manager.

"Hell no. They'll shut us down and search the entire warehouse. It'll take days. Our fruit and vegetables will spoil. And who knows what else they will find. Remove the mortar and repair the crate. When it is picked up for delivery, have the driver followed. I want to know who is behind this. I also want you to search for any other crates from the supplier of the saw. If there is a mortar, there are bound to be shells too. Let me know if you find them."

"What do you want me to do with the mortar in the meantime?"

"Put it in the trunk of my car under the spare tire in place of the jack. I'll deal with it."

Countryside, Algeria

It was early morning, well before sunrise. Si Larbi walked across a field to a line of railroad tracks dividing the countryside. He knelt and put his ear to one of the iron rails. He could hear the clicks of an approaching train in the distance. Satisfied, he stood up and motioned toward the field. A dozen Mujahideen fighters carrying picks and crowbars rose up from their hiding places and moved toward the tracks. They loosened the spikes holding the track down on the wooden ties and removed a rail. Si Larbi was not worried that the train's conductor might see the missing rail. The train was coming off a mountain and would be moving too fast to stop in time.

Once the rail was removed, Si Larbi and his men moved back to their hiding places in the field where they waited. As planned, the train sped across the countryside. When it hit the section of the missing track, the train derailed. The locomotive's wheels dug into the ground and tipped the iron beast on its side. The cars behind followed, crashing into the back of the engine one after another. It was a massive pile-up.

The Mujahideen again rose up from their hiding places and ran forward, armed with rifles and submachine guns. They fired at anyone stupid enough to stick their heads out of the passenger cars or caboose where French security guards were riding.

The Mujahideen searched through the wreckage until they found what they were looking for - a boxcar filled with weapons and ammunition. The FLN was severely in need of more weapons. Their numbers were multiplying as the French methods of putting down the revolt became more and more extreme. Violence begat violence. It was a never-ending circle of aggression that worked to the rebels' advantage.

The rebels pried open the boxcar door and prepared the fire their weapons. It wasn't necessary. The two soldiers guarding the cargo had been crushed by the heavy crates and were already dead. The shipment was loaded onto horses and donkeys. Si Larbi gave one final signal to his men. The Algerian rebels set the train ablaze and disappeared into the early morning twilight. It was a good day's work for the FLN and still before breakfast.

Paris, France

Rabah Hannachi, more boy than man, sat on a bench in an underground metro station on the eastern side of Paris. Hannachi had first met Messali Hadj, the charismatic rebel leader when he was only thirteen and had been following him ever since. It took two years before he was allowed to join the Mouvement National Algérien (MNA) that Messali had founded and another year before he could join the Organisation Speciale (OS), the paramilitary wing of the MNA. He was sixteen now and nervous.

The most important mission he had been given up to this point had been as a covert lookout for French weapon convoys rolling out of the Port at Algiers. But the MNA had taken heavy losses over the last two years during the Café Wars. The FLN, a competing underground organization, had killed most MNA operatives in both Paris and Algiers using a combination of bombs and drive-by shootings. Hannachi was one of the few that had survived. He had been blessed by Allah and selected for a very important mission by Messali himself. It was a great honor, but he was understandably anxious.

Hannachi followed Saadi to a nearby mosque. He didn't wait for Saadi to finish his visit. Instead, he headed back to the train station to study its layout and make preparations. Hannachi had been following Saadi for an entire week and knew his routine. That was Saadi's third visit to this mosque.

Hannachi believed Saadi would come back to the train station when he finished his midday prayers. He knew which train he would take to get back to his apartment and would wait for him on the platform. He didn't know why Saadi was in Paris. It didn't matter. His orders were to kill him.

Saadi had been the FLN mastermind behind the sirens – three young Algerian women dressed and made up to look like Europeans. The sirens had placed bombs throughout Paris and Algiers. Under Saadi's tutelage, they had killed hundreds of MNA operatives, along with thousands of civilians. They struck fear into the French and made them pay for their continued enslavement of Algerians. Messali did not allow women into the MNA because he felt it went against the teachings of Mohammad. Saadi had no such scruples and had decimated his enemies using the three women that he had trained personally. Saadi was also the architect behind the attempted assassination of French Colonel Marcel Bigeard several months earlier. The attack had failed and embarrassed Saadi.

Hannachi reached into the pockets of his jacket. In one hand, he felt the grenade, and in the other, he held the semiautomatic pistol that his older brother had given him for his sixteenth birthday. Either one could do the job. He wasn't sure which he would use. He would need to wait until Saadi showed up and look for the right opportunity. He had several opportunities earlier in the day but had trouble mustering the courage to act in time. The opportunities had passed. He felt guilty for having failed. But not this time, he thought. This time he would act.

It was almost a half-hour after midday prayers, and Hannachi began to worry. Maybe Saadi had taken a taxi or used some other way to get back to his apartment. Perhaps he would fail once again. He was relieved when he saw Saadi walking down the stairs and onto the platform. Hannachi turned away so he would not be seen. He didn't think that Saadi knew what he looked like, but he wasn't taking any chances.

Saadi walked up to the edge of the platform near the rails. The train would be arriving soon, and he wanted to make sure he got a seat. It was a long ride back to his apartment.

Hannachi studied Saadi at a distance. He was tall and slight of build. Hannachi realized that he now had three options to kill Saadi: the pistol, the grenade, and the train. He could move up behind Saadi and at the last second, push him onto the tracks as the train pulled into the station. It would look like an accident. He was sure that Saadi would not survive the impact, but he questioned whether he had the muscle and weight to push a man the size of Saadi. And what if Saadi grabbed him on his way over the edge of the platform and pulled him onto the tracks with him? Hannachi was not afraid to die, but he didn't want to waste his life when it was not necessary. As a jihadist, Allah had work for him.

He decided on the pistol. It was the surest way to get the job done. It was a small-caliber pistol, but his brother had told him that small bullets worked best for assassinations. He would wait until the train arrived so the noise of the train braking would cover up the gunshots. *Two shots in the back of the left side of the chest and a coup de grace in the forehead or temple once Saadi had fallen to the ground,* thought Hannachi. He would move up behind him to be sure he wouldn't miss. It would be easy.

Hannachi felt a change in the air before he heard the approaching train. He estimated it would arrive within the minute. The waiting passengers moved toward the edge of the platform in anticipation. He moved behind the pillars. There were several people around Saadi. They would mask his movements as he walked in closer, but they could get in the way. It couldn't be helped. He was committed.

The brakes squealed loudly as the train pulled to a stop. Hannachi pulled the pistol from his pocket but kept it low by his side. The train doors opened, and the passengers inside the compartments exited while the passengers on the platform waited to board. Hannachi moved up to within three feet behind Saadi. *That's close enough*, he thought. *I can't miss.*

The last of the passengers disembarking stepped onto the platform, and the crowd waiting inched forward. Hannachi raised the pistol and pointed it to the back of Saadi's head. *It's now or never*, he thought. *Do it.* He pulled the trigger. Nothing happened. He pulled the trigger again, and still nothing. He was sure it was loaded. He had pulled the clip out and saw the bullets. It suddenly occurred to him what had happened. It was a single-action semiautomatic, and in his excitement, he'd forgotten to chamber a round. Squeezing the trigger did nothing. *You idiot*, he thought as Saadi stepped forward through the doorway of the train. *I'm losing him.*

Saadi was ten steps away now. If Hannachi could chamber a round, there might still be time. He pulled the gun's slide, cocking the hammer back, and released it. The slide pushed a bullet into the chamber. It was ready now. He raised the pistol again and aimed. There were passengers in front of Saadi. The train door alarm sounded, signaling that the doors were closing. Hannachi fired. He hit a woman, holding the hand of a toddler, in the side of the head. She crumpled to the floor of the train car. The child bawled. Saadi heard the gunshot, turned, and saw Hannachi. He ducked before Hannachi could fire again. The doors started to close. The wounded woman's arm blocked the doors from closing. The doors opened again. Hannachi looked for Saadi but couldn't see him in the crowd, some kneeling to help the woman, others moving away as they saw the gunman. *He's gone*, thought Hannachi. *No. He's in there. Somewhere.*

Saadi was on his knees hiding below the line of the windows, using the crowd of passengers as cover. Seeing that the woman's arm was keeping the door from closing, he reached over and pulled it inside. The doors started to close again.

Hannachi reached into his other pocket, pulled out the grenade. He pulled the safety pin, and the spoon flipped off, arming the weapon. He tossed the grenade in through the doorway just as the doors closed.

Passengers screamed as they saw the grenade bouncing across the compartment floor. The train started to move out of the station. The grenade rolled under a bench and spun around like a top on the smooth floor. Passengers ran to the opposite ends of the compartment. Saadi knew there wasn't time for him to escape. He knew explosives well. He knew what was about to happen and what it would mean for those trying to flee. He climbed onto the bench above the grenade and laid flat, making sure his arms and legs were not sticking over the edge. The grenade exploded. Splinters of steel flew in all directions.

The windows in the compartment shattered outward, pelting Hannachi's face and body.

Hit by shrapnel, passengers inside the train screamed and fell to the floor. Saadi flew three feet up into the air and came back down on top of the bench. The bench had a metal core to give it strength and had stopped the shrapnel from passing all the way through. Saadi was stunned from the concussion of the blast, and his ears were ringing. The train stopped with a jolt. *Get up*, he thought. *The police will be coming. You can't be here when they arrive.*

Saadi forced himself to rise. There was a stream of blood flowing down the center of the compartment. He stepped on something as he moved toward the doorway. He almost fell. He looked down at a man's severed hand beneath his foot. He shook off the shock and reached for the emergency door release. He pulled it down. Nothing happened. The doors were jammed closed from the blast. He grabbed the edges of the doors and pried them open. He stepped out of the compartment and came face to face with Hannachi.

Hannachi's face was covered with small cuts from the shattered glass. He was bleeding heavily and started to panic. He saw Saadi stepping from the train compartment. He raised his pistol and fired wildly at Saadi.

Saadi considered taking cover back inside the compartment but knew he would be trapped and at the mercy of the assassin, then the police. As Hannachi started firing, Saadi ran forward straight at him like a charging bull.

Hannachi was horrified to see Saadi moving toward him. It didn't help his aim. He fired three shots in Saadi's direction. One grazed the top of Saadi's scalp splitting it open. Saadi didn't stop. He grabbed Hannachi around the waist and tackled him to the ground. He grabbed for the gun in Hannachi's hand. They struggled. Saadi was infuriated. Hannachi was frightened. Saadi could see it in his eyes. Saadi bent Hannachi's hand, so the barrel of the pistol was pointed at Hannachi's face. He forced Hannachi's finger to pull the trigger. The gun fired. The small-caliber bullet entered through Hannachi's left eye and bounced around inside his skull. There was no exit wound. Hannachi went limp and died.

Saadi struggled to his feet. He could feel the blood running down his back from the head wound. It wasn't fatal, but it burned. He would need stitches to stop the bleeding. He moved toward the stairwell. He heard footsteps coming down the stairs. He laid flat against the wall at the base of the stairs as two policemen ran out of the stairwell toward the train. He waited until they were gone and peeked around the corner. The stairs were clear. He ran up them and out of the station. He was free and alive. It was God's will, thought Saadi as he disappeared into the crowd.

TWO

November 3, 1956 - Paris, France

It was Brigitte's first day back in the office since returning from Egypt. She had been an embedded journalist with the British, French, and Israeli armed forces fighting the Egyptian military for control of the Suez Canal. She was excited to start writing. She had a multitude of notes from her time reporting on what was now known as "The Suez Crisis" and was planning a series of in-depth articles about the short-lived war. Everyone in the office greeted her with a smile and an obligatory, "Welcome back." The staff at the magazine where she worked were predictable but sweet. She didn't mind. They were busy, and so was she.

She popped her head into the office of her editor, Damien Archambault. He wasn't in. She was a little disappointed. She liked Damien. He had saved her ass on numerous occasions, and in exchange, she had been loyal to him and the magazine. After her popular articles on the siege at Dien Bien Phu, she had received quite a few offers from competing magazines and newspapers. She politely turned them all down. To reward her, Damien had given her an office. She loved her office. It was quiet, which was unusual for a journalist's workspace.

She grabbed a cup of coffee, her third of the day, and headed down the hallway leading to her office. She was surprised to see the door open and a young woman sitting in her chair talking on the phone as she stared out the window. Brigitte's window. The woman was turned away from the door and didn't notice Brigitte as she entered. Brigitte could tell she was young by the way she dressed and the cut of her hair. It was a style more for attracting men than professional.

Brigitte waited patiently as the woman finished her phone call, which appeared to be a request for an interview of a low-level government official. It wasn't going well. The young woman was speaking rapidly as if the person on the other end of the phone might hang up at any moment. A few moments later, they did.

"Shit," said the young woman as she swung around in the chair to hang up the phone.

"Call 'em back," said Brigitte.

The young woman turned and saw Brigitte standing next to the door. "Oh, my God. It's you," said the young woman, shocked. "You're Brigitte Friang."

"Yep. Last time I checked," said Brigitte giving the young woman a look as she was expecting something.

The young woman froze, not knowing what Brigitte wanted. Brigitte could see her struggling, her mind racing for the answer. "You're in my chair," said Brigitte.

The young woman jumped up and said, "Oh, my God. You're right. I am so sorry."

"That's alright," said Brigitte sitting down. "You must be new."

"Ah, yeah. About two weeks. Damien didn't have a place to put me, so he said I could use your office while you were away."

"That was awfully nice of Monsieur Archambault."

"Who?"

"Your editor, Damien Archambault."

"Yes. Right. Of course. Monsieur Archambault asked me to call him Damien."

"That's because you have perky tits," mumbled Brigitte turning away to hang up her coat.

"Excuse me?"

"I said you have nice hair."

"Oh, thank you."

"So, what's your assignment?"

"My assignment... oh, ah... I was supposed to interview the Assistant Deputy Transportation Director about the proposed metro line to the East End. It's quite controversial. They scheduled the demolition of a historic library building to make way for an entry point."

"That does sound controversial. So, what happened?"

"He said no."

"And that is okay with you?"

"Well, no. But what am I supposed to do?"

"I don't know. But quitting doesn't seem like a good strategy if you want the interview. What did you use for leverage?"

"Leverage?"

"Yes. He's probably not going to give you an interview because he's a nice guy. You're a journalist. That means trouble."

"So, I'm supposed to blackmail him?"

"Don't be dramatic. He's in the same boat as you."

"What do you mean?"

"He's a low-level bureaucrat that wants to be a mid-level bureaucrat. Help him, and he'll owe you a favor that you can use later when he is more powerful and what he says really matters."

"How am I supposed to help him?"

"You're a journalist from a powerful magazine. Tell him he walks on water, and you're going to make him famous."

"How?"

"Do you remember seducing the captain of the football team?"

"I don't know what you are talking about."

"I think you do."

"Alright. Maybe I did flirt a little in school."

"It's the same thing. Only, I think you would do much better if you just went down to his office and asked in person."

"The guards will throw me out."

"No, they won't. You're a journalist. Nobody's looking for trouble. Remind them of that and make sure you quote the constitution."

"You really think I can do it?"

"With those tits… yeah. I think so. Now, get the hell out of my office. I have work to do."

"Thank you, Mademoiselle Friang."

"You're welcome… What's your name?"

"Noelle Paquet, but you can call me Ellie."

"Don't even think of calling me Brig until you've been here a year. Now shoo. My typewriter calls," said Brigitte with a snarky smile and a sweeping hand gesture.

Ellie grabbed her things and left, as Brigitte loaded a blank page into her typewriter.

Brigitte was putting the finishing touches on her first article when Damien entered. "I see you've kicked out Ellie," he said.

"Did she think you screwing her was going to earn her my office?"

"I don't know what you are talking about."

Brigitte stopped typing and turned to give Damien a sarcastic look. "What do you want me to say?" said Damien with a shrug as if admitting she was right.

"Nothing. You just did."

"We just got word of a bombing at a metro station. I thought I'd offer it to you first."

"A welcome home present?"

"Oh yeah, welcome home. Do you want the story?"

"I've got ten good articles, maybe more from my Egypt trip. When am I supposed to finish those if I am running all over the city?"

"I don't know. At night?"

"And when am I supposed to sleep?"

"Sleep is overrated."

"Do you think the bombing is connected to the FLN?"

"I don't know. Maybe. That's what you've got to find out."

"Alright. I'll look into it."

"Good. Why don't you take Ellie with you?"

"Go to hell, Damien. If I want a puppy, I'll buy one."

"Give her a break, Brig. You were a new reporter once, weren't you?"

"Fine. She can be my assistant."

"Call her whatever you want. Just make sure you impart some of that Friang wisdom upon her."

"She gets no story credit. I don't share my byline."

"Sounds fair," said Damien handing her a slip of paper. "Here's the address of the station."

Brigette grabbed her coat and purse. Damien followed her out.

She passed the bullpen where Ellie was sitting. "You're with me. Let's go," said Brigitte, not slowing down.

"Really?" said Ellie, excited.

Ellie turned back to Damien, who winked at her. She smiled back at him and followed Brigitte out of the office.

Paris, France

Saadi hailed a taxi. Even wounded and in pain, he was careful not to go directly to his apartment. He had the driver drop him off several blocks away. He took the extra precaution of writing down the driver's name and threatening him and his family if he ever mentioned anything about Saadi to anyone.

Samiah, Saadi's newest siren, was waiting for his return. She was dressed, and her hair was styled like a European. She hated the look and longed for her hijab. The dress she wore revealed too much of her chest and legs. The bright-colored fabric clung to the curves of her breasts and hips. It was shameful.

She had been trained by Saadi as an assassin but failed to kill French Colonel "Bruno" Bigeard while jogging along the Mediterranean coastline several months earlier. It wasn't her fault. Her bullet had been well-aimed and landed less than an inch from his heart. But Bruno was a hard man to kill, as previous attempts on his life had demonstrated. Still, she felt that Saadi was disappointed in her and longed for another opportunity to prove herself worthy.

When Saadi entered, she saw that he was wounded and went to work without being told what to do. "What happened?" said Samiah retrieving the medical supplies from the bathroom.

"Ambush at the metro station. I think he was from the MNA. One of Messali's men. No, not a man. A boy, really. Messali must be getting desperate to send one so young after me. I could see his hand shaking right before he fired."

"He shot you?"

"Yes. Then I killed him."

"You are safe. That is all that matters. Praise Allah."

"Yes, God is great."

She opened the medical kit and poured alcohol on the wound. Saadi flinched. He didn't want to show weakness in front of the girl, but he couldn't help his reaction from the sting of the alcohol on the open wound. "I need to close the wound to stop the bleeding. This is going to hurt," said Samiah as she threaded a needle.

"Do your job, woman."

Samiah stitched his wound closed.

Paris, France

Brigitte and Ellie, with their press credentials around their necks, walked down the stairs leading to the metro platform. It was crowded. Technicians inspected the crime scene, and police interviewed witnesses. Medical workers treated victims for minor cuts from flying glass and shrapnel from the grenade. Hannachi's body lay on the ground. Firemen retrieved bodies from the train. Ellie looked down at several sets of red footprints that had stained the concrete and said, "Is that blood?"

"Yes. Watch where you step," said Brigitte. "The police can ban you from a crime scene if you mess with evidence."

Ellie looked like she might get sick. "Stop it. You're a professional. This is the job. Do it," snapped Brigitte. "Find victims to interview first, then the police. Make sure you get contact information if they will give it to you so we can follow up. You need to establish a relationship of trust and caring first. Ask them how they are doing and empathize with them when they show emotions. Once they know you are not a threat, you ask what happened. Don't lead the conversation in any direction. Just let them tell you what they know. Your job is to listen and take notes. Pay attention to details. Just remember... the real key is to let them come to you. People want to tell their story. You just need to help them do it."

Ellie nodded and moved off. Brigitte wanted to get a fresh look at the crime scene before she started asking questions. She didn't want Ellie getting sick at what promised to be a gory setting. She walked past Hannachi's corpse. She noticed the gunshot wound in his face and the cuts on his face from flying glass. *He must have been standing and facing the train when the bomb went off. That's why his face was cut from the shattered glass. He was shot after the bomb blast,* she thought. She looked at the pistol still in his hand. *Maybe he was the bomber and committed suicide. But why?* She saw the shell casings near the body and looked back at the train. There were bullet holes in the sheet metal. *He was shooting at someone. Maybe the bullet that killed him wasn't from his gun. Maybe he was shooting at the bomber, or perhaps he was the bomber's intended target?* She considered for a moment and looked back at the bloody footprints leading away from the body. *Or maybe he was the bomber, and his target wasn't dead from the blast?*

There was only so much she could learn on her own. She needed to fill in the blanks. She interviewed the police officer in charge, a fireman, and several victims. It was all beginning to make more sense. *The dead man had shot at a man inside the train. He missed and killed a woman. He threw a grenade into the train as it began to leave the station. His target survived the blast. The assassin shot at him again but didn't kill him. They struggled for the gun, and the assassin was killed with his own pistol. The target ran off before the police arrived. It looks like an FLN or MNA assassination attempt,* she thought.

She was searching the crowd for her next subject to interview, when she saw a sketch artist making a drawing of a man that looked familiar. A woman with bandages on her face was describing the man. Brigitte walked over to get a better look at the drawing. It was a drawing of Saadi. "Excuse me. I'm a journalist covering the story. Who was this man?" said Brigitte motioning to the drawing.

"He killed the guy that threw the grenade. He ran off before the police arrived," said the woman.

Brigitte studied the drawing more closely. She knew this man. This was the man that had tried to kill Coyle and her at a Parisian hotel a few months ago. She had only caught a glimpse of him, but the artist's sketch had jarred her memory. She was sure it was him. They had barely escaped with their lives. The man had disappeared into the crowd. Several months had passed without incident. She thought the man had returned to Algeria or was maybe hiding in another city. A shiver ran down her spine, and she thought, *This is the man that wants to kill me. He's still in Paris.*

November 20, 1956 - Paris, France

Brigitte was cooking a turkey with all the trimmings. It was Thanksgiving in America. She wasn't a good cook when it came to American food, but she wanted to do something special for Coyle. She figured if she just put a lot of butter on everything Coyle would like it. *Americans like butter,* she thought. *It's something they share with us French.*

She understood the sacrifice of being away from one's home country on the holidays. She had missed dozens of holidays herself and had always felt a little depressed each time. Tradition was grounded in strong emotion coupled with memory. But the more one tried to make a foreign country feel like home, the more one missed their real home. This Thanksgiving was no exception.

Coyle was quiet and pensive as the smell of the turkey cooking wafted through the apartment. It had been years since he was back in America. He was forgetting what it was like and wondered how much things had changed.

He had made new friends overseas, like Bruno and, of course, Brigitte, but it wasn't the same. As much as they all tried to break it down, there was always a wall of commonality between them. They would laugh off the misinterpretation in their languages. Idioms were especially curious. The struggle for understanding was tiresome at times. Coyle longed for a normal conversation with another American like the ones he used to have with his friend Earthquake McGoon before he died during the siege at Dien Bien Phu. He missed McGoon and was sure he would have livened up the Thanksgiving holiday.

It wasn't that Coyle was miserable, living in Paris. It was a great city, and he was with Brigitte. They liked to take long strolls together along the Seine. Winter was quickly approaching. Most of the foliage had turned dormant, and the trees had lost their leaves. Paris was beautifully stark, with its overcast skies and stone bridges. The distinctive architecture stood out even more without the color of the other seasons. Nature was asleep, but the city was still very much alive. Paris, like no other city, could pull off that dreary time between fall and winter.

Coyle hovered in the kitchen, sneaking nibbles of mashed potatoes and cranberry sauce with his finger. Brigitte finally kicked him out in mock anger. He went out for a walk while she finished cooking.

Coyle wanted to watch an American football game. Instead, he settled for a rugby game in the park across from their apartment. It wasn't the same. He didn't understand the rules. But he liked the roughness between the players. He wondered if slugging one's opponent was allowed and thought to ask Bruno next time he saw him.

Bruno. Where the hell is Bruno? he thought. *The war in Egypt was over now. He should be coming home soon.* Bruno was a paratrooper. Coyle doubted that the French army would leave Bruno and his men in Egypt now that a ceasefire had been called. There was still a war in Algeria to be fought, and the elite paratroopers were too valuable for peacekeeping. Coyle liked Bruno. He didn't trust him with Brigitte, but he liked him nonetheless. They had fought side by side, and that created an unbreakable bond between them. Sure, Bruno could be obnoxious and even rude at times, but he was a true warrior, and one had to make allowances. Deep down, Coyle admired Bruno and was in awe of his combat skills and his bravery.

Of course, Coyle was no slouch himself when it came to fighting. He had proven his bravery in the War of the Pacific, the Korean War, the Chinese Revolution, and the First Indochina War, not to mention the Algerian War and the Suez Conflict. *Holy shit, that's a lot of wars,* he thought. *How the hell did that happen? No man should be allowed to fight in that many wars. War changes you, and not in a good way.*

His stomach growled. He wondered if Brigitte had put out some pickles and olives as appetizers like his mom used to do. He headed back to the apartment.

Supper was ready when he returned. As she placed the various dishes on the table, Brigitte considered whether she should tell Coyle about the man in the police drawing. Coyle had been with her when he tried to kill her at the hotel. *He deserves to know,* she thought. But then she thought about Coyle's reaction to the news or, better yet... his overreaction. Things were just getting back to normal after Egypt. She and Coyle were both back to work. It felt good. Normal. If she told Coyle about the man, he would become overly protective and make her job more difficult. It would cause friction between them. Besides, what did she really know beyond a police sketch that may or may not have been the assassin that tried to kill her? She thought it was better to let things play out for a few days and see what happened. After all... she could take care of herself.

They sat down and toasted the holiday with a buttery chardonnay Brigitte had purchased at the wine shop down the block. *More butter,* she thought as she took her first sip. The table was so packed with serving plates Brigitte had set up a serving table for the turkey. After a quick prayer thanking God and asking for his protection of troops and loved ones, Coyle got up to carve the turkey. It was a man's job. At least that was the thinking of the day. Which made sense because it required upper body strength and a bit of savagery.

"I thought it might be nice to ask Bruno to dinner on Christmas Eve if he's back," said Coyle.

"Bruno?" said Brigitte, hesitant.

"Yeah, why not? If he's back."

"I am not sure he will accept."

"Why won't he?"

"We had words that last time I saw him in Egypt."

"About what?"

"Nothing really. You know Bruno. He can be such a pill at times."

"Yeah, but that's never stopped you two from being friends."

"Well, some friendships run their course, and then they are over."

"You really think your disagreement was that bad?"

"I don't know. Can we talk about something else?"

"Sure. How about them Red Sox?"

"What?"

"Nevermind."

They ate the rest of the meal in silence.

Paris, France

Saadi walked to the corner newsstand and purchased a magazine that showed a photo of the assassination at the Metro station. He opened the magazine to the story and saw that Brigitte Friang had written it.

Under orders from the FLN, he had tried and failed to assassinate Brigitte and her boyfriend. It was one of the few times his bomb had failed to take out its intended target. He was disappointed and took the failure personally. He knew the botched mission had damaged his reputation with the other FLN leaders. He needed to kill Brigitte Friang to make amends and clear his conscience.

He considered how he might find her. He knew where she worked at the magazine. He could bomb the building. But he was concerned that her death would be minimalized among the deaths of so many other magazine employees. That was not what he wanted. He wanted everyone, especially the FLN leaders, to know that Brigitte Friang was his target and he was the one that killed her.

After a little more thought, he decided the best way to find her was to lure her to him. It would be easy. She was the journalist assigned to the Paris bombings. When a bomb went off, she was sure to show up. He would be waiting and follow her when she left the crime scene. Once she was alone, he would tend to unfinished business.

Algiers, Algeria

Colonel Trinquier entered an office at Brigade Headquarters. He saluted his commanding officer - General Jacques Massu - sitting at his desk, talking to a man with his back turned to Trinquier. "Have a seat, Colonel," said Massu.

As Trinquier moved to sit, he saw that the man was Abraham Toledano. Toledano politely nodded to Trinquier, who looked like he had swallowed a pool ball as he sat down. "I assume you know Monsieur Toledano?" said Massu.

"Yes, of course," said Trinquier nodding back to Toledano while wondering how in the hell he had finagled a meeting with a commanding general.

"Monsieur Toledano is a representative of the Pieds-Noirs in his district. I am curious if you knew that before you burned down his forest?"

"No, sir. I did not."

"I thought not. While I am sure your intentions were well-founded, I believe you owe Monsieur Toledano an apology."

"Sir, if I may explain…"

"No, you may not. What you can do is fucking apologize."

"Yes, sir," said Trinquier, then turned to Toledano. "Monsieur Toledano, I apologize for my misunderstanding. I hope my actions did not inconvenience you or your family."

"Did not inconvenience you or your family… An interesting choice of words, Colonel. You burned down my forest!"

"Yes, and I am quite sorry for that."

"Monsieur Toledano, I have already taken the matter up with the Interior Ministry. They are prepared to offer you the use of a nearby forest to compensate you for your loss until your trees grow back," said Massu.

"Until my trees grow back? It took four generations for that forest to grow."

"Then I imagine you will be using the adjoining forest for quite a long time."

"Perhaps it would be better if the Interior Ministry sold the adjoining forest to my family at an appropriate discount?"

"Perhaps. I can ask."

"Please do, General."

"In the meantime, please accept our profound apology to you and your family."

"Of course. We are all on the same side," said Toledano, then turned to Trinquier, "Mistakes will occasionally happen. But it is good that they don't happen too often."

Toledano rose and was escorted to the door by Massu. He left, and Massu closed the door. "What in the hell were you thinking, Roger?" said Massu.

"We were hunting the Mujahideen in his forest. He would not cooperate."

"So you burned his forest down?"

"He's a coward."

"He's the reason we are fighting this war. Do you have any idea how much that man pays in taxes, not to mention his political contributions?"

"No. But he is a Jew, so I imagine it is not much."

"Don't be an ass, Colonel. You are on thin ice as it is."

"Yes, sir."

"The reason you could not find the Mujahideen was because they were no longer there."

"What do you mean?"

"They've moved… to Algiers."

"All of them?"

"As far as we can tell, yes."

"How do you know?"

"Our intelligence shows a vast increase in food purchases almost overnight. They estimate twenty thousand more people living in Algiers in just this last week."

"How is that possible?"

"I don't know, but I expect you to find out. Your brigade is being recalled to the capital, effective immediately. Get a grip on the situation before it gets completely out of hand, Colonel."

"Yes, sir."

Algiers, Algeria

A furniture moving truck pulled into a dark warehouse. The driver jumped out of the cab and closed the warehouse rollup door. A man appeared from the shadows and walked over to the electrical breaker panel on the wall. He threw the power switch for the lights. The interior of the warehouse was illuminated. The man was Si Larbi.

The warehouse was empty, apart from several tables. One of the tables held dozens of neatly folded blankets, while another had a stack of Khubz at-tajín: a flatbread of wheat semolina, yeast, water, and salt. There were also several empty tables. Si Larbi nodded to the driver that the warehouse was safe and that he should continue.

The driver walked to the back of his truck and opened the cargo door. Inside the truck, thirty Mujahideen fighters, each holding a weapon, sat on the wooden floor of the truck's cargo compartment. They climbed out and formed a loose semicircle around their new commander - Si Larbi. He was well known among the Mujahideen.

Si Larbi spoke with authority, "You'll stack your weapons on the empty tables. Remove the magazines and open the chambers before setting them down. We don't need any accidents from a weapon discharging. You will be issued new weapons and ammunition once you enter the Casbah. Each of you will pick up a blanket that you will take with you to your new accommodations. You can also pick up a piece of Khubz at-tajîn for nourishment. I know it's been a long trip for many of you," said Si Larbi. "You will each give me your name, and I will give you the address and the password you will use to gain entry once you meet your contact in the Casbah. You will each eat in the home of an assigned family. This may or may not be the same place where you sleep. If anybody asks, you are a relative visiting the family from out of town and hoping to find work in Algiers. You will need to get your story straight with your family on the first night. Do not wait. You are to take no action against the French on your own. You will only fight under direct orders or if it looks like you may be captured. You may also defend the family that feeds you. They are doing God's work and deserve your protection. Your missions will be assigned by your unit commander and conveyed to you through a coded message based on various sūrah and āyāt in the Quran. Your contacts will explain how to decipher the messages you receive. Each method will be unique, so if one of you is captured by the French, you cannot reveal the method of deciphering the messages of your fellow soldiers. The Casbah is a short walk from this warehouse. Make sure you have nothing on you that may identify you as a Mujahid. You will leave in groups of two or three in ten minutes intervals. Eat quickly. God is great. May he be with you."

The group of fighters repeated the phrase "God is great" and began stacking their weapons.

Algiers, Algeria

It was late in the afternoon, and the shadows were long from the buildings surrounding a square. There were shops and cafés around the edge while fruit and vegetable vendors filled the center of the square. Over a hundred Algerians and European tourists negotiated their purchases with vendors. It was the Arabic tradition to barter. Not doing so made one a fool.

A squad of French policemen operated a checkpoint at the entrance to a long alley leading up to the Casbah – the 17th-century walled fortress, home to seventy thousand Algerians and dozens of mosques, the religious and cultural center of Algiers.

The Algerians that lived and worked in the Casbah lined up on both sides of the checkpoint, waiting to be inspected as they entered or exited the ancient citadel. It was bothersome to be treated as criminals in their own country, but they used the time to gossip with their neighbors or read the local Arabic newspaper.

Sitting at a café across from the checkpoint, two Algerian men watched. They both had pistols at the ready, hidden inside folded newspapers laying on the table.

A woman wearing a full burka moved into the checkpoint. A young policeman moved to inspect her and was unsure what to do. "What am I supposed to do with this one?" said the young policeman to a nearby sergeant.

"Whatever you do, don't touch her unless you want to start a riot. The ones wearing burkas are married to fanatics. It's a sin for another man to even see the skin of a married woman," said the sergeant.

"So what? I just let her go?"

"If you're smart, yeah. Don't worry about it. A husband would never let his wife carry a weapon. It's against their culture."

The young policeman waved her past the checkpoint. She walked up the cobblestone path into the Casbah.

Once out of sight, the woman wearing the burka ducked through a doorway and entered a riad – a traditional, multi-storied house with an interior courtyard. Two more women were waiting inside. They helped the woman lift up her burka, revealing a submachine gun hanging between her legs. They loosened the twine wrapped around the gun's barrel and attached to a leather belt around her waist. They placed the submachine with dozens of other weapons she had smuggled past various checkpoints throughout the day. She let her burka fall back down over her legs and straightened the fabric. The two women kissed her for luck and wished her a blessing from Allah. She went back out the doorway and down the alley.

Algiers, Algeria

Two French policemen hauled a drunken Pied-Noir from a German restaurant in the European Quarter of Algiers. He was cursing at them until one of the policemen rapped him on the side of the head with his wooden Billy club. "Shut up and behave yourself, or you'll get more of it," said the policeman.

They hauled the man to their police car and placed him in the backseat. One of the officers rolled down the window. "What the hell are you doing?" said the other officer.

"If he pukes, I don't wanna clean it up," said the officer.

"Good thinking."

"You hear that, you drunken fool. If you get sick, put your head out the window. We don't want you messing up our patrol car."

The drunken Pied-Noir grunted. The officers shut the back door and climbed into the front.

An Algerian man on a bicycle pedaled up beside the driver's side and rapped his knuckles on the window. The policeman rolled down the window and said, "What the hell do you want?"

The Algerian man pulled a machine pistol from his jacket and fired through the window. Each officer received a spray of four bullets. The policeman behind the wheel slumped over dead. The policeman on the passenger side was badly wounded but still alive. He opened the door and stumbled out onto the street. The Algerian took aim and shot him in the head, then rode off on his bike.

The Pied-Noir in the back looked over the seat at the dead policeman in the driver's seat. He was frightened by all the blood and whimpered. The backdoors would not open. He crawled through the open window to escape the carnage. He couldn't get away fast enough.

Algiers, Algeria

The police checkpoint at the bottom of an ally leading up to the Casbah was busier than usual. The people going in and out were frustrated by the long delays they had to endure. The police occupying the checkpoint didn't seem to care. They just did their job searching people and checking their documents at the same rate, no matter how long the lines.

A whisper moved through the crowd of Algerians waiting in line and gathered around the checkpoint. People moved off rapidly. Within a minute, no more lines were going in or out of the checkpoint, and no Algerians were in sight. The police exchanged a nervous glance.

Three metal balls rolled and bounced down the cobblestones from the ally above. As they picked up speed, the police saw that the metal balls were grenades. They dove for cover.

A policeman knelt behind a rain barrel. A grenade bounced and wedged itself between the barrel and the building. The explosion killed the policeman and wounded two others hiding nearby.

Another grenade rolled past the corner of a building where two more officers had hidden for protection.

The grenade exploded, wounding one and killing the other.

The final grenade rolled under a vegetable cart and exploded, sending green beans, red peppers and squash flying through the air.

Once the chaos was over, no Algerian moved to help the wounded police officers. It wasn't that they didn't have compassion for them, but they could not be sure who was watching. Algerians collaborating with the French were treated harshly by the FLN; they were seen as traitors of their own people and country.

Eight Mujahideen fighters armed with rifles and pistols, and lead by Si Larbi, emerged from the alleyway above the checkpoint. They descended on the surviving policemen and killed them. Si Larbi signaled dozens of Mujahideen waiting in the alleys outside the Casbah checkpoint. They rushed forward, pushing handcarts filled with weapons, many too large or heavy to be smuggled past the checkpoint, including large mortars, anti-tank guns, and crates of ammunition. Any FLN leader or Mujahideen fighter whose face was known to the French, and prohibited from entering the Arab community for fear of being arrested, moved past the breached checkpoint. They entered the Casbah unimpeded.

Si Larbi was satisfied with the attack's results. It sent a strong message to the people of Algiers. The Mujahideen now owned the Casbah, not the French.

Algiers, Algeria

A French policeman directed traffic on a busy street corner. An Algerian man dressed in a suit waited on the street corner until the policeman signaled that it was okay to cross. Taking his queue, the Algerian walked across the street. When the French policeman turned to direct traffic in the opposite direction, the Algerian changed his course and walked up behind the policeman. He pulled out a pistol and fired a round in the policeman's back. The policeman fell into the street. Traffic stopped. The drivers were in shock at what had happened. Pedestrians scattered for cover. The Algerian walked over to the mortally wounded policeman squirming on the ground and fired two more bullets, killing him. Then the assassin ran over to another man on a motor scooter and jumped on the back. They sped away back toward the Casbah.

Algiers, Algeria

Henri Lenore, the police prefect of Algiers, sat behind his desk, speaking by phone with the Minister of the Interior in Paris. "I have lost five percent of my police force to death and injuries caused by the FLN in the last two weeks. Another fifteen percent have surrendered their badges or are no longer willing to go out on patrol. I cannot blame them. The streets are no longer safe. My men are targets," said Lenore.

"It is your duty and the duty of your men to protect the citizens of Algiers," said the Minister.

"I understand my duty, as do my men. But we are no longer facing an underground organization of thugs. We are facing a well-trained and well-armed army. We cannot protect ourselves, let alone the civilians in Algiers. You must do something immediately, or I will be forced to resign my post as prefect," said Lenore, hanging up the phone in a huff.

He was beyond caring about his career. The lives of the men he commanded were at stake. He had to make a stand for their sake and the sake of the citizens of Algiers. He was indignant. He rose from his desk, grabbed his jacket, and walked out of his office, slamming the door shut for good measure.

Lenore left the prefecture, purchased a newspaper from a paperboy, and walked to his favorite café. He sat grumbling to himself. The waiter came over immediately. Lenore ordered a coffee and two croissants. He opened the newspaper and read the headlines – Seven Police Killed In One Day. It was a mockery. The waiter served his coffee. "And my croissants?" said Lenore, impatient.

"Right away, sir," said the waiter as he moved off toward the café's kitchen.

A moment later, a waiter placed a basket of croissants on the table and continued walking past. Lenore looked up from his paper to see that the man was not the waiter that had served him and continued to walk around the corner of the restaurant. Lenore shrugged. It was not important. He folded his newspaper, took a sip of coffee, and reached for his croissants. Inside the basket were two croissants and a grenade missing its pin, and its spoon flipped open. The explosion killed Lenore instantly, plus three other patrons. The waiter that had served the coffee only lost an arm.

THREE

December 24, 1956 – Paris, France

The wide boulevards of Paris were lined with restaurants and cafés. This wasn't one of them. This was a neighborhood bistro where the food was good, and the liquor was cheap. There was a thick haze of grey cigarette smoke that hung over the tables where customers dined for hours on end. Talking. Laughing. Teasing. It was the Parisian way.

Lieutenant Colonel Marcel Bigeard sat alone at a table in the corner of the bistro. His commander, General Massu, had given him one week's leave, and he was intent on making the most of it before returning to duty in Algeria.

He was drunk. It was not an easy feat, even for him. Bruno, as he was called by his friends and the men under his command, was in great shape, and his body processed alcohol very efficiently. But he was determined to get completely plastered, and his perseverance had won out. Chalk up another victory. Mission accomplished. Bruno didn't believe in doing things half-way, and the room was starting to rotate.

He had asked the waiter to remove the extra chairs so nobody could sit down. He was a well-known war hero from the siege at Dien Bien Phu. Strangers had a bad tendency of sitting down uninvited to pry loose a story of one of his many exploits. He liked telling stories and the free drinks they would buy him, but he wasn't in the mood. Not tonight. It was Christmas Eve, and he was feeling sorry for himself. Not because he was alone. He liked it that way when he was really sloshed. Nobody could understand his drunken slurs, anyway. No. His desire to be alone was founded in something much more severe than annoying fans. It was founded in betrayal.

He had left Egypt just in time to make it back to Paris for the holidays. Bruno was the commander of a battalion of French paratroopers. They had been fighting in Egypt to secure and protect the Suez Canal after the Israelis had invaded the Sinai. He and his men had captured all of the objectives assigned to them. Many of his men had died, and even more had been severely wounded. That wasn't what bothered him. He was used to death and pain. It wasn't that he was cold and unfeeling. He understood the need for sacrifice in the time of war. He was willing to give his life for France, and so were his men. But he refused to see that sacrifice wasted.

After only two days of fighting, France's ally – Britain – buckled under international pressure and called for a ceasefire. The job of securing the Canal Zone was left undone. Bruno hated leaving anything unfinished. He didn't understand what had happened. They were winning. With another twenty-four hours, they could have secured the entire Canal Zone from the Mediterranean Sea to the Gulf of Suez.

But what irked him most of all was that Egyptian President Nasser remained in power. Although it was never disclosed directly, Bruno knew that the real purpose of France's invasion was not the protection of the Suez Canal but to bring about the destruction of Egypt's army and the overthrow of Nasser. Nasser had been supporting the FLN by giving its leaders a haven in Cairo. He had also been providing funding, training, and military supplies to the rebels. Without Nasser's help, the Algerian rebellion would collapse.

After Bruno and his paratroopers had captured a strategic bridge and Port Faud's waterworks, it would have taken little effort to pick up his entire battalion and drop it on Cairo. The Israelis, British and French warplanes had decimated the Egyptian air force. The Egyptian army was busy executing a fighting retreat back down the Canal Zone. Bruno knew the Egyptian civilians in Cairo would fight back, but they had proven to be vastly inferior against his aggressive and well-trained paratroopers. "The hell with the British, we could have taken Cairo by ourselves," said Bruno a little too loudly.

Heads turned. People whispered. "We bleed for you, and you never let us win," he blurted out in a drunken slur.

More heads turned. More whispers.

Bruno thought for another moment and decided the real blame was on the Americans. They were Britain and France's ally. While he didn't expect America to join the fight, he saw it as disloyal to threaten France and Britain with sanctions and financial ruin if they did not pull out of Egypt. "Fucking Americans," said Bruno. "They put their noses where they do not belong."

He was pretty sure it was the alcohol talking, but he also felt like it had to be said. He ordered another Chartreuse from a passing waiter. The manager came over and asked if he would prefer some coffee. Because of his notoriety, Bruno was good for business. But too much Bruno was like letting a bull loose in a china shop.

Bruno stood up, wavering a bit. The manager wondered if he had made a big mistake. Even drunk, the manager was pretty sure Bruno could kill him with one blow. Bruno reached into his pocket and pulled out a wad of money. The manager waved off Bruno insisting that his meal and drinks were on the house. "For your service to France," said the manager.

Bruno snarled, then saluted the manager and wobbled out the door, bumping into a table on his way out. The patrons thought it novel that the great war hero had knocked over their drinks.

Outside the bistro, Bruno looked around. He wasn't sure where to go. He couldn't go back to the military airbase while he was still drunk. He would be arrested and spend Christmas in the brig. He might even get demoted, although he doubted it. His reputation as a warrior made him beyond that sort of thing. The main reason he didn't want to go back to the airbase was he didn't want any of his men to see him in his inebriated state. It would set a bad example.

He thought about going to Brigitte Friang's apartment, but then he remembered that he and Brigitte had had a falling out in Egypt. After leading him on, she had chosen the American pilot, Tom Coyle, over him. "Fucking Americans," he said to himself once again.

He walked down the street toward the Seine River and came upon Notre-Dame. He loved the 12th-century cathedral with its twin stone towers and rose-colored, stained glass windows. It was not the gaudy Eiffel Tower or the crowded Champs-Élysées that Bruno thought of when he was overseas fighting France's wars. It was Notre-Dame. It was the heart of Paris and felt like home.

He moved to the front doors to go inside but then thought better of it. It would have been crowded with parishioners attending midnight mass, and he was very drunk. Not a good combination. He was Catholic like most French but did not like attending religious services. As a warrior, he had done things. Things that he understood were necessary but not things he was proud of. *Sins?* he thought. *Perhaps. But when judgment day comes, God will surely understand. After all, I am a man of war.*

Instead of going inside, he walked around the side of the building. He sat down on the paving stones and leaned his back up against one of the tall stone buttresses. Just being next to God seemed enough and comforted him. It was cold. The heavy clouds promised snow. That didn't bother him. He had his coat, and he had slept in much worse conditions when he was fighting the Nazis in Northern France. As he dozed off, he thought about Brigitte and their last conversation. He had scolded her for being wishy-washy and told her he was through chasing after her. He whispered to himself, "What have I done?" and fell asleep.

Colombey-les-Deux-Eglises, France

Dressed in his most elegant uniform, Massu felt honored to be spending Christmas Eve with General de Gaulle and his family. Not many had even visited La Boisserie, the family's nine-acre estate one hundred and twenty miles outside of Paris. The grounds and manor house were locked away behind ivy-covered walls built for privacy. Massu was one of only three guests - two generals and one history professor from the Sorbonne University. De Gaulle was not a fan of politicians. He had too much respect for the truth and loathed self-interest above country. Even as president, he rarely listened to the counsel of his cabinet. He always did what he thought best for France.

General de Gaulle was surprisingly private about his family. Some supposed it was because of his daughter Ann, who suffered from Downs Syndrome and held a special place in the general's heart. But in reality, it was de Gaulle himself that was rather shy, especially after stepping down as President of France years earlier. He had miscalculated and thought the people would demand his return. They did not. It seemed even war heroes had an expiration date when it came to politics. But unlike brass, their golden luster often returned over time.

De Gaulle greeted Massu with a hearty handshake and said, "So, Massu, are you still stupid?"

"Still a Gaullist, General," replied Massu.

"And here I thought you would grow more intelligent with age."

"Little chance of that."

"And how are things in Algeria?"

"Intense. While we were in Egypt, the FLN used the opportunity to reorganize and redeploy their Mujahideen forces."

"To Algiers, I would imagine."

"You still have your spies, I see."

"No. No. No spies. Just common sense. The rebels cannot win against a modern army. They must hide among the population and fight an urban war as the French resistance did with the Nazis during the occupation. What better place than Algiers?"

"It's going to be the devil rooting them out."

"Yes, I would imagine."

"We never should have given them breathing room."

"Yes. Yes. Too bad about the Suez Crisis. It was a debacle in the making. One should never trust the British."

"...or the Americans."

"Joined at the hip, I think."

"I'm not so sure anymore. The Americans were very angry with the British."

"Do not fool yourself. America needs Britain to keep its foot in the European door and to stand against the Russians."

"... and France?"

"You know how I feel. France needs to find its own way. Independence is the only way to true freedom. Our future is in Europe, not America or Britain."

"You do not consider Britain part of Europe?"

De Gaulle simply smiled in response.

"When are you coming back to the government, General? France needs you," said Massu.

"I am done with all that. A father needs to know when it is time for his child to venture on their own. My time has passed. France will do fine."

"I doubt that. Not with those idiots in parliament running things."

"I told them we needed a strong executive branch. They didn't listen."

"You should have stopped them while you had a chance."

"I am a soldier. I obey," said de Gaulle with a shrug. "Do not worry so much, Jacques. For history to be written, it has to be lived first. The story of France is not over."

"A soothing thought for Christmas Eve, General?"

"Yvonne won't allow me to be melancholy around the holidays. She says it spoils the goose and frightens the children."

Paris, France

Coyle supervised the loading of pallets filled with spools of barbed wire into the back of the Fairchild C-119 Flying Boxcar he had been assigned. He wanted to ensure that the pallets were well secured and didn't shift during the flight. His cargo boss was new and young – two things Coyle was not fond of when it came to cargo bosses. A loose load during a flight could cause havoc with the plane's balance and even punch a hole in the aircraft's aluminum skin.

Coyle didn't pay much heed to what the French Air Commander had told him during his employment interview. He knew that the number of C-119s in the French Air Force was limited, and he wasn't in the mood to train on another model of aircraft if he wrecked this one. He liked the C-119s. They were powerful for a cargo plane, and he had grown accustomed to their quirks. They were like a well-worn pair of cowboy boots… comfy. He just couldn't let 'em go.

He was checking the knots that the cargo boss had used to tie down one of the pallets. Knots were a big deal to Coyle. The new cargo boss was using a trucker's hitch knot, which was fine for most loads, but when Coyle wanted to ensure security, he liked to use a figure-eight loop with a half-hitch bight. The figure-eight loop was just as strong at the trucker's hitch, if not stronger, but it helped the rope retain its strength. The only problem with the figure-eight loop knot was that it was impossible to untie with loads over one thousand pounds. You'd have to cut it loose with a knife. That was fine with Coyle if it kept his plane safe. Besides, his contract never said anything about paying for cargo rope. Coyle retied the knot.

He heard a knock on the side of the aircraft's hull and looked up to see Bruno standing beside the cargo doors with his duffle bag. "Permission to come aboard," said Bruno.

"Permission granted," said Coyle with a smile.

"I see they don't trust you to fly human beings anymore."

"Trust me? Hell. I asked to fly this stuff. I don't have to feed it, and it doesn't puke on my deck if I hit turbulence. Where the hell have you been? Brigitte and I wanted to invite you over for Christmas Eve."

"Brigitte wanted to invite me?"

"Well, maybe it was my idea. I can't believe you two ain't talking."

"Yes, it seems strange."

"I ain't gonna pry, but I hope you two work it out."

"You want us to work it out?"

"Sure, why not? Just keep your mitts off her."

"Mitts?"

"Hands. Keep your hands off her."

"Yes. Of course. She is your woman. I respect that."

"And I appreciate it. So, where are you heading?"

"Algiers. I was hoping to catch a ride with you if you have room."

"You probably don't want to ride back here with barbed wire. Those spools can get a little prickly if ya rub up against them. The French Air Force is still too cheap to give me a navigator. Why don't you ride with me in the cockpit?"

"I would like that. We can catch up, as you say."

Algiers, Algeria

Achiary sat in the backroom of a French bistro listening to his fellow French-Algerians squabble amongst themselves. They were a rabble, but he needed them to accomplish his objectives. The tide was turning against the Pieds-Noirs – European colonists living in Algeria. The native Algerians were gaining more civil rights and power.

Achiary was not a reasonable man. Most things were black or white. There was no middle ground with Achiary, especially when it came to Algeria. He didn't see the point of being civil when his freedoms were being assaulted, and his livelihood was being threatened. He was willing to fight and die for both. That didn't make him bad. It just made it difficult to deal with him. It was the secrets he kept that made his morals questionable.

He was the founder of the Ultras – an underground paramilitary organization bent on keeping Algeria French territory. To Achiary, giving rights to native Algerians was taking away rights from the Pieds-Noirs. The Pieds-Noirs were French citizens and enjoyed full protection under French law. The native Algerians were considered second class citizens by most Pieds-Noirs and many Frenchmen. The Algerians had few rights, and that was the way Achiary and his fellow Pieds-Noirs wanted to keep it.

But not all Frenchmen felt the same. Parisians were especially sensitive to the native Algerians treatment under French law. Slowly and steadily, the Algerians had been making progress in their struggle for civil rights, including the right to vote.

After World War II, the native Algerians had obtained the right of representation in the newly created Algerian Assembly. However, the elections were always rigged by the Pieds-Noirs and French authorities willing to accept bribes and cooperate with their schemes. The results were that all of the Algerian Nationalist movements were prevented from winning seats in the Assembly. The Algerian Assembly was nothing more than a façade to appease the masses.

Many Algerians could see a day when they would be given real power and even French citizenship. The Pieds-Noirs knew that would be a day of reckoning, and they would do everything in their power to see that day never came. That's why Ultra was created, to turn back the tide of change and maintain the status quo.

Achiary waited patiently as several Pieds-Noirs vented their frustrations. He knew it was important that his fellow conspirators felt like their complaints were being heard. One sheep farmer complained that nine of his sheep had been taken from his lower pasture in the past weeks. He imagined it to be the Mujahideen trying to feed their troops in the field. A restaurant owner complained about the rising taxes placed on all Algerians to pay for the half-million French troops stationed in Algeria. Nevermind that it was the Pieds-Noirs that had demanded the French army do something about the unrest.

Achiary saw all of this as quibbling. It didn't matter. The FLN was growing in number. They were the real threat. It was true that the Ultras would also increase in number as FLN terrorist attacks grew. But the Pied-Noir population was much smaller than the native Algerians. They were outnumbered nine to one. Time was not on the Pieds-Noirs' side. They needed to do something radical and quick.

Achiary had heard enough. He gave a nod to several members of the group, who then called for him to give his opinion on what they should do. More members called for Achiary to speak. He rose at their request, a seemingly unwilling participant. "There is only one way to deal with this growing Muslim hindrance. We must send a strong message to the politicians in Paris that the French citizens of Algeria will not tolerate these encroachments. We will not sit idly by and watch everything our families have worked for be destroyed. Algeria is France and nothing else. They must hear us and know we will not be silenced. We must roar like a lion."

The crowd cheered. They were with Achiary. He chose to say no more. He understood the sacrifices they must make, even if they didn't.

Algiers, Algeria

Achiary led ninety Ultras, armed with clubs and
crowbars, into the square at the base of the Casbah.
Some had pistols hidden under their shirts just in case.
Others carried placards and banners that read –

ALGERIA IS FRANCE,
COLON FAMILIES DEMAND PROTECTION
and
PARATROOPERS FOR FRENCH JUSTICE

The Algerian business owners saw the group of angry
Europeans approaching and rushed to close their
shops and restaurants. Patrons and tourists
disappeared down alleyways. The square emptied.

The police saw the protestors and stood their
ground at the checkpoint. The Pieds-Noirs would not
be allowed into the Muslim quarter even though the
police were vastly outnumbered. A messenger was sent
to the nearby police prefect requesting back up.

The Ultras chanted slogans and shouted insults
against the Muslims. Several Ultras grabbed tomatoes
from an abandoned vegetable cart and hurled them at
police and Muslim residents standing on balconies and
peering out of their windows. They, too, quickly
disappeared. Achiary signaled to several men with
crowbars. They pried open the metal grids and rollup
doors protecting the windows and doors of shops and
restaurants. Paving stones were pried loose from the
street and hurled through shop windows, scattering
glass shards and knocking over displays. Several men

lit the gasoline-soaked rags in Molotov cocktails. They threw them into buildings and at parked cars. Muslims living in the apartments above the square fled. Firefighters were called but refused to enter the area until the angry protestors had left. The police were helpless and watched as the square burned. The message to the politicians in Paris was sent – the Pieds-Noirs of Algiers demanded the French government send in the paratroopers or they would take justice into their own hands.

Algiers, Algeria

Bruno sat with Trinquier and Major Paul Aussaresses – the head of the Brigade's Intelligence Unit – listening to Massu standing in front of a map of Algiers. "Messieurs, we have been given new orders from Paris. The 10th Para has been reassigned solely to Algiers. The war has dragged on long enough. The French people are losing their patience. We are to do whatever is required to quell this uprising. That means destroying the FLN by all means necessary."

"If we can find them," said Trinquier.

"Well, that is the good news. While we were away on our little adventure in Egypt, the leaders of the FLN spent their time consolidating and repositioning their forces. They are in Algiers. More specifically, they are in the Casbah."

"Along with seventy thousand native Algerians that all look alike," said Bruno.

"Yes. And I think it is safe to assume their fellow Algerians are helping to hide them within the Casbah. They are co-conspirators, if you will. And from this point forward, any co-conspirator is to be considered a combatant, equally guilty under the law."

"What does that mean?" said Bruno.

"It means… the gloves come off. We cannot find the FLN because the people are helping to hide them. The people who know where rebels are. It is their duty to reveal the leaders and members of the FLN to us. If they fail to reveal the information by their own free will, we are now authorized to use all means necessary to compel them to give us the information we need."

"Does that include torture?" said Aussaresses.

"All means necessary. I think your orders are clear enough," said Massu. "Obviously, French citizens are exempt from these new guidelines."

"And if we find a French citizen that we believe has information about the whereabouts of the FLN?" said Trinquier.

"Then we will deal with them on a case-by-case basis. But I want to make myself crystal clear. It is time to win this war, and now we have been granted the tools to do so. Use them liberally. The longer this war drags on, the stronger the FLN will become. We had them on the run before we left for Egypt. Let us repeat our past successes and finish this business in a timely manner."

"And we are guaranteed immunity?" said Aussaresses.

"Absolutely," said Massu. "Now for the battle plan. We are going to lay siege to the Casbah. I want it completely cut off from the outside world. No leaks. Once that is accomplished, we will perform random searches of houses and buildings for weapons and evidence of the FLN. When we find such evidence, all occupants of the house or building will be brought in for questioning, and they will not leave the interrogation until we are given a name and location of an FLN member."

"Does that include women and children?" said Bruno.

"All occupants. The Algerians are hiding the FLN. Once word gets out that the treatment of co-conspirators will be just as harsh as the rebels, the people living in the Casbah will be reluctant to help the FLN. Their hiding places will dry up, and they will be forced into the open where will squash them like the bugs they are."

"What about residents that work outside the Casbah?" said Bruno.

"We will set up checkpoints where everyone will be required to show their documents and be thoroughly searched before entering or exiting the Casbah."

"That includes women?"

"Especially women. I think we all know it is the women that have been used to smuggle weapons into the area."

"The Arab men aren't going to like Frenchmen touching their wives and daughters."

"Good. The more they dislike the treatment they are receiving, the sooner this will all end. There will be no exceptions. Everyone will be searched. In addition to the searches and checkpoints, we will have multiple patrols checking documents to ensure there are no breaks in our perimeter. Now for assignments... Major Aussaresses, your men and you will continue to be in charge of all interrogations and intelligence operations. Colonel Trinquier, your men and you will be in charge of all territory within Algiers outside the Casbah. Colonel Bigeard, your men and you are to be given the plum – the Casbah. You will be responsible for rooting out the FLN leaders and their Mujahideen fighters hidden within the fortress."

"I don't understand. Why the change?" said Bruno, hesitant. "My men and I have been having great success fighting the Mujahideen in the countryside. Wouldn't it make more sense for us to continue that effort and let Colonel Trinquier have the Casbah?"

"I would be fine with that, General. My men are ready and willing," said Trinquier.

"Normally, I would agree with you both. But time is of the essence. Colonel Bigeard, your battalion's reputation for aggressiveness is what this operation needs. I was impressed with your actions in Egypt. You and your men accomplished all of your objectives. We need that same esprit de corps to ferret out the FLN. I am sure Colonel Trinquier and his men can handle the rebels in the rest of Algiers. Besides, we have our orders. The paratroopers are to stay within Algiers. The rest of the French army will deal with the Mujahideen in the countryside and other cities."

"Yes, sir," said Bruno and Trinquier.

"I want all of our troops repositioned, and the Casbah closed off within one week. We have a tremendous amount of work do, Messieurs. Let's get to it."

The meeting was adjourned. Trinquier hung back to talk with Massu once the others had left. "Why the long face, Roger?" said Massu.

"I'm just wondering if you have lost confidence in me, General?" said Trinquier.

"You still don't see it."

"See what, sir?"

"We are entering new territory with the interrogations of a mass number of civilians. When it is over, there will be investigations into what we have done."

"But you said we are authorized to carry out such interrogations."

"We are... by the current government. But how long will the new PM last? And what happens when he is gone? Mark my words, anyone in government that gave us permission to carry out these interrogations is going to have a very short memory when the accusations go public... and they will go public, Roger. If Colonel Bigeard is the one carrying out the searches and apprehensions, the politicians in Paris are going to be hesitant to accuse a popular war hero of any wrongdoing. It's not politically expedient. Bruno is our insurance."

"I see," said Trinquier.

"Really, Roger... You need to take more of a long view of events if you ever plan to be a general."

"Of course. I appreciate the guidance, sir."

January 7, 1957 – Algiers, Algeria

General Massu was at the head of the 10th brigade of paratroopers as they marched through the streets of Algiers carrying their submachine guns and grenades strapped to their chest harnesses. Bruno and Trinquier followed, each at the head of their individual battalions. It was more like a parade than an invasion, but the message was clear for all of Algiers-- the paratroopers were here, and they meant business. The Pieds-Noirs and French tourists cheered as the paratroopers marched past. The Algerians watched in silence.

While Massu did not like politics, he understood them. He knew that this war would be a test of will rather than strength. The FLN could continue to draw upon the Algerian population for recruits as long as they remained popular. That was the key in Massu's mind. The French paratroopers needed to show the Algerians that siding with the FLN was a losing proposition that would only bring death and misery to them and their families. It was the people of Algiers that would betray the FLN. Once that happened, the war would be over, and things could return to normal. Life would go on under a French government. It was all so clear in Massu's mind what needed to be done.

Massu, Trinquier, and Bruno were patriots and were willing to die for France. However, they differed in their understanding of what patriotism meant.

Massu saw patriotism as the preservation of French culture and ideals. He knew that politicians came and went like laundry; first clean, then soiled, then clean again. He also knew that the French people could be manipulated, especially by the media and therefore were not to be trusted with anything as precious as the Republic. He saw himself as a lighthouse, steady and strong in the storm.

Trinquier saw patriotism as carrying out the true will of the French people. He and his men were a cog in a vast machine called France. An extension of democracy and the constitution. He believed in duty and obeyed the orders of his commanders without question or doubt.

Bruno saw patriotism as a duty to protect his country and the men under his command. He was a tool of the government to be used when diplomacy failed. And like any tool, they needed to be used properly and with purpose. He understood that sacrifice was sometimes necessary. He followed his commanders as long as they obeyed French law and did not waste the lives of his men.

All three men were dedicated warriors and loved their country.

January 9, 1957 – Algiers, Algeria

Paratroopers quickstepped into the burnt-out square below the Casbah. A truck pulled to a stop in front of the repaired police checkpoint. The paratrooper engineers unloaded spools of barbed wire and fencing as the police and Algerians looked on. The police sergeant in charge of the checkpoint was relieved by a French paratrooper lieutenant. The police closed the checkpoint with many Algerians still in line waiting to cross. The police returned to their prefect, grateful to no longer have to face the dangers of the FLN in the Casbah.

The paratroopers set up 30-Cal machineguns surrounded by two layers of sandbags on both sides of the checkpoint. The machinegun nests were meant to deter anyone from attempting to cross or any attacks by the FLN. More sandbags were used to create walls at the checkpoints so that undercover FLN members could not signal their comrades. The checkpoints had a menacing look about them and seemed impenetrable.

The stone wall that surrounded the Casbah citadel was an ideal barrier and was capped with loops of barbed wire. Concertina wire – triple loops of barbed wire stacked as triangles – was laid at the base of both sides of the wall to prevent ladders or ropes from being used to scale the wall.

The paratroopers laid out concertina wire and fencing across the alleyways leading in and out of the Casbah, sealing them off. Occupants of buildings on the edge of the perimeter were forced to use side entrances, keeping them within the boundaries of the neighborhood and within the paratroopers' perimeter of barbed wire and fencing.

There would be far fewer checkpoints under the paratroopers' watch than when the police were in charge. The reduced number of checkpoints created long lines of Algerians trying to move in and out of the Casbah. It was a tight mousetrap. Some people waited three or four hours before being allowed to cross. Everyone was searched. Paratroopers used mine detectors to check for weapons. They were exceptionally thorough with any woman wearing niqabs or burkas. The troops didn't need to touch the woman unless something was detected. She was then led to a private area and inspected by a French woman.

The perimeter was closely guarded by squads of paratroopers that were careful to mix their scheduled patrols. Each patrol was dealt with like a fire mission with half the paratroopers moving into an area and taking up defensive positions while the other half checked documents and inspected the fencing to ensure there were no breaks in the perimeter. There would be no surprise FLN attacks against the paratroopers. They were trained to defend themselves far better than regular French troops or the police.

Movement within the neighborhood was severely restricted by the patrols of paratroopers. Documents were required of any person on the street. Those that attempted to avoid the patrols were run down, arrested and taken in for interrogation. Age, sex, and even nationality were no exceptions when it came to showing proper documents. No excuse was tolerated.

French interrogation facilities were so crowded it could take two to three days before a person was interviewed and released. And for those with the wrong answers... much longer. It was a miserable time for the Algerians in the Casbah, and that was precisely what Massu wanted. The more pain the civilians felt, the sooner they would reveal the FLN hideouts, and the war could be brought to a successful conclusion.

It took almost a week to completely seal off the Casbah. But when it was finally done, Bruno was confident that he had confined the FLN behind the perimeter around the Arab quarter and restricted their access to the rest of Algiers. The paratroopers were ready for the second phase of their operation, which would be by far riskier.

January 13, 1957 - Algiers, Algeria

Bruno skipped the paratroopers' morning jog. They would need all their strength over the next few days. He had his men gathered in an empty warehouse where he could speak with them in secrecy. The doors and windows were shut tight, and guards were placed to ensure privacy. Maps of the Casbah were handed out to the squad leaders. He moved to the front of the room and spoke, "I regret to inform you that the morning jog has been canceled."

A cheer went up. "Fortunately, I was able to procure your morning onions."

The crowd groaned as sacks of raw onions were brought into the room and passed out to the paratroopers. Bruno started the morning meal with a big bite of his onion and said with a smile, "Breakfast of Champions, yes?"

The paratroopers grumbled, then ate their raw onions as they listened to their commander, "At O-Five hundred this morning, we will begin the next phase of our operation to root out the FLN from the Casbah. Until our initial search is completed, nobody is to be allowed into or out of the Casbah. Our searches of buildings and houses will be random, so the FLN leaders will be unable to predict where we will show up next. They will attempt to move their forces to safer hideouts. That is when we will catch the rats before they scurry away. Any person found without identity documents is to be immediately arrested and brought to interrogation."

"What about women and children?" said a lieutenant.

"No exceptions. Women and children are to be searched and will be required to show their documents. While many of the people in the Casbah are not directly helping the FLN in their rebellion, everyone knows what is going on and where many of the insurgents are hiding. Make no mistake... everyone is complicit."

A sense of excitement rippled through the ranks as the paratroopers realized they were finally being unleashed to win a war by all means necessary. "General Massu had made it clear that no person or building in the Casbah is to be exempt from search. If weapons or insurgents are found, all building occupants are to be detained immediately and brought in for interrogation."

"What about searching the mosques and madaris?" said a sergeant.

"Especially the mosques and madaris," said Bruno. "We will assign special squads to double back and perform surprise repeat searches of high target structures and areas. Nobody is to be seriously injured unless they resist. But that doesn't mean you need to be gentle either. You are authorized to use all means necessary to bring the residents of the Casbah to heel if any organized opposition is detected. This is a military operation and is to be carried out with aggressive professionalism."

Bruno let the last phrase sink in before continuing, "We are the elite. France needs us now more than ever. Our homeland is under attack. We shall defend it with honor and our lives if necessary," said Bruno snapping to attention and saluting. "Vive la France."

"Vive la France," shouted the paratroopers standing and saluting.

The paratroopers surrounded the base of the Casbah early in the morning before the people had awakened. The battalion was augmented by the police force. Groups of policemen armed with rifles and shotguns were placed at every possible exit from the hillside citadel. No one would be allowed to leave the Casbah for the next two days.

When the raids began, locked doors to buildings and houses were kicked in without warning. Surprise was the paratrooper's best approach to catching the insurgents and their collaborators. Occupants were escorted into the main room, where they were guarded while the search was carried out. The paratroopers took to heart their orders not to be gentle. Furniture was broken. Cookware and vases were smashed. Shelves were toppled. Rugs and tapestries were torn. Any loose floorboards were pried up. Hidden doorways were forced open. Every possible space was searched for weapons and contraband.

As the French crackdown grew and more insurgents were arrested, the FLN leadership spread the word throughout the neighborhood that any Algerian helping the French would be treated as a traitor and dealt with harshly. The people of the Casbah were caught between a rock and a hard place. They had allowed the FLN into their homes and businesses. They had fed them, hidden them, and protected them. FLN reprisals against their own people were more dreaded than the French interrogation rooms.

The FLN leadership had their hands full. Moving their Mujahideen troops during the search was risky. The likelihood of being stopped in the street and asked for identification papers was much higher, with thousands of French paratroopers roaming the neighborhood. It was even difficult to send a message by courier. But leaving their men in place was a surefire method of getting caught up in the sweep. The French were very thorough, and fewer hideouts were available. More and more of their men were being arrested by the minute as the search continued.

The results of the two-day search were impressive. One thousand five hundred FLN members were arrested. Thousands of collaborators were taken in for questioning. Tons of grenades, rifles, pistols, and ammunition were confiscated.

It was a deep blow to the FLN, but their big fear was what would follow as their members and the civilians that protected them were being interrogated by the French. Many would break down under coercion or torture. They would reveal the whereabouts of the FLN leaders and their followers. No one was safe.

Didouche, Bitat, and Boulaïd were members of the executive council that ran the FLN. Ben Bella, considered by many to be the group leader, had been captured the previous year when the French intercepted an airplane in which he was traveling to a peace conference. The plane had been forced to land on French soil, and he was arrested. While Didouche, Bitat, and Boulaïd did their best to plan and coordinate FLN operations, none had the military experience of Bella. There were talks about breaking Bella out of jail in Paris, but they were just revolutionary pipe dreams. The human cost of a raid on the high-security prison would have been enormous.

Didouche, Bitat, and Boulaïd were meeting in the Casbah to continue planning several missions when the French search operation began. Their immediate reaction was to flee. As the day progressed, they made their way to the Northern end of Casbah, where they had often used a little-known underground passage between two warehouses, one on either side of the citadel wall. They were surprised to find that the French were aware of the passageway and had posted a squad of paratroopers inside the warehouse waiting for whoever might show up. The three FLN leaders barely escaped detection and left the area immediately.

They tried several other escape routes they had previously used and found all of them guarded by paratroopers or police. "We could fight our way through," said Didouche.

"With what? We have no weapons," said Bitat. "The French have confiscated them."

"Not all of them. We can always find weapons."

"Perhaps… but they are paratroopers. Elite fighters."

"They are men and bleed just like we do."

"Maybe a diversion would work," said Boulaïd.

"Like what?" said Didouche.

"I don't know. I just thought of it. What about a fire?"

"A fire in the Casbah? This place will go up like a tinderbox. We could lose half our men, and only Allah knows how many civilians," said Bitat. "What about taking a couple of policemen hostage and using them to negotiate our freedom? It's worked before."

"I don't know. Do the paratroopers really care about the lives of a few policemen?" said Boulaïd. "It's us they want."

"I think we should gather as many men as we can and whatever weapons we can and try for a breakout. We can go someplace where the police are guarding the wall. It'll be easier. The police are lousy fighters," said Didouche.

"I agree. A breakout makes the most sense. Besides, we need to get as many fighters out as we can before they are captured," said Bitat.

"All right. I agree too. A breakout. We should send messengers to our largest groups of fighters," said Boulaïd.

"If they're still free," said Didouche.

"That's a big if," said Boulaïd.

"It's a chance we will have to take," said Bitat. "We give our men one hour to rendezvous. Those that make it go with us. And those that don't will just have to fend for themselves. Agreed?"

Didouche and Boulaïd nodded their consent.

Five messengers were sent. The young boys that carried the messages ran through the Casbah and hid whenever they encountered French patrols. The largest groups of Mujahideen fighters were housed in warehouses and factories. For some, it was already too late. They had been rounded up. Some had fought with the few weapons they had on hand. Most died in the attempt to keep their freedom.

The paratroopers were well trained in urban warfare, and most had just returned from the battle for Port Suad in Egypt. Nothing taught a soldier better than actual experience, and the paratroopers had plenty.

Hocine was eight years old when he pleaded to join the FLN as a fighter. His request was refused, but the cell leader he petitioned liked him and offered him a position as a messenger. His friends were impressed when word got out that he had been accepted into the FLN ranks. He had stretched the truth about his new position and said he was the leader's assistant. Fortunately for Hocine's reputation, the cell leader didn't refute his claim. Hocine was one of the messengers selected for this vital mission. He was given a coded message to deliver to the Mujahideen leader in a sardine factory.

When Hocine arrived, he saw that the factory was silent and empty. Not even the factory workers were inside. He wondered if maybe the Mujahideen were hiding. He called out into the interior of the building. He heard no response.

When he turned to go, he ran smack into a French paratrooper. The soldier looked like a giant and grabbed him by his shirt. Hocine was caught. He had heard the rumors of what the French did to the FLN members they captured. He would be tortured. Maybe his nails would be ripped from the tips of his fingers, or maybe he would be shocked with a car battery until he bit his tongue off. He began to cry.

The paratrooper searched him and found the encoded message in the rim of his baseball cap. The paratrooper couldn't read it, but he also knew that it might not be necessary to translate the message to catch his prey. After all, they had already rounded up the Mujahideen in the building. Somebody had sent them a message. That's who the paratrooper wanted.

Hocine was locked in a janitor's closet. The only light in the little room came from a small skylight. Hocine thought he might be able to fit through the opening if he could climb up and open the window. He climbed the supply shelves. Even standing on his tippy toes, Hocine couldn't reach the window from the top shelf. He found a box of paper towels, moved it under the window, and climbed on top of it. It was just enough to help him reach the window. He was in luck; the latch was not locked. He pushed open the skylight window, reached over the edge, and pulled himself up. He was a good climber. He had practiced on grandmother's fruit trees, and his muscles were strong for a boy his size.

Hocine climbed out onto the roof. He moved to the edge and looked down. The street in front of the factory was empty. The French paratroopers were stupid not to have left a guard out front and even more foolish for leaving a boy like him alone. He shimmied down a drainpipe until he was only a few feet above the cobblestone and jumped. He landed on his feet. He didn't waste any time. He took off running back to the rendezvous point. The FLN leaders needed to know that the Mujahideen in the sardine factory had been captured.

Four paratroopers hidden around a corner watched Hocine run down the street. "Anybody up for a little jog?" said the paratrooper that had caught Hocine.

The paratroopers followed Hocine at a distance. The boy was quick, but the paratroopers were in great shape from their morning runs with their commander.

When Hocine arrived at the rendezvous point, he was out of breath. His mouth was parched. A Mujahideen gave him a sip from his goat-skinned water bag. Boulaïd walked over to the boy and said, "How did it go? Did you deliver the message?"

"No. They weren't there. The French paratroopers captured them. They caught me too, but I escaped," said Hocine proudly.

"You were captured by paratroopers?" said Boulaïd realizing the implications of the boy's story.

"Yeah. But I'm okay. They didn't do anything to me."

Boulaïd moved to a window and looked out. He could see dozens of French paratroopers taking up defensive positions around the building they were in. It looked like it might be an entire company. They even had a 30-Cal machinegun they were setting up. "We're surrounded," said Boulaïd. "A company of paratroopers, maybe more."

Didouche and Bitat moved to the window and looked out to see for themselves. Boulaïd's observation was confirmed. "Prepare to fight," said Didouche.

"We're dead men," said Bitat.

"Shut up," said Boulaïd.

"Once we engage the French in the front, we will head out the back. We collapse like a balloon but don't stop firing until you are given the order to redeploy," said Didouche to the Mujahideen. "We fire on my command."

But Didouche never gave the command to fire. A stream of machinegun bullets shattered a window and hit him in the neck and shoulders. He fell dead. Hocine's eyes went wide. He had seen a man die before, but never with this much blood and never this fast. One second the man was talking, and the next, he was dead. Hocine's eyes welled up with tears. *How did the French paratroopers find us?* he thought. More windows shattered as the rate of French fire increased. Hocine curled up in a ball in the corner of the room.

The Mujahideen returned fire. The paratroopers' aim was far more accurate than the Mujahideen's. One by one, the Mujahideen fell dead. A bazooka shell blew the door off its hinges. It wouldn't be long before paratroopers made their final assault.

Bitat and Boulaïd exchanged a knowing look. They were leaders. It was essential for the success of the war and Algerian independence that they escape. They moved toward the back of the building and looked out the windows. They were in luck. No French in the alley behind the building.

They bolted through the back door and ran down the alley. When they reached the end of the alley and turned the corner onto the street, they saw four paratroopers aiming their submachineguns at them. The two rebel leaders threw up their hands and surrendered.

Algiers, Algeria

The French interrogation center was filled with a series of small concrete cells plus several larger rooms used for the actual interrogations. There were drains at the bottom of each room to make cleaning easier. At times the interrogations could get messy, especially when electricity was used. People tended to relieve their bowels when the electricity was turned off, and their muscles relaxed.

The walls of the center were thick to keep the Algerian heat out and to keep the prisoners from tunneling. There were firing slits along the outer walls of the second story. Suspects were held offsite in local jails and a central military prison at HQ until they were called in for their interviews. After that, they were kept in cells until they were released or executed. It was all very controlled and organized.

There were few windows in the building and even fewer doors. Access was limited. Soldiers armed with submachineguns guarded each entrance, and light machine guns were positioned on the four corners of the roof. The building was isolated from the surrounding buildings and had clear fields of fire in all directions. Two platoons of paratroopers traded off guard duty. Attacking the interrogation center with anything less than an entire battalion of well-trained soldiers would be suicidal.

Major Aussaresses peered through a peephole in a cell door with his one good eye. He had lost his other eye during an assassination attempt at his favorite restaurant. Surprisingly, he didn't mind the missing eye as much as he thought he might. It gave him a menacing look that fit his current duty assignment as commander of the brigade's intelligence group. Besides, the women he dated found his leather eyepatch strangely erotic.

Inside the cell was a fifteen-year-old Algerian girl. She had been picked up in the Casbah during a check for identification. She had identification, but her name was on a list, which meant she was required to come in for interrogation.

Her headscarf and outer dress had been removed by the guards to prevent her from hanging herself. She was left wearing her undergarments – loose trousers and a thin blouse made of cotton. She was standing defiant in the middle of the bare room with a single light bulb and no windows. "Interesting," said Aussaresses after closing the door on the peephole. "The young girls usually curl up in the corner holding their legs closed. Not this one. This one seems ready to fight. I like that."

"That won't last long once we start interrogating her," said a French sergeant.

"Yes, but we may be missing an opportunity."

"Opportunity?"

"You really are a blunt instrument, aren't you?"

"Yes, sir. I am. Isn't that what you want?"

"At times, yes. But I think this one will require some finesse. Where did you say you picked her up?"

It was later in the day. The girl continued to stand in her cell. It was a matter of pride. She would only touch the floor during prayer. Even through the concrete walls, she could hear the faint call of the muezzin from a nearby mosque. She was unsure of the direction of Mecca but did her best to guess and kneeled in that direction during her prayers. If she were wrong, Allah would forgive her. She was sure of it.

The door opened. A young Algerian man, slightly older than her, entered with an empty toilet bucket. She moved to the opposite side of the cell out of his way. She was embarrassed that a man was allowed to swap out her toilet bucket. He did his job quickly, avoiding eye contact. She glanced at his face. His beard was just starting to appear on his acne-covered face. He wasn't overly handsome. In fact, he was rather plain-looking. He walked back through the doorway and began to close the door when she said, "Why am I being kept here?"

He stopped for a moment, looked at her incredulously, and said, "You think I know?"

"You work for them, don't you?"

He was embarrassed. He shut the door. She was angry with herself. She had pushed him. She shouldn't have done that. She needed his help.

He came into her cell again when it was mealtime. He opened the door, walked in, and held out the metal tray that held a stale piece of French bread with tiny bugs in it, a slice of moldy cheese and a tin cup of water. She looked down at the food on the tray. It was disgusting.

"You should eat," he said. "It's all you are going to get until tomorrow."

She decided he was right. Besides, she was starving. She took the tray from his hand and said, "Thank you."

"You're welcome."

"I'm sorry what I said earlier."

"No. You were right. As much as I hate it, I do work for them."

"Why?"

"After my father died, I needed a job to support my family. This was all that was available in my neighborhood."

"You live around here?"

"Yes. A few blocks away, near the square."

"What is your name?"

The young man considered for a moment. "It's against the rules to talk with prisoners," he said. "I've already said too much. I could lose my job."

"I understand. I don't want to get you in trouble," she said, looking at him with her soft brown eyes. "My name is Inara."

He nodded, left the cell, and closed the door.

Later that night, Inara's legs finally gave out. She sat on the freezing concrete floor. She was exhausted, cold, and hungry. She couldn't see it, but her face was stained with trails of dried tears. It was only the first day, and she was already depressed and lonely. She had heard stories of Algerians being locked away in the French interrogation sites for weeks, even months. She didn't know how they could possibly survive. The light bulb above burned all night, making it hard to sleep.

The door opened again. The young man entered with a blanket in his arms and made a shushing gesture.

He handed her the blanket, "I'm sorry, Inara, but I have to pick it up before the morning rounds, so the guards don't see it. But at least it will keep you warm for a few hours, and you can get some sleep."

"Thank you," she said and meant it.

"I overheard some of the guards. Your interrogation starts tomorrow."

"Good. I will finally be over this and can go home."

"I don't think that's going to happen."

"What do you mean?"

"I don't think you are the kind of person that will easily breakdown and tell them something they want to know."

"I'm not. I will never help the French."

"Then we will see each other a lot," he said with a gentle smile. "I must go. May Allah protect you, Inara."

"And you… for your kindness."

"My name is Halim," he said, closing the door to the cell as he left.

She placed the blanket on the floor, laid on one side of it and folded the other side over her body. She was finally warm and fell quickly asleep.

In the morning, Halim retrieved the blanket but promised to bring it back that evening if possible. Inara thanked him again. He pulled an apple from his pocket and handed it to her. Her eyes welled up with tears.

"You will need your strength today," he said and left.

She curled up in the corner and set the apple on top of her knees. She resisted eating it, even though she was starving. She gazed at the apple as if it was the most precious thing she had ever been given. She lasted twelve minutes before devouring every last bit of it.

Two French paratroopers entered Inara's cell and picked her up by her arms. They were rough in how they handled her as she was escorted down the hallway. She saw Halim mopping the floor of a cell as she moved past its open doorway. He glanced at her for only a moment, then looked away. She felt hurt but understood. There was nothing he could do against the two giant paratroopers that were carrying her.

She was placed in a room with a pulley mounted in the ceiling. Her hands were bound, and she was hoisted up by her arms. She had to stand on her tippy-toes to keep pressure off her wrists. The two paratroopers left and closed the door behind them. She waited and tried not to cry. She didn't want to give her interrogator the satisfaction of knowing that she was frightened. She needed to be brave. She needed to be defiant.

A French corporal entered carrying a car battery. He set the battery down on a table and hooked it up to a voltage regulator. He twisted the dial to increase the voltage and picked up the two leads with an alligator clip on the ends. He touched the two leads together. Sparks flew. That part was for his subject – Inara. He set the clips down and walked over to Inara. Her arms were incredibly sore, and she thought of asking him to let her rest them for a few moments. But she knew deep down that was not going to happen. This was a room of pain and terror.

He said nothing. He just stared at her. She could feel his eyes perusing the outlines of her body. He still said nothing as he walked over, picked up a bucket with water, and threw it on her. She gasped. It was freezing, and her clothes were drenched. Her cotton blouse and trousers clung to her body. He smiled as he moved closer. She could smell the sour wine on his breath. He still said nothing as he reached up and touched her. "Good skin," he finally said.

Now, there was fear in her eyes...

The two paratroopers returned Inara to her cell and closed the door. She sat on the floor. Her clothes were still wet, and her blouse had been ripped open. Her nipples were still burning from where the alligator clips had been attached. Her eyes were blank as if her mind was someplace else. Her body was shaking violently – half from cold, half from shock.

After a few moments alone, the cell door opened. Halim slipped inside and closed the door most of the way so he would not be seen but could still get out. "Are you okay, Inara?" he said, trying not to look at her naked body through her wet clothes.

She said nothing. "Inara?" he said again.

Still nothing. "You're freezing. I'll get you a blanket," he said and moved back toward the door.

"No," she said with her eyes pleading. "Just hold me."

Halim nodded and sat down beside her. He put his arm around her in an attempt to warm her. He was unsure where to put his hands, not wanting to offend her. She laid her head on his shoulder and closed her eyes. "I'm so sorry this happened to you, Inara," said Halim. "The French can be such bastards."

"It's not your fault, Halim. I chose my path," she said quietly. "I need you to do me a favor."

"Anything."

"I need to get a message to my uncle."

"Your uncle?"

"Yes. He and his men are hiding in the Casbah. I must warn him. They must move before it is too late."

"Did you tell the French where they are?"

"No. But I will. I know that now. It's only a matter of time until they break me. Will you do it?"

"Inara, I want to. I do. But if the French catch me, I'll be in here just like you. Maybe even worse."

"I understand. I know it is a lot to ask."

Halim considered for a moment and looked down at her face. The tears stains had been washed away. She was beautiful and pure. "Alright. I'll do it," he said with a gentle smile.

Inara was alone and asleep on the floor. Halim had brought a blanket for her before he left. Her muscles were sore, but she was warm. For that, she was grateful. She heard yelling from the hallway and cell doors opening and slamming shut.

The door to her cell opened. It was Halim. He had an orange in his hand. She smiled. She was glad to see him. "How are you feeling?" said Halim.

"Better. Thanks to you," she said.

"I thought you might like an orange for a change," he said, handing her the orange.

"Thank you," she said and kissed him on the cheek.

He blushed. "Did you get the message to my uncle?"

"I took care of everything."

"Thank you so much. May Allah bless you."

"I've got to get going. My shift starts soon. I need to take the blanket again."

"Yes. Of course. Will you come back?"

"You know, I will."

She smiled and handed him the blanket. He folded it up and opened the door. There was more commotion down the hallway. Inara looked out the doorway and caught a glimpse of her uncle being dragged into a cell by two paratroopers. "Oh my God, they caught him. They caught my uncle," she said with a gasp.

"Yes... and the bastards staying with him. Fourteen in all. It was a good catch. I'll probably get a promotion."

Everything suddenly clicked in Inara's mind like a piece finding its place within a puzzle. "You told them. You told the French," she said, tears running down her face.

"No. You told them. I just helped speed things up."

"How could you do that? You're Algerian."

"Don't be a fool, Inara. Not all Algerians want independence. My family is Harki. We fight on the side of the French. Look at everything the French have done for Algeria. We were a bunch of desert tribes fighting for wells and scraps of land before the French came. Now we have hospitals, schools, and roads. The people are crazy to want to leave France."

"What have I done?"

"It's okay, Inara. You can't go back to your family now. You betrayed them. You're one of us," said Hamil closing the door. "The French will release you soon, once you agree to spy for them. Then we can be together."

It took Inara the good part of an hour to break her wooden sloop bucket and free a wooden shard. It was long and pointed like a chisel. She knew that cutting her wrists would be useless. The guards would find her and save her. She needed a method much more immediate and definitive. The wooden shard was perfect.

She knelt and said her final prayer to Allah, asking that her death be quick. She stood up and placed the tip of the wooden shard at the base of her neck. She closed her eyes and fell forward. She fought her instincts to throw out her hands to save herself from falling on her face. The base of the shard hit the concrete floor and pushed the tip through her throat, piercing her windpipe and slicing one of her carotid arteries. She didn't feel any intense pain. It was more like confusion as the oxygen and blood were prevented from entering her brain. It was over in two minutes. She was dead.

When Hamil found her a few hours later, he cried. He liked her, maybe even loved her. Aussaresses was disappointed. He believed she had more to tell. Such a lovely young girl.

FOUR

January 23, 1958 - Paris, France

Brigitte sat in her office, staring at her typewriter. She had just finished her fourth article on the Suez Crisis and was designing the fifth article in her mind. It was hard to focus. She needed a break. *Coffee*, she thought. *Coffee is always a good idea... and a croissant with honey... another good idea.* Before she could get up to hunt for her snack, Damien entered. "Good news. De Gaulle's secretary just called. He's accepted your request for an interview."

"I have no idea what you are talking about. I never requested an interview from de Gaulle," said Brigitte.

"You didn't?"

"No. I am swamped as it is. Why would I want to start another story, especially about de Gaulle?"

"Okay... maybe I did... on your behalf."

"What? Why would you do that, Damien?"

"I heard he was a fan of your work. And like you said... you're swamped. So I thought you could use a little help."

"By piling on more work?"

"It's an interview with de Gaulle, Brigitte. The general hasn't given an interview to anyone in almost a year."

"Yeah, because he's out of politics. He retired."

"He resigned. And many people think his resignation was a mistake."

"You mean Gaullists think it was a mistake."

"It doesn't matter. He's news, especially when things are heating up down in Algiers. Did you know the paratroopers raided the Casbah?"

"I read the paper, Damien. Why do you suppose de Gaulle agreed to an interview? Do you think he's considering coming out of retirement?"

"I don't know, but I think you should find out. The interview is on Tuesday. Shall I cancel it?"

"You are really bad at bluffing, Damien. We should play poker sometime."

"So you will do the interview?"

"Yes. Tom's going to kill me."

"Trouble on the home front?"

"What home front? Between his flying and my writing, we haven't seen each other in three days."

"Well, that's not good."

"Really, Damien?"

"I should probably stay out of relationship advice, huh?"

"Good call. Have someone fetch me a coffee and croissant, will ya?"

"Fine. I'll put Ellie on it."

"You really don't know anything about relationships, do you?"

"No. I really don't," said Damien, exiting.

Colombey-les-Deux-Eglises, France

De Gaulle had chosen his study for the interview with Brigitte. It was filled with photos of the general commanding French forces and the dozens of awards he had received as president. For the interview, de Gaulle wore his uniform with medals, including his Grand-Croix of the Légion d'honneur – France's highest military award. It was impossible for Brigitte not to be impressed. "General de Gaulle, do you regret resigning your office after the formation of the Fourth Republic?" said Brigitte.

"Regret? Heavens no," said de Gaulle. "It has been one of my greatest blessings. After a lifetime of service to my country, my time is finally my own. It's been wonderful. I have time for my family. Time to write my memoirs. I even have time to read my history books. I have so many, you know?"

"But don't you miss it?"

"Miss what? The squabbling? The backbiting? The political arena is not a Sunday stroll in the park, Mademoiselle. I would rather face a brigade of tanks than a quorum of ministers. My time in government was not for me. It was for France. I don't miss it. Not at all."

"Many of the Pieds-Noirs are concerned that France is abandoning its commitment to Algeria."

"I understand how they feel. The current government can't seem to make up its mind what it wants about anything. That is the problem when you do not have a strong executive branch, as I suggested when the Fourth Republic was being formed. There is no true leader to stay the course. Just the whims of the electorate. But look... Algeria has been part of France

95

for over one hundred and fifty years. The Pieds-Noirs came to Algeria based on a promise that France would protect them. They built their businesses and raised their families in Algeria. For them, there is no other life. It is their home. We should respect that. France has benefited from their toil. Their exports bring in millions of Francs. Their wheat makes our bread. They are truly the breadbasket of France. In turn, France protects Algeria. France builds roads, harbors, and airports like a good father takes care of his child. The French need Algeria, and the Algerians need France. The French people have not forgotten Algeria even if the politicians are wavering."

"And what of the Algerian Independence movement?"

"There will always be detractors in any society. It is inevitable that we do not agree on everything. But there are also many things that we do agree upon. There is always common ground if one is willing to look."

"And the FLN?"

"In a democracy, there are ways to voice the desire for change. Revolt is not a proper forum. The FLN is deceiving the Algerian people. It is making France look like a drunken father that beats his children. But the reality is quite different. France loves Algeria as it loves itself. They are one and the same. I believe it is just a matter of time before all sides in this conflict sit down and work out a diplomatic solution that may not please all parties but will satisfy them. War is such a waste. Nobody wants it."

"And what if France needs its old general once again?"

"Of course, I will always answer the call if France needs me. I would give my life for my country. But others are much better suited for the affairs of state. You must remember... I am a general, not a politician."

Algiers, Algeria

The leaders of the FLN were limited as to how they could respond to the French raid in the Casbah. Most of their weapons had been confiscated during the random searches, and they were continually on the move to evade capture. It was difficult to even communicate with their men, let alone organize any kind of counterattack. There were able to place a few bombs here and there, but the buildings were so close together in the Casbah that it was difficult not to hurt sympathetic civilians. Now more than ever, the FLN needed the help of the Muslims living within the walls of the citadel.

Outside of the Casbah, the FLN was having more luck. Those FLN leaders not in the Casbah took over command of the Mujahideen outside the walls. They were still free to move around as long as they avoided the roving French patrols and checkpoints.

Even Saadi, still in Paris, took over the planning of the bomb attacks in Algiers and around the country. It was a big job. Well-placed bombs were always a primary point of attack for the guerilla army. He had developed a secret army of bombmakers and more of the European-looking sirens that placed his bombs in several Algerian cities. He communicated by phone using a coded language he had created from scratch and was not based on anything the French had used before. In Paris, one never knew who might be listening in on phone conversations. The revolution continued, and the Pieds-Noirs became the focus of the FLN's rage.

Algiers, Algeria

Abraham and Victor Toledano arrived in Algiers in the late afternoon after having driven the family's Mercedes Benz since early that morning. Abraham had a meeting dinner scheduled with a deputy minister of the interior to discuss the disposition of government land for reparation of the fire that destroyed his forest. Victor had other plans and went to wash the dust off the car once he dropped his father off at the government building.

Although many Jewish families were living in Algeria, Abraham had insisted the girls that his sons courted came from good Jewish families with no mixed blood. Good Jewish family meant "moneyed" in Abraham's mind, so that narrowed the list quite a bit. Victor had briefly dated a young woman, Miri Kodish, while she was visiting her cousins on a horse ranch near the Toledano estate.

After a brief but fiery triste, which included a romp in a hayloft, Miri had returned to Algiers, where she lived with her family. Victor visited her every time he and his father came to the capital. Tonight was no different. He cleaned himself up in a gas station bathroom after he hosed off his father's car. He didn't want to waste any time going back to the hotel before he picked up Miri.

They had a quick supper with Miri's family. That was required for any young man wanting to date Miri.

It was not that they rejected any of her suitors, Miri was a smart girl and had good taste in men, but traditions had to be maintained. Victor knew he was pushing it when he said that the movie they were going to see together started soon. Her father grumbled until he enquired about which movie he had selected, and Victor told him The Ten Commandments. The director was Cecil B. Demille, a practicing Jew, according to Miri's father. Victor knew he wasn't but didn't say anything. Her father was satisfied, and that was all that mattered at the moment.

Victor and Miri were whisked out the door and headed into the European quarter where the movie was playing. He parked the car across the street from the theater, bought tickets for the balcony, and ran inside with Miri just as the newsreel was about to start. Victor ran back out to the lobby and purchased some buttered popcorn, a Dr. Pepper soda, Black Jack Taffy, and a candy necklace for Miri, which he knew she liked. He sat down with Miri just as the movie was about to begin. He put the candy necklace around her neck, and she couldn't be happier. That's when the bomb went off under the seat beside her, killing them both.

The bomb had been fabricated by the FLN and placed under the seat during the newsreel by a young Algerian woman with a European-style hairdo and dress. It was meant to kill Pied-Noir and French citizens on vacation. The timer was set for ten minutes so the bomb would go off at the beginning of the movie when the theater was most crowded. The balcony was chosen for placement because it was hoped that the concrete slab would crack and fall on the patrons below. It didn't. Even without the balcony falling, the bomb served its purpose well. Twelve people were killed, and another twenty-six were seriously wounded. It was a strong statement for Algerian independence. The FLN would make the Europeans pay with their lives and the lives of their children until they left Algeria for good, hopefully taking the Pieds-Noirs with them.

Abraham was horrified when he was dropped off at his hotel and heard news of the bombing. He knew Victor and Miri were going to that particular movie. He hoped against hope that their urges for each other got the best of them, and they decided to skip the film entirely. That, of course, was not the case, and later that night, he was asked to identify the body of his son. He was shattered. He didn't know how he was going to tell his wife.

After making arrangements for his son's body to be shipped home, Abraham picked up his car and drove all night. He did not want his wife to hear the news of her son's death from anyone but him. She would need him, and he would be there for her.

As the grief welled up inside him, he pulled the car over in the desert before the foothills where he and his family lived. He was alone. He stepped out of the car and fell to his knees, and cried like he had never cried before. He yelled into the night and cursed God's name.

Algiers, Algeria

The leaders of the FLN were becoming more frustrated by the day at the paratroopers' invasion of the Casbah. They had to spend most of their time moving from one hiding place to another to keep ahead of the French house-to-house searches rather than carrying out their own attacks.

The talk in the coffee shops was one of despair and helplessness. The people of Algiers were watching their hopes of an independent Algeria vanish as the FLN members were being hunted down. Each day brought new reports of rebels being captured both in and out of the Casbah. Those that fought were killed by the well-trained and aggressive paratroopers.

Si Larbi was particularly irritated by the FLN's inability to carry out its primary mission. The people could see that they were failing and, without the people's backing, the FLN would lose its power, and its supply of new recruits would dry up. Something needed to be done to counteract the French raids and show the people that it was the FLN that was still in charge of Algiers.

Si Larbi asked for a meeting with Ramdane. It was dangerous to get together; they were two of the top FLN leaders in Algiers. If one was caught, it would have been disastrous, but if both were captured, it would have been catastrophic. But they needed a new strategy, as the current strategy clearly was not working. Ramdane accepted.

They met on the rooftop of a tannery where the leather was soaked in lye to make it more pliable. The stench was harsh and stung their eyes. While uncomfortable, this also made it an ideal place to meet in secret. French troops, even paratroopers, had little desire to search a tannery. "I say we attack a French checkpoint and break the siege," said Si Larbi. "If we can get some of our Mujahideen outside the walls of the Casbah, we would be free to carry out further attacks."

"No. The paratroopers are expecting us to make such an attempt. We are better off staying where we are and waiting them out. This can't last forever," said Ramdane. "In the meantime, our attacks in the countryside are becoming more successful. Our Mujahideen units move freely. The paratroopers cannot be two places at one."

"If we do nothing, we will lose the people. We will be forced to abandon our position in the Casbah and give up all that we have gained."

"I agree. It's a difficult situation. But we must be patient."

"Screw patience. My men are ready to attack."

"If we lose your Mujahideen, we lose the war. The leadership of the FLN will not allow that to happen."

"This is not what I signed up for."

"Actually, it is exactly what you signed up for – to obey the orders of your superiors."

"As long as my superiors are not cowards."

"You sound like a petulant child, not the leader of God's chosen army."

"You think this is what Allah wants? Cowering like frightened children from the French?"

"Look... Maybe there is something we can do that will not cost the lives of your men but will still show the people that the FLN is in charge."

"Like what?"

"A general strike. We shutdown Algiers for an entire week. The French would be powerless without the Algerians. We are the backbone of Algeria. A strike would show the world who really runs Algeria."

"Do you think we can pull that off?"

"I think the people still fear us. We get the word out that anyone not participating in the strike will be punished severely by the FLN. I think they will obey.

"I like it. Little risk, big reward. How long do you think it would take to get the word out?"

"Two, three days tops, but we need to let the media know what we are doing. It needs to be clear this is the FLN taking action."

"I agree."

January 28, 1957 – Algiers, Algeria

The word of the strike spread quickly throughout Algiers. The people were ready to strike a blow against the French. A general strike seemed like such a simple protest, but the message was powerful. The people had prepared by stockpiling food and supplies. The French citizens and European tourists had no idea what was about to happen.

On Thursday morning, as the sun rose, Algiers was silent. There was no smell of bread baking. No coffee brewing. There was no tapping of hammers or sawing of wood in the workshops. No school children skipping to their classes. The buses didn't run, and neither did the taxis. Hotel workers failed to show up, and the guests' rooms remained unkept. Even the police force, which was mostly made up of Algerians, was a no show.

The traffic snarled with no officers to direct it through intersections. Without the Algerians, Algiers didn't function, and the French could not properly govern. Only the call to prayer by the muezzin high on the minarets could be heard throughout the city.

Algiers, Algeria

Bruno and Trinquier sat in General Massu's office, offering their reports on the strike. "The Casbah is, for all practical purposes, shut down. The FLN has threatened to unleash the Mujahideen on anyone that dares to break the strike. Compliance is one hundred percent. The people stay in their homes and pray," said Bruno.

"It is the same for the majority of Algiers outside the Casbah except for a few Pied-Noir owned shops and restaurants run by families. They are exclusively in the European quarter where the Pieds-Noirs hold most of the power," said Trinquier. "Still, without the help of the Algerians for delivery, most will soon run out of goods and food to sell. My intelligence informs me that wine and flour for the bakeries will be in short supply in a matter of days."

"No wine or bread… God, help us," said Massu with a dry tone.

"The bright side is that the strike is harder on the Algerians than it is on the French and Europeans," said Bruno. "It cannot last long."

"It does not matter, Gentlemen. This strike cannot stand. We must break it now by all means necessary. Do I make myself clear?"

"Yes, General," said Trinquier.

Bruno did not respond. It annoyed Massu. "Colonel Bigeard, you have reservations?"

"I'm not sure I understand, General. The strike will collapse on its own within a few days… a week at the most. The average Algerian lives from day to day. They have no savings to buy food if they do not work. And what little food they do have on hand will be gone within the week. Their families will go hungry," said Bruno. "There is no need for violence against civilians. Let's not forget we still need their cooperation to ferret out the FLN and their Mujahideen."

"This strike is meant to make a mockery of French administration. It is illegal. The Algerians are defying the law. If we let this go unpunished, what will be next?"

"Fair enough. But perhaps violence is not the only answer."

"Really, Colonel? I am sitting here wondering if you are too soft for the task at hand."

"General Massu, I am a patriot and will obey your commands as ordered. But someday, this war will end, and when it does, France will still need to govern the Algerians. I believe that will be a much simpler process if we do not have a history of massacring them."

"Fine. What do you purpose?"

"We force them to return to work."

"... and imprison those that do not?" said Trinquier.

"Precisely," said Bruno.

"And if your plan fails?" said Massu.

"We will always have your methods as a failsafe."

"Alright. We'll try your way, Colonel Bigeard. You've got forty-eight hours to end the strike by peaceful means," said Massu. "I suggest you both get to it."

Bruno and Trinquier saluted and exited.

Algiers, Algeria

The silence of the city of Algiers was broken by the march of paratroopers' boots entering the commercial districts. Every fourth paratrooper was armed with a crowbar and bolt cutters.

Entering a square, a platoon of paratroopers broke into fire teams of four. Three paratroopers to stand guard and deal with any resistance, while the fourth paratrooper cut the locks on the roll-up doors of restaurants, coffee houses, and shops. The front door was pried open with a crowbar.

With his unit commander, a corporal, watching, a paratrooper attempted to cut the lock from a roll-up door on a boutique dress shop. The lock was too strong. "Can't cut it open, Corporal," said the paratrooper. "Lock is too thick."

"Alright, private. Move to the next one; I'll handle this one," said the corporal signaling to the driver of an armored car parked in the square.

The private moved off to the next shop with his bolt cutters and crowbar. The armored car backed up to the roll-up on the dress boutique. The corporal removed a chain with a hook on the end from the back of the armored car. He hooked the chain to the edge of the roll-up door and signaled the armored car driver to take up the slack. The armored car crept forward until the chain was taught. The corporal threw his arm down as a signal to gun the engine. The armored car lurched forward, yanking the roll-up door from one side of its wall mounts. The door hung from the wall mounts on the opposite side. The corporal repeated the process.

The owner of the shop arrived just as the armored car yanked out the remaining wall mounts dragging the door into the street. "What in the hell do you think you are doing? You have no right," said the owner.

"I have my orders," said the corporal. "If you don't like them, you can take it up with our brigade headquarters. I am sure they will give you a sympathetic ear."

"What am I supposed to do? My shop will be looted by the time I get back."

"I agree. It's quite a problem. I suppose you could open for business."

"I cannot. The Mujahideen will burn me out if I open."

"We will protect you from the rebels."

"Are you and your men going to stand guard in front of my store all night?"

"I doubt it. But we will patrol the area and shoot anyone making trouble."

"That is the French solution to everything. To shoot anyone causing a problem."

"It's quite effective. Look, you've got a choice... stay closed and let the looters take your merchandise or open for business. It's up to you."

The owner had little choice. Like most of the owners, he opened for business and hoped the Mujahideen would understand that the French had forced him to break the strike.

Squads of paratroopers searched neighborhoods and rounded up children who were forced to return to their schools. If the parents stood in the way, they were arrested and spent the night in jail before they were released. If a child was found missing when the roll was called each morning, paratroopers were dispatched to the family home, and the parents were again arrested to spend another night in jail. It was effective. The schools filled up after only a few days.

Factory and workshop owners were forced to give the paratroopers the names and addresses of all their employees. If someone did not show up for work, the paratroopers were dispatched, and the worker spent the night in jail without pay or an evening meal. Most workers only lasted one night and returned to work the next day.

After forty-eight hours, the strike broke as most Algerians returned to work and school. The restaurants were opened, and the hotel beds were made.

The FLN leadership was forced to make a decision on retaliation against the population of Algiers for disobeying their edict. If they let the Algerians go unpunished, they lost the authority to enforce their will, but if they punished the Algerians, they could lose their support or worse... turn the citizens to the French cause. They chose the former, and their hold over the citizens of Algiers was significantly reduced. The French had won the round.

FIVE

Paris, France

Saadi sat on a bench in the park across from the building where Brigitte worked. He was reading a book and enjoying his time outside. He had so little time to enjoy things nowadays. He was always plotting and planning. He glanced at his watch. It was almost time...

Brigitte exited the building with Ellie. They talked shop while Brigitte waited for a taxi.

Saadi could see that the young girl was soaking up the words of her mentor. He considered walking up and shooting them both with the pistol he carried in his coat pocket. A simple assassination would be very efficient but lacked the drama that the FLN needed to keep their cause on the front page of the newspapers and magazines. Saadi knew very well how to orchestrate such drama.

A taxi pulled up, and Brigitte climbed in. Ellie waved goodbye as the cab pulled away. Ellie walked down the street toward the nearest bus stop.

Saadi considered the pretty young woman for a moment, then followed her as if an idea had occurred to him.

Paris, France

It was early morning and cold. Coyle and his co-pilot finished the preflight checklist. Managing the startup of a C-119 was a complicated affair with the checking of lever settings, flipping of switches and coordination with the engineer who monitored the aircraft's gauges. The French Air Force did not provide a navigator on cargo flights between Algiers and Paris. It was a well-known route and considered a waste of manpower. The cargo hold was filled with supplies considered too urgent to send by ship across the Mediterranean. The small fleet of C-119s regularly ferried supplies and weapons to the troops in Algeria. The ongoing war was a ravenous beast.

Brigitte sat in the navigator's chair and wrote in her notepad. She lived by bullet points, each one a separate thought. Most reporters scribbled all over their notepads, using up every available space on a piece of paper. Brigitte was much more organized and liked to keep plenty of white space on notes so she could add to the page later if a thought occurred to her. Today, her bullet points were the various angles on the story she would write about the ceremony she and Coyle would attend – the traditional laying of the wreath on the monument of the unknown soldier in Algiers. She usually left this type of thing to other reporters. It was soft news. But this year was different.

The Prime Minister, Guy Mollet, had been making gestures toward reconciliation with the FLN. There were even rumors of secret peace talks. This infuriated the Pieds-Noirs, who saw any discussions with the rebels as treason. They feared that Mollet would negotiate away Algeria, giving more power to govern to the Algerians. The Pieds-Noirs were determined that France should remain in charge. Brigitte was sure there would be a lively protest around the monument.

"How are we doing on time?" said Coyle.

"We're fine," said Brigitte, glancing at the watch he had given her. "...Or were you just asking because you wanted me to look at my new watch?"

"A little of both. Your wrist makes it look good. Did I tell you it's from Switzerland?"

"Several times."

"The Swiss know how to make watches."

"...and hide money."

"I wouldn't know about that. I was hoping we could grab a bite to eat before the ceremony."

"That would be nice. I know of several good restaurants along the coast."

"Actually, I've already got a place picked out."

"Really?"

"Yup. Are you strapped in?"

"Snug as a bug."

"Alright. Here we go," said Coyle, checking out the side window to ensure that nobody was near the prop as he fired up the pilot-side engine.

Algiers, Algeria

The restaurant Coyle had picked out specialized in seafood and had a patio overlooking the coastline. Coyle was not big on seafood, but he knew Brigitte loved it. He wanted her in a good mood. Things had been strained between them in the last few months. They were both busy, and what little time they had together often ended up in little squabbles. Nothing earth-shattering; more the chores of living together and the little insecurities that come with any relationship.

Coyle could see Brigitte relax as she breathed in the ocean air. The Northern coast of Algeria was much like the French Riviera on the opposite side of the Mediterranean. Even in February, when most of France was cold and grey, the Algerian sun was warm, and the sky was clear except for the occasional cloud. Brigitte saw Coyle twiddling his soup spoon in his fingers. "Nervous?" she said.

"Me? No. Just hungry."

She placed her hand over his, and he gave up the spoon to intertwine their fingers. It felt good just to sit and enjoy the view. "I often forget that this is what life is supposed to be," she said.

"Yeah. Life gets in the way of moments like these."

"I would love to live by the sea."

"Me too. Maybe we could look into it after we…"

"After we what?"

"Nothing. I don't imagine Damien would appreciate you being out of Paris too long unless you are on assignment."

"No. He probably won't."

"Do you ever see yourself giving up journalism and maybe trying something else?"

"Like what?"

"Oh, I don't know… maybe raising a family?"

"Children?"

"Well, yeah… I mean, a few kids would be nice."

She smiled and said, "Of course, I think about it. How could one not? I am a woman. But I love my work too."

"I know. But maybe you could replace it with something more important."

"More important?"

"I didn't mean more important. Your work is obviously very important. It's just that…"

"Just what?"

"It consumes you. You give everything to your writing."

"Everything?"

"Almost everything. I know that is why you are so good at it. You need to focus on your career if you are ever going to make something of yourself."

"I think I have already made something of myself."

"Yeah. That's my point. I mean… where do you go from here? How do you top jumping out of a plane with a bunch of paratroopers? How do you top reporting on war?"

"You don't. That's why I do it. It is the ultimate."

"So what about a family? Could that replace it?"

"Honestly… I doubt it."

"Yeah, but even this war will end. Then what?"

"I wait until the next one."

"That's kind of sad… that there will be a next one… war, I mean."

"Yes, but it is a reality. It seems there is always a war to fight."

"That seems wrong."

"Perhaps. I think that is why my writing is so important. The people must understand what France sacrifices when we go to war. I bring attention to that."

"What about writing your memoirs? You've certainly led an exciting life."

"Memoirs are for the old and grey. I still have plenty of life to live. I'm not ready to be put out to pasture."

"I wasn't saying that. We were talking about family."

"No. You were talking about family."

"Well, somebody had to."

"Why? What is wrong with the way things are? We are in love. What's wrong with that?"

"Nothing. It's great. I suppose I just think about how beautiful our children would be."

"Yes. They would be beautiful. And I want children, Tom. I really do, but when the time is right."

"And when might that be?"

"I don't know. Not now. I'm not ready."

"We're not getting any younger, Brigitte."

"You mean I am not getting any younger?"

"I didn't say that. But I think we both know there is only a window of opportunity for you to have children."

"Relax, Tom. I assure you... I still have time."

"I know you do. I just don't want work to get in the way of what is important."

"You mean important to you?"

"Important to us."

"I wasn't intending on planning out my entire life this morning."

"Neither was I. I just think about the future. About us."

"I do too. But, Tom... we have time."

"Do we?"

"Maybe we should change the subject?"

"Maybe we should."

There was silence. Neither wanted to talk. They stared out at the ocean with thoughts boiling in their minds. Every subject of conversation seemly trite. Coyle glanced at his watch and looked a bit uneasy.

"What's wrong?" said Brigitte. "I thought we were spending the morning together."

"We are. We're here, aren't we?"

"Yes. And it's lovely," said Brigitte, softening. "You know what I like."

Coyle smiled. "Thanks. I try."

"Yes. That's what I love that about you… that you try."

"How could I not? My girlfriend is the beautiful and famous Brigitte Friang."

"Yes, she is. And don't forget that… even when I am old and grey."

They laughed. Something caught Coyle's eye at the edge of the patio. "There's something I probably should have told you…"

"What's that, Darling?"

"I invited Bruno to join us."

Brigitte's eyes flared in anger. She turned around to see what Coyle was staring at… It was Bruno standing at the entrance to the patio, searching the crowd. "You didn't."

"Yeah, I did," said Coyle raising his hand so Bruno could find them.

"Why would you do that?"

"You guys are such great friends. I know how much you mean to each other. This argument you have been having… it's not worth it. I'm sure of it. You should talk."

"You should keep your nose out of other people's business."

"What are you talking about? You're not other people. You're my girlfriend. I love you."

"Well, you have a horrible way of showing it," said Brigitte rising from the table as Bruno approached. "I'll find my own way back to Paris."

Brigitte walked past Bruno without saying a word or even making eye contact. Bruno look confused and looked at Coyle. Coyle just shrugged as Bruno came to the table. "I thought she had forgotten about the argument," said Bruno.

"Obviously not," said Coyle.

"So, what happened?"

"I may have exaggerated the whole – she's over it thing."

"Oh, Coyle. This is bad. You should know her better than that."

"Yeah, I should. But I don't. Brigitte is not the most open woman."

"Yes, but that is what makes her so great. She carries her own water."

"Carries her own water?"

"Yes, yes. She doesn't burden others with her problems. She handles them herself."

"So basically, you are saying she doesn't need a man."

"Well… not for solving problems. There are other things that a man can do."

"You don't need to make a list. I am well aware of what I can do for her."

"I'm just trying to help."

"Yeah, well… as you can see, it's not a good day to help. I hope you like swordfish."

"It's okay."

"Good cause that's what you're eating for lunch."

Bruno sat down where Brigitte had been seated. He looked at the glass of white wine Brigitte had been drinking. There was lipstick on the rim. He rotated the glass to avoid the lipstick and took a sip. "Not bad," said Bruno tearing off a piece of bread, making himself at home. "She always did have good taste in wine."

Coyle just sad silent, wondering where he went wrong.

The square in front of the monument was crowded with tens of thousands of Pied-Noir protestors and Algerian nationalists, shouting at each other angrily and waving placards. Both sides were passionate in their cause – the Algerians seeking freedom, the Pieds-Noirs seeking the status quo.

Achiary was at the front of the largest group of Pieds-Noirs. He had placed his gang of Ultras throughout the square to whip up the Pieds-Noirs. He wanted as much confrontation as possible from the protest. The more violent, the better. The Pieds-Noirs were slowly losing the attention of the media as the war droned on. He needed the front page to drum up support from the electorate and keep the French politicians from submitting to the will of the native Algerians. Algeria must remain part of France if the Pieds-Noirs were to survive.

Brigitte rode in the backseat of a taxi driven by an Algerian. She was thankful she had left the restaurant early, even though it was because of another disagreement with Coyle. Men can be so dense, she thought. Some things can't be fixed. She had work to do and was in no mood for drama, especially with Bruno in the mix.

A large group of Pieds-Noirs on foot walking toward the square spilled off the sidewalk and into the street, blocking the taxi. The taxi driver was agitated and honked his horn to clear the way. An angry Pied-Noir turned, slammed his fists on the hood of the cab, and shouted a string of curses at the driver. Brigitte could see the anger in the man's face. It was beyond reason. After venting his frustration, the man moved to catch up with his group.

The taxi driver refused to go any further. Brigitte protested and even offered to pay him extra. He was adamant. Resigned, she opened her purse to pay the fare. He refused to take any money since he had not completed the journey. She could see that he was embarrassed by his cowardice. She nodded agreement and got out. Not wanting to drive any closer to the protest, the driver turned his taxi around the narrow one-way street and drove back in the wrong direction. Brigitte continued toward the square at the end of the street. She was cautious but moved quickly.

Entering the square, she could see that the protest was much larger than she had imagined. It was, after all, just another photo opportunity for the Prime Minister to show he cared about Algeria. It was to be a gesture of reconciliation. She knew from a series of interviews she had done that the Pieds-Noirs saw it as capitulation. The Pied-Noir leaders feared that France was sliding down a slippery slope. While Algeria was smaller in population than France, the Pieds-Noirs were the largest voting bloc in their country and united in their cause. Their vote could make or break a bill before parliament and carried an inordinate amount of sway. They only cared about one issue – that Algeria remained part of France. This, too, gave them power. They were willing to support the issues of any politician that supported their core concern.

The nine million native Algerians that occupied most of the country were not French citizens, even though their land was considered part of France. This inequality was a significant cause of tension between the two sides. The only real voice the Algerians were allowed was to protest, and when that didn't work... to strike. The native Algerians were the backbone of Algeria's workforce. When they struck, the country ground to a halt and exports stopped producing much-needed tax revenues. Crops weren't harvested. Lumber wasn't milled. Mines produced no ore. The seaside hotels that the Europeans loved so much emptied for lack of service. It was economic suicide, but it was effective, and the French took note.

The crowd in the square was still mixed with pockets from each side. As the temperament grew more heated, the protestors shifted to separate into sides. This made the demonstration even more dangerous as each side grew in mass and their voices united. Protestors moving through the crowd to reach their side were pushed and shoved by the opposition. Fists flew. Placards were used as clubs. It was like running the gauntlet.

Brigitte wanted to get a good view of the Prime Minister as he laid down the wreath. Hopefully, she could snap a few photos from the camera Damien had given her. She wasn't a great photographer when it came to composition, but she felt she could capture the feeling of the moment. The technical aspect of photography was easy for her, and her photos were rarely out of focus or exposed wrongly. Damien had offered to send a photographer with her, but she refused. It was just one more thing to keep track of while trying to capture the story. She worked better alone.

Studying the mob, Brigitte figured she was safer on the side of the Pieds-Noirs since her skin was fair. Nobody cared to ask about one's politics that day. Color determined which side a person belonged to. She moved along the edge of the square. Skirmishes broke out as the crowd continued to divide. Anyone unlucky enough to be on the wrong side was beaten. She reached the edge of the main body of Pieds-Noirs.

She needed to cross the square to reach the monument. She waded into the horde of irate men. She could feel the anger in the crowd and began to wonder if moving through it was such a good idea. She was small in stature compared to the men around her. They weren't watching where they were stepping as they moved back and forth. Her feet were stepped on several times by men weighing twice as much as her. For once, her slender figure was a disadvantage. She couldn't see beyond their shoulders and heads. She seemed powerless as she tried to push her way through the throng. She felt lost, with no way out.

After lunch, Bruno and Coyle took a taxi to the location of the ceremony, where Coyle hoped to find Brigitte and apologize. He still wasn't sure what he had done wrong, but he knew it really didn't matter. Brigitte would make sure he understood what he had done and promise to never do it again. He was feeling very emasculated. He didn't like it.

It wasn't that he was too proud to admit he was wrong. It was that he felt like he was wrong all the time lately. He felt like he was losing his confidence. He knew that his self-confidence was one of the things that Brigitte loved about him, but it seemed like she went out of her way to point out what he was doing wrong and rarely complimented him anymore. The more he tried to make things right between them, the more it felt like she was going out of her way to find things that were wrong. He knew she still loved him; otherwise, why did she stay with him? Brigitte was not the type of woman that would let sentiment get in the way of what she wanted. He was sure of that. He knew he could fix their relationship. He just didn't know how.

Bruno and Coyle were both surprised by the size of the protest in the square as they stepped from their taxi.

"Merde," said Bruno.

"Yeah. Double merde," said Coyle.

The cursing and shouting between the two factions grew in volume as the sides coalesced. The more they united, the more enraged they became. They whipped each other up, pushing their angry rhetoric toward the opposition further and further. "Brigitte is in there someplace," said Coyle, worried. "We've got to find her now."

"We need higher ground," said Bruno looking around."

They moved to a nearby lamp post. Bruno shimmed up and looked out on the crowd. "Do you see her?" said Coyle.

"Not yet. It's mostly men. They're taller than her," said Bruno.

"She'll probably be heading toward the monument. Look for a gap in the crowd. That's probably her."

"Yes, yes. I'm looking. I don't see anything."

Brigitte wanted to reach the opposite side of the street. She was forced to move as the crowd moved like being caught in a series of waves in the middle of the ocean. It took all her strength to keep from falling as men pushed and shoved. She had no choice but to ride it out.

A column of police holding shields and long hickory batons quick-stepped into the square to separate the two sides of the crowd. The protestors' anger turned against the police.

This was the opportunity Achiary was looking for. The press might not care about a confrontation between the protestors. That happened whenever there was a demonstration, and many editors considered it old news. But an assault against French authority such as the police force was sure to make headlines.

Achiary used hand signals to direct his Ultras to confront the police line. He had instructed them on what to do. The Ultras advanced toward the police, shouting and cursing, pushing against police shields, setting an example for the other protestors, stirring them into a violent frenzy.

Achiary signaled a truck driver parked at the edge of the square. The driver released the tailgate and tipped his truck bed, filled with rocks and broken bricks. The load spilled out of the back of the truck bed onto the street. The protestors grabbed greedily from the pile of rubble and moved toward the police line.

Skirmishes between police and protestors broke out as some of the demonstrators tried to break through the line. Police officers used their batons to beat anyone who attacked them. Bones were broken. Skulls were cracked. Blood flowed. The police were vastly outnumbered, and the line they formed was two-sided, making their numbers appear even smaller.

Unable to break the police line, the Algerians threw overripe tomatoes at the Pieds-Noirs. The Pieds-Noirs retaliated by throwing back rocks, broken bricks and pieces of paving stones dug up from the street. The Algerians raided trash bins and crates of empty soda bottles in nearby alleyways. Bottles, garbage, and rocks flew back and forth across the police line, occasionally hitting one or more of the police officers.

Bruno continued to search the crowd for Brigitte. It was an impossible task as the numbers of protestors swelled to over one hundred thousand. The violence on both sides of the line was growing in ferocity. More objects flew through the air.

An Algerian man knelt down and used a well-worn bow to launch flaming arrows into the air. Several Pieds-Noirs were struck by the arrows, and their clothes caught fire. It was difficult for the police to see where the arrows originated since the archer was below the heads and shoulders of the men around him. The arrows just magically appeared out of the Algerian side as they sailed over the police line to land on the opposite side. Once the archer had launched three or four arrows, he would pick up the bow and move to another part of the crowd. He kept one step ahead of the police.

Just as things looked like they couldn't get any worse, the Prime Minister's motorcade drove into the square.

"Ah, balls," said Bruno.

"What is it? What do you see?" said Coyle, anxious.
"The Prime Minister's motorcade just entered the square."
"That can't be good."
"No. It won't be."

The police moved their line to make an opening through the Pied-Noir side of the crowd as the motorcade pulled to a stop. The Pied-Noir mob roared in anger. The Algerians cheered and chanted slogans of support as the Prime Minister emerged from his limousine.

The Prime Minister's security team used their shields to form a protective turtle around the Prime Minister like the Roman legions of old. They moved into the crowd in unison with shields on the side and above, the Prime Minister walking in the center. They had practiced many times for such an occasion and moved as a well-trained unit.

The Pieds-Noirs threw rocks and bottles at the shields as the Prime Minister and security team advanced toward the monument. The Algerian threw tomatoes and garbage at the Pieds-Noirs to avert their attention away from the Prime Minister.

With the police line weakened, the Algerians and the Pieds-Noirs pushed towards each other, neither backing down. Many had wooden clubs. Others had knives, clawed hammers and small hatchets.

An Algerian reached over the police line and grabbed a Pied-Noir by the shirt collar, trying to pull him over to the Algerian side. The Pied-Noir pulled out a knife and sliced the Algerian's hand. The Algerian let go of the shirt and pulled his bloody hand back over the line.

Brigitte realized that things were quickly spiraling out of control. She was in the middle of a sea of frustration and anger. She could see herself tripping or losing her balance, falling to the street and being trampled by the mob. She had to find a way out. "Come on, Brig. You've been in much worse situations. Time to suck it up and get moving," said Brigitte to herself, beating down her fear as she had done many times during battle.

She was determined not to be pushed around anymore and find a way out. She pushed up on her tippy toes and looked out the best she could over the heads of the men around her. She saw the top of the monument. The crowd was moving in the wrong direction. She turned toward the memorial. She pushed and shoved, trying to make a way through the wall of men, but the crowd was too compressed. The men lunged forward, almost knocking her to the ground. It only made her more determined. She started stomping men's feet with the heels of her shoes. One man went down, grabbing his foot in pain. She used the side of her shoe to scrape down another man's shin. He, too, collapsed down, grabbing his shin. Several more men tripped over the two men on the ground and fell. Brigitte stepped over them all and continued her stomping and scraping campaign.

At the top of the lamp post at the edge of the crowd, Bruno spotted a gap opening up in the sea of heads and said. "I think I may have spotted her."

"Where?" said Coyle.

"Two o'clock, about two hundred yards."

"Keep your eyes on her. Don't lose her. I'll go into the crowd. You guide me."

"Are you sure that's a good idea?"

"No," said Coyle as he moved into the crowd.

Coyle kept pushing and shoving his way through the mass, looking back at Bruno's hand signals for direction and distance.

Brigitte was still making headway, but slowly. She hadn't realized the strength required to break a man's toes. Boots were especially tough. She kept at it. More men fell like toppled trees from a lumberjack's ax. As soon as a man fell, Brigitte used his body as a stepping stone. Foot by foot, she made her way toward the monument.

An empty soda bottle flew through the air and smacked Coyle on the side of the head. It didn't break, but he staggered from the impact.

Bruno saw that Coyle was in trouble. He jumped down from the lamp post and ran into the crowd. Anyone that stood in his way received a punch in the gut or a cuff on the chin. Bruno was strong and did not tire as a normal man might. His fists were merciless, his blows powerful. It didn't take him long to reach Coyle. "Are you alright?" said Bruno.

"Yeah. Just a little dazed," said Coyle rubbing the side of his head.

"Follow me. I've got a good idea where she is at. Stay close."

"Don't worry about me. Just find Brigitte. I'll be right behind you."

Bruno continued to fight his way through the crowd. Men much larger than him fell by the wayside. A few tried to fight back, throwing punches. Bruno could take a punch. Pain just made him more determined and focused. He fought back using his legs to trip his opponents, throwing them to the ground. Coyle stayed right behind him. They kept moving forward.

Brigitte was exhausted. She had stomped so many feet, she could barely lift her legs. She was unsure where she was at. The wall of men closed in on her. The mob lunged. She tripped and fell. She tried to climb back up to her feet, but she didn't have the strength. She curled up in a ball and wrapped her arms around her head to prevent it from being kicked or stepped on. It was the only thing she could do. She was helpless.

Just as she about to give up hope, Bruno burst through the wall of men around her. "Brigitte?" said Bruno looking down at the ball of a woman on the ground.

"Oh, thank God, Bruno," she said, reaching up to his face. "I'm so sorry."

"Let's get you up and out of here."

Coyle burst through the opening Bruno had created and saw Brigitte wrapping her arms around Bruno. Hugging as if her life depended on him. Kissing him on the cheek. "Brigitte, are you okay?" said Coyle.

"Yes, yes. I just need to get some air. I can barely breathe."

"It's alright. We'll get you out of here. Bruno, lift her up on my back. I'll carry her. You make a hole."

Bruno used his elbows to make more room, thrashing against the men around them. They moved.

He lifted Brigitte up and put her on Coyle's back. He turned back the way they came. "No," said Brigitte. "Move toward the monument. It's closer."

Bruno nodded and changed direction. He punched and kicked his way through the crowd. Coyle and Brigitte followed close behind, tussled as the mob moved back to seal the hole.

Their little convoy made it to the monument just as the Prime Minister and his security team arrived. He looked panicked and confused as one of his advisors handed him the wreath. Brigitte reached into her purse, pulled out the camera and shot a perfectly focused photo of the Prime Minister holding the wreath with the enraged crowd around him shaking their fists and screaming profanities. It made the front page of her magazine.

Algiers, Algeria

Brigitte, Coyle, and Bruno sat in a café along the Mediterranean. Coyle had a towel with ice in it pressed against his head where the bottle had hit him. Bruno was soaking both his hands in a champagne bucket filled with ice water. His knuckles were raw from throwing punches.

Brigitte wolfed down a plate of soft cheese with bread. She seemed overly animated for a woman that was almost crushed to death. She talked fast, jumping from one subject to the next, "I am sorry for being such a grouch lately. I don't know what has gotten into me. I think it's my workload. I'm still writing my articles from the Suez Crisis, and Damien has me running all over the country covering stories. I don't understand why he can't use someone else. This is political coverage. I'm a war correspondent. I should be in Algeria with you guys. This is where the action is at. I mean, think about it. We could go to dinner together. Drink wine every night if we want. And the sun. It's so beautiful down here. God knows I could use some work on my tan."

Bruno and Coyle exchanged a look like maybe she had gone off the deep end. "It's so good to be friends again, don't you think?" she said, not waiting for a reply. "We're like the Three Musketeers. All for one and one for all."

Paris, France

Guy Mollet was not happy as he read Brigitte's article on the riot in Algiers. His photograph on the front cover was especially humiliating. The whole debacle made him look like a fool, and he knew he would pay the price at the upcoming election. The Prime Minister of France was made or unmade on the streets of Algiers.

He had underestimated the Pieds-Noirs' determination and swore to himself that he would not make the same mistake twice. To stay in power, he needed to end the war quickly. His first move was to replace the current Governor General of Algeria with Robert Lacoste. He authorized Lacoste to use all means necessary to re-establish order in Algiers and the countryside.

Algiers, Algeria

Robert Lacoste was a seasoned politician and a warrior. He had fought with the French Resistance during the Nazi occupation in World War II. He was a socialist who knew how to get things done. Lacoste was familiar with the Algerian problem and went to work immediately on arriving in Algiers.

His approach to the war was to use both carrot and stick. He realized that Algerians would never be happy under French rule unless they were adequately represented in the government. He devised a program to Algerianize his administration. This was the carrot. He surmised that it would be difficult for the native Algerians to complain if they were being ruled by their own officials. He also knew that the Pieds-Noirs would object to this program and do their best to see it undermined. He needed to work quickly.

In addition to reorganizing his government to be more inclusive, Lacoste created new social programs designed to make life easier for many of the Algerians, including more hospitals and schools. He also beefed up the civil rights of Algerians by making the laws more equal and selecting more of the lower court judges from Algerians.

The stick part of his plan was to use Algerians to fight Algerians. Not all Algerians wanted independence from France. In fact, a large portion of Algerians liked the improvements the French had made in their country. The trains and buses ran on time and didn't break down. There were schools and universities for their children. There were hospitals and clinics with well-trained doctors and nurses. Things ran smoothly under French law and order. Inter-tribal conflicts were not tolerated under the French, and while the native Algerians were second class citizens, at least they were treated equally among themselves. This was seen as a significant improvement over many other North African countries.

Lacoste authorized the recruitment of one hundred and fifty thousand Harkis – native Algerians that fought for the French. In truth, most Harkis did not care much for politics. What they cared about was money to feed their families. The French paid well. This made them loyal. The fact that they were occasionally allowed to rape and pillage native settlements in the countryside was a bonus. The French authorities could be counted on to turn a blind eye to their ruthless behavior as long as they produced results, and no French citizens were harmed. The program worked, and the number of raids on French facilities and outposts went down.

The Harkis were especially good at infiltrating the Mujahideen camps and gathering intelligence. After all, they were native Algerians that spoke the language, dressed the same as the Mujahideen and could mingle in with the other fighters without being noticed. Many Harkis had family and friend connections that would vouch for them as they attempted to enter the Mujahideen ranks. The Harki spies would tip off the French commanders when Mujahideen raids were planned. The French would organize ambushes. The French often had trouble discerning who was Harki and who was Mujahideen. They had a bad tendency to shoot first and ask questions later.

The Harkis were not beyond using their new positions to settle blood feuds that went back decades. During raids on villages supporting the rebels, old adversaries of the Harkis were hunted down and shot to settle a score. While French commanders did not encourage this kind of activity, they did little to stop it, as long as the Harkis continued to be useful.

Ten of thousands of Algerians sympathetic to the rebels were rounded up and relocated to internment camps near the big cities and French military bases, where they could be watched more easily. Entire villages were moved from the countryside and detained in barbed-wire compounds until the end of the war. The French did their best to keep families together, but it wasn't always possible. Many Algerian children ended up in orphanages. It was part of a pacification program to deny the rebels the support they so desperately needed to continue their fight.

Being a Harki meant that your family and property were protected by the French. It also said you were a target of the Mujahideen and FLN. Many Algerian families would have one member join the Harkis while another joined the Mujahideen or FLN. The crossing of alliances ensured the family's survival no matter who eventually won the war. The French found that keeping a Harki in the area where they grew up and had contacts was the most productive. This meant that brothers and cousins would often fight each other during battles and then celebrate with each other when they returned home for holidays or weddings.

The Harkis were often used for false-flag operations when the French wanted to convince the locals that the threat of the Mujahideen was real, and they should help the French army stop them. If the village elders refused to help the French, the French would send in the Harkis disguised as the Mujahideen to raid the village.

If a particular village elder had been adamant about staying neutral in the growing conflict, he was targeted for assassination by the Harkis during the raid. The French would arrive and drive the Harkis off by firing their weapons over the Harkis' heads. It was a well-choreographed and effective charade. Every village raided by the Harkis joined the French struggle against the Mujahideen.

While most of the Harkis were from the countryside, many were city dwellers. There was a large Harki force used by the French paratroopers to penetrate the FLN in Algiers. Unlike the Mujahideen commanders who would accept almost any Arab with a rifle and a will to fight the French, the leadership of the FLN was much more wary of outsiders. Volunteers needed to prove themselves loyal and were often required to kill a Frenchman before they were accepted into the FLN ranks. These requirements were slackened as the FLN members were hunted down by the French paratroopers and infiltrated by the Harkis.

Paris, France

Coyle picked up and examined his flight manifest from the transportation office at the airfield. He was surprised by what he saw on the cargo schedule and said, "Mines?"

"What's so unusual about carrying mines?" said the sergeant.

"Nothing. But an entire shipment of them? That's a lot of mines."

"Yeah. Well... you're gonna be making a lot of supply runs over the next few months. The engineers

133

are building two defensive lines on the Tunisian and Moroccan borders. Over twelve hundred miles of high-voltage electric fence and two million mines. It's supposed to stop the Mujahideen from reinforcing their troops by cutting off their training camps in bordering countries. They're calling it the Morice Line after the defense minister."

"Can't the Mujahideen just go around like the Germans did with the Maginot Line?"

"I don't know. Strategy is above my pay grade. I just ship the stuff."

"Why don't they ship this stuff by boat instead of using aircraft in short supply?"

"In a hurry, I guess."

"You French sure like building things."

"It keeps us busy."

Coyle shrugged and left the office. He walked down the tarmac to his C-119. The cargo crew was busy loading stacked crates filled with mines in the aircraft's hold. "Make damn sure that stuff's tied down good," said Coyle to his cargo boss.

"Will do, sir," said the cargo boss.

Coyle would do his own inspection once they were done loading. He wanted to give his crew the chance to do it right, then he showed them if they did it wrong. But he wasn't going to take any chances either. This was the type of cargo that could kill you if it shifted in flight.

Border, Algeria, and Tunisia

A well-protected convoy of military trucks pulled to stop at the border between Algeria and Tunisia. The crates of mines were unloaded and immediately put to use.

An eight-foot fence made from long strands of electrical wire pulled taut between insulated posts extended for as far as the eye could see. The Harki work crews were heavily defended as they dug shallow holes and placed the layers of mines stretching forty-five feet on either side of the fence.

Once correctly placed and packed tight with dirt around the edges, an engineer would activate the mine by carefully unscrewing the arming cap. He would gently bury the rest of the mine and its pressure switch with loose dirt and sand until no longer visible.

This mind-numbing procedure continued day after day, week after week, month after month until the Morice Line was finished. Occasionally at night, the crews and engineers would hear one of the mines explode, or the lights in the camp would flicker from a nearby voltage fluctuation. They would smile and crack jokes - one less Mujahideen to worry about.

SIX

February 15, 1957 – Paris, France

A city bus drove down a tree-lined boulevard in a neighborhood of three-story apartment buildings. Most of the buildings in Paris were low-rise. Parisians disliked tall buildings that blocked out the sun in the winter months and stifled the cool breezes in the hot summers. For decades there had been a moratorium on new construction over one hundred and twenty-one feet in height. It gave a city the size of Paris a small-town feeling and created great views of the Eifel Tower, the city's tallest structure, from most rooftop gardens.

Samiah sat in the back of a bus where she could observe both doors as passengers got on and off. The bus slowed for the next stop and pulled to the curb. Several people got on, including Ellie, who was on her way to work. She sat across the aisle from Samiah. Samiah studied Ellie's face and makeup. Her skin was very fair and flawless. Her hair was neatly brushed. She was beautiful. Samiah took note of Ellie's tight sweater that accentuated her breasts and slender waist. Normally it would have been a sin to notice such things, but Saadi had explained that learning how to look and act European was part of Samiah's education.

The bus continued down the boulevard for several more blocks. Saadi sat at a bus stop and waited. The bus arrived. Samiah climbed off and sat next to Saadi without saying a word. He could see Ellie sitting in her usual seat by the window. As the bus pulled away from the curb, Saadi glanced at this watch. He scribbled the time in a notebook below a column of similar time notations for the same bus. They rose together and walked off. This was the fourth time they had practiced a run through. The timing was critical.

Samiah waited near the front counter of a neighborhood store as Saadi picked up a loaf of fresh bread, a bottle of olives, a can of coffee and some cheese. As he approached the cash register, Samiah asked Saadi for a chocolate bar. He refused.

Seeing her disappointment, he explained that he didn't want her to get fat. Her attractiveness was part of her disguise, especially when it came to disarming men or nosey police officers. The cause had spent a great deal of money buying European style clothes, shoes, jewelry, and makeup for her. The least she could do was give up her precious chocolate bar. She felt embarrassed that she had even asked.

Upon entering Saadi's apartment, Saadi walked into the back bedroom while Samiah went to the kitchen with the groceries. She placed the coffee in the cupboard and made a plate of bread slices, cheese, and olives. She walked to the back bedroom with the plate of food, knocked lightly, and entered.

Saadi was busy, sitting at a table, soldering two wires together attached to a timing mechanism. A package of plastic explosives had already been assembled and placed inside an empty tin of biscuits.

Samiah moved to set the plate of food down on the table. Saadi's eyes flashed with anger. Samiah withdrew the plate and set it on a nearby nightstand. She had been warned not to touch or place anything on his work table. Saadi considered beating her as a reminder, but there was work to be done. She was a smart girl but often forgot the simplest things. That was dangerous in their line of work. He would talk to her about it later.

Paris, France

Samiah rode on the bus with a shopping bag in her lap. Inside the bag was the biscuit tin that hid the bomb. The bus was filling up with passengers quickly. She was concerned that Ellie's seat would be taken or worse, someone would sit next to her, and she would be unable to activate the timer on the bomb without being seen. There were only a few stops more before Ellie's stop. There was little Samiah could do to control the situation. Allah would be angry if she didn't complete her task. Saadi would be furious.

The bus stopped, and several more passengers stepped on. A young man moved to the back of the bus where Samiah was sitting. She placed the bag on the seat next to her, ensuring that the man would not sit there. Instead, he moved to sit where Ellie usually sat. "Excuse, please," said Samiah. "My friend will sit there."

The young man, irate, looked over at Samiah. She smiled and batted her long eyelashes twice. He smiled back and said, "Of course. I can find someplace else... especially if your friend is as cute as you." She faked a blush. He moved forward and sat next to another passenger.

Saadi sat on the park bench across from Brigitte's workplace, reading the same book as before. It was poetry by his favorite Islamic author. He glanced at his watch. It was time.

Brigitte and Ellie exited the building. Ellie treasured her time with Brigitte. She was a fountain of knowledge and told the greatest stories of her travels. Ellie especially liked it when Brigitte talked about the paratroopers. Ellie was disappointed when her bus arrived before Brigitte could hail a taxi. She considered waiting for the next bus so she could talk with Brigitte. As the bus passed, a taxi behind it pulled over. Ellie quickly said her goodbyes and ran for her bus pulling to the curb in front of the bus stop. Brigitte climbed into her taxi.

As the taxi hung a U-turn and headed in the opposite direction toward Brigitte's apartment, she looked over at the man sitting on the bench reading a book. The man lowered the book revealing more of his face. Brigitte knew that face – it was the man from the police sketch, it was the man that had tried to kill her and Coyle.

Saadi did not try to hide his face from Brigitte. He wanted her to know who had killed her young protégé. He smiled as Brigitte drove away in the taxi and Ellie stepped onto the bus. Saadi knew that he and Brigitte would meet again soon enough, after the explosion when she went to investigate the murder of her co-worker. Saadi would be waiting. She would not escape. Tragedy would be piled on tragedy. The media would devour the story. Everyone would know that the FLN bombed the bus and killed Brigitte Friang.

Brigitte's mind raced. What is he doing here? She thought. What was he planning? She looked back to ensure he wasn't following her. He wasn't. She watched as he rose from the bench and walked down the street in the opposite direction, the same direction as the bus Ellie was on. Brigitte tried to put together the pieces of what was happening. What was his target? The office building where she worked? Maybe a nearby restaurant or boutique? She was unsure of everything. He is a bomber. He likes to make big statements. There was no logic. No connection. Then it hit her… Ellie. The man had seen them together. She was on a public bus. She still wasn't sure. Some of the pieces fit, some did not. It didn't matter. There was no time. "Turn the car around," she said to the driver.

The driver shrugged and obeyed her request. Passengers often changed their destinations. "I'll triple your fare if you can catch up with that bus," said Brigitte, pointing.

The driver gunned the taxi's engine. The car lunged forward. Brigitte was thrown back in her seat.

Saadi saw Brigitte in the window of the taxi as it sped past him. His expression darkened. He looked at the bus in the distance, then down at his watch. He calculated coldly. Was there enough time for her to warn the people on the bus? It was going to be close. But Brigitte might also die in the blast. It could look like an accident. She just happened to be there when the bomb went off. That wasn't what he planned. It wasn't what he wanted. He ran down the sidewalk toward the bus.

Ellie sat in her usual seat across from Samiah. She had noticed the shy girl riding next to her several times but said nothing. Ellie saw the shopping bag on the seat next to Samiah. "Buy something good?" said Ellie.

"Sweets for my boyfriend," said Samiah placing the bag back on her lap.

"Boyfriend. Must be nice."

"It is. He is very handsome and cares for me deeply."

"Sounds like a prince. Does he have a brother?"

The taxi caught up with the bus. "Honk your horn and pull up alongside," said Brigitte rolling down the back window.

"Is everything okay?" said the driver concerned.

"No. It's not. We need to stop that bus."

"Why?"

"There's a bomb on board."

"A bomb?!"

The driver slammed on the brakes. The taxi skidded to a halt. "What the hell are you doing?" said Brigitte. "People are going to die if we don't stop that bus."

"I'm no hero."

"Obviously not."

"I'm sorry. I have a family," said the driver as he jumped from the taxi. Brigitte sprang out of the backseat and climbed into the abandoned seat behind the wheel. She threw the car in gear and floored it. The cab sped after the bus. She pressed on the horn and held it down.

The driver of the bus looked in his side mirror at the taxi coming alongside his bus honking its horn. "What the hell?" he said, ignoring the crazy woman behind the wheel.

Ellie and Samiah heard the taxi's horn. The cab was on Samiah's side of the bus. She looked out and saw Brigitte trying to wave the bus down. "What is it?" said Ellie, unable to see.

"I think someone is getting married," said Samiah stalling for time.

Ellie was suspicious and moved across the aisle to look out the window. She saw Brigitte holding up her notepad with the word "BOMB" scribbled in big letters. Ellie's eyes went wide. She turned to Samiah, "There's a bomb on the bus. We've got to get off."

Ellie ran up the aisle, screaming at the driver, "Stop the bus. There's a bomb on board!"

The driver hit the brakes, slowing the bus and pulling to the curb.

Brigitte could see the bus slowing down and shouted, "That a girl, Ellie."

Samiah saw Saadi's plan unraveling. She loved Saadi and could not stand to fail him. She said a quick prayer to Allah as she opened the lid on the biscuit tin. She reset the timer to zero.

The bus stopped, and the driver opened the doors. Ellie moved into the closest doorway.

Samiah flipped the activation switch. The bomb went off. She died instantly.

Brigitte watched in horror as the bus's windows shattered outward and the sheet metal side panels were ripped apart by the explosion. The shockwave hit the taxi. Brigitte's experience in a war zone kicked in. She turned away as the windows exploded, sending glass shards toward her. The taxi tumbled across the street onto the opposite sidewalk, where it landed on its side.

Brigitte was knocked unconscious for a few moments. She woke and gasped for air. She could feel the blood trickling down her neck from the cuts on the back of her head. She put her hand on the back of her head to gauge how serious the wounds were. There was a lot of blood, but it wasn't life-threatening. She turned herself around, stood up, and pulled herself out of the broken side window and onto the sidewalk.

A woman on the sidewalk ran to help her. A gunshot rang out, and the woman fell face-first on the concrete. Behind the woman at a distance was a man standing with a pistol in his hand pointed at Brigitte. It was Saadi. He fired twice. Both shots missed Brigitte. Saadi ran toward her to close the distance before firing again.

Brigitte's reacted from instinct. She dove behind the taxi putting it between her and her assassin. She knew she couldn't stay hidden long. He was closing in fast and would likely flank her at point-blank range before shooting again. She didn't know from which side he would appear. She looked over at the remains of the burning bus. Thick smoke billowed out and was moving across the street in her direction. It was creating a smokescreen. If she could reach the opposite side of the bus without being noticed, she would buy herself some time. She kept low and ran toward the front of the bus. The smoke folded in around her. She coughed from the stench of burning flesh.

As she rounded the front of the bus, she saw what remained of the driver hanging from over the broken front window. He was clearly dead, and his clothes were burning. She had seen brutal violence before in battle, so it wasn't a shock. She kept moving. What she saw next stopped her cold in her tracks...

Ellie laid face down on the sidewalk. Her left leg was shattered and torn below the knee, and her left hand had been blown clean off. The hair on the back of her head was singed. Her clothes were torn and smoking. She was motionless.

Brigitte gasped. She moved closer and saw blood spurting from a severed artery in Ellie's hand. That meant that her heart was still beating, but Ellie would bleed out and die if nothing was done to stop the bleeding. Brigitte realized that the assassin had probably already reached the taxi and discovered that Brigitte was gone. He would be coming. She had to make a decision and make it fast – save Ellie or save herself. She didn't want to die but couldn't leave Ellie.

She moved to Ellie's side. Ellie still had her purse on her shoulder. Brigitte detached the shoulder strap and wrapped it around Ellie's forearm to create a tourniquet. The bleeding slowed. She could hear the sirens of fire trucks and police cars approaching from a distance. Brigitte pulled her belt from her skirt and made a tourniquet above Ellie's left knee. She slowly turned Ellie over. To her surprise, Ellie's face was almost untouched. Her back had been facing the explosion when the bomb went off, and she was thrown clear of the bus. As far as Brigitte could tell, she was the only survivor. Passersby, not seriously injured by the blast, were approaching the wreckage to see if they could help. Ellie's eyes fluttered open. "Hey, kiddo," said Brigitte trying not to cry.

"What happened?" said Ellie.

"You've got yourself your first exclusive."

"Yeah?" said Ellie, strangely hopeful.

"You bet. It's all yours."

Ellie smiled weakly. Brigitte didn't notice Saadi moving up behind her with his pistol pointed at her head. It was a good thing. He might have fired sooner had she tried to flee. Instead, he moved closer and closer, decreasing the distance between them, so he was sure not to miss.

He had lost another one of his sirens, and he was angry. He thought about calling Brigitte's name so she would turn around and he could shoot her in the face, but he didn't want to take any chances of her trying to escape. He would end her life here and now. He took final aim at the back of Brigitte's head and squeezed the trigger.

A rock slammed into Saadi's arm, causing him to miss when the gun went off. Another rock hit him in the side of the head. He was stunned.

The passersby were picking up rocks from a garden and hurling them at the man with a gun. More rocks hit Saadi. He whirled around and fired three wild shots at the gathering mob, wounding one teenager in the side. The crowd ran for cover, some dropping their rocks.

Brigitte stared Saadi in the eyes when he turned back to her and Ellie. "Fuck you, you merciless prick," she said defiantly, putting herself between Ellie and Saadi.

Saadi took aim and squeezed the trigger. His pistol clicked empty. He couldn't believe it. He reached into his pocket and pulled out several spare bullets. He opened the pistol's chamber and started to reload when several more rocks hit him. He turned to see the mob closing in on him. He could hear the police sirens down the street. He was out of time if he was going to escape. He cursed and ran off. The mob chased after him throwing their rocks to ensure he didn't return and following him to see where he went.

Several police cars and a firetruck arrived. The police chased after Saadi, and the mob following him. One fireman ran to help Brigitte and Ellie while the other used hoses to put out the bus fire.

Brigitte wept with gratitude. Ellie would live.

Paris, France

The neighborhood hospital was overflowing with wounded from the bus explosion and the shooting spree that had followed. All the passengers on the bus, except for Ellie, had died. But there were still plenty of people on the sidewalks and in nearby cars that had been badly hurt from the blast. The hospital morgue was over capacity as many mortally-wounded were brought in only to be pronounced dead on arrival by the doctor assigned to triage.

Ellie laid in a hyperbaric oxygen chamber with her head sticking out the hole on one end. She was asleep, drugged heavily. Brigitte sat beside her. The stump that was once Ellie's hand was wrapped tightly with bandages while the remaining tissue and bone on her leg were exposed to the high-pressure oxygen being pumped into the enclosure to promote blood flow and healing. It was a long shot. The doctors treating Ellie had informed Brigitte that there was a good chance that they would need to amputate, but they wanted to give her every chance of saving her leg.

Damien entered, carrying two cups of coffee. He handed one to Brigitte.

"You're a lifesaver," said Brigitte softly.

"Tell her that," said Damien motioning to Ellie. "You should go home and get some sleep."

"No. I want to be here when she wakes up."

"She looks like such an angel laying there. It's amazing that her face was untouched."

"You know she's really going to need your support."

"I doubt that. She broke up with me earlier this week. Said she wanted to make it on her own without my help."

"So, why are you here?"

"Just because she broke up with me doesn't mean that I stopped caring."

"You know you're really not the shit you pretend to be."

"What can I say. I'm in love with the girl. Maybe now she'll want me back."

"And you'd have her?"

"Of course. She still has her best parts."

"I take back the part about you not being a shit."

"Good. I'd hate you to think I was getting soft," said Damien. "How are things with Tom and you?"

"I don't know. It's hard. We both work so much."

"He's in Algiers?"

"Yes. He'll be back tomorrow. He offered to return tonight, but I told them there was little he could do and that I had you to keep me company."

"Lucky girl. I'm such a good conversationalist... and card player," said Damien pulling a deck from his pocket. "Mille Bornes?"

"No way. I need my paycheck. I've seen you cheat."

"Only when my opponent is drunk, and I know they won't mind," said Damien pulling a whiskey flask from his other pocket and sweetening both their coffees.

Brigitte looked back at Ellie. "So damn young. So much pain," said Brigitte as a tear rolled down her cheek.

"She's gonna be okay, Brig. She's a fighter like you," said Damien. "She'll adjust. It'll just take some time."

"I suppose. At least she's alive."

Paris, France

It was raining heavily. Hidden by an umbrella and the collar of his coat, Saadi stood at a newsstand staring at a police sketch of his face on the front page of every newspaper. Many people had seen his face after the bombing of the bus, and the sketch had been greatly improved. There was little doubt it was him. He was a hunted man.

The citizens of Paris were demanding justice, no matter the cost. The police seemed more determined than ever. They had set up roadblocks and checkpoints all over the city. It was almost impossible for him to move about. He knew if he stayed in Paris, it was only a matter of time before he was caught. He considered moving to another big city in France like Marseille or Lyon, but he knew that his bombs would have less of an impact on the media. This was Paris. The darling of Europe. Her rape was a slap of reality that could not be ignored.

The Battle for Algiers was heating up. The leaders of the FLN had asked him to return to the capital, where his unique skills were needed to fight the French. He had refused up until now. With the righteous suicide of Samiah, he was alone now. There was nobody to help him deliver his bombs, and his face was too well known to be an effective courier. There were attractive Muslim girls he could recruit in Paris, but they didn't seem to have the same devotion to Allah or dedication to the independence of Algeria. They had been seduced by the meaningless baubles of the city's boutiques and the long leisurely lunches of the Parisian cafés. It was time to go home and rebuilt his team of female operatives.

His mission to kill Brigitte Friang had failed again, and he felt angry. He didn't understand why Allah could let that happen. Allah was all-powerful and all-wise. The Friang woman must have some other purpose to have escaped him not once, but twice. His faith was strong. As much as he hated to leave her death undone, he knew he must accept God's will.

Getting out of France and back to Algiers would not be easy. Of course, he would disguise himself, but the police had been trained to look beyond the façade. He could make his way down to the coast by train and stowaway on a cargo ship in one of the Mediterranean ports. He decided to carry a bomb with him even though it increased his risk if searched. If caught, he would take the honorable way out like his dear Samiah had done. His last breath would be one of fire and mayhem. He would strike one last time at the French lion.

Saadi noticed the kiosk owner glancing discretely in his direction. It was possible that the man was just minding his newspapers and magazine, making sure that Saadi was not reading for free or possibly stealing his inventory. But Saadi could see that it was more than that. He recognized Saadi's face. And why shouldn't he? It was on the front page of every newspaper. Saadi also noticed the phone hanging on the back wall of the kiosk. He knew that as soon as he left the stand, the owner would use it to call the police. There was little chance that the police would arrive in time to find him, even if they were in the neighborhood. But this kiosk was near Saadi's apartment, and he needed time to pack his things before leaving. He could not risk the police doing a door to door search or setting up multiple checkpoints which he would need to pass to escape their web. Unfortunate, thought Saadi. The man is just doing his duty as a citizen. He has nothing personal against me, nor I against him.

Saadi set down his umbrella, picked up one of the papers, and tucked it under his left arm. He reached into his left pocket and retrieved a handful of coins. He held the coins out as if not knowing which coin was which or how much was needed to pay for the paper. Saadi said nothing and kept his reach short because of the newspaper under his arm. The kiosk owner was forced to lean out of his stall window to select the right coin. With his right hand, Saadi reached into his pants pocket and removed a gravity stiletto. He allowed his hand holding the knife to fall to his side. He pressed the release button, and the seven-inch, double-sided blade effortlessly slid out of the handle and locked in place. One powerful thrust into the left side of the man's chest was all that was required. The blade entered the man's heart and stopped it from beating. He gasped as he fell back into his chair and slumped over. Saadi wiped the blood from the blade on a newspaper. He held the knife up, pressed the release button, and the blade once again disappeared into the handle. He tucked it back into his pocket, picked up his umbrella, and walked away unnoticed in the rain.

February 24, 1957 – Algiers, Algeria

Saadi wanted to make a strong statement on his return to Algiers. The FLN had conducted multiple bombings in Algiers and around the country during his absence. The bombs were effective at killing large numbers of French citizens, but Saadi felt they lacked finesse. They were one-off attacks. He felt the current campaign was missing the opportunity to strike true terror in the hearts and minds of the populace – the idea of uncertainty, that anyone could be killed at any time.

The FLN leadership had given Saadi his choice of female recruits. He was impressed with the lineup of girls that had been ordered to meet with him in an empty workshop in the heart of Algiers. The pool of candidates had grown vastly since picking his first three operatives several years ago.

He still wanted to keep his group of sirens small – no more than three. It took time to train them to properly activate his bombs while placing them in the correct spot for maximum effect. But he decided to develop a second group of operatives that he could use for assassinations or diversions. They would not require as much training.

For both groups, he selected the smartest and most attractive girls. He also looked for girls that were virtuous and had strong faith in Allah. The girls he chose would need to change their outward appearance to be effective, but their hearts needed to remain pure.

He needed Allah's help to carry out his will. He was to be a mentor and steward over these girls. They were to become an elite army of God's servants. They were exceptional, and he would protect them as much as he could. If their lives were sacrificed, then it was God's will.

He talked with each girl that garnered his interest. He asked them about their schooling, their families, and their faith. He studied their eyes and expressions as they conversed. He wanted girls that already understood how to flirt and use their good looks to get what they wanted from a man. They would need to use every possible means to outwit the French soldiers and police.

He selected three girls to place the bombs and seven others to carry out assassinations and help with diversions. An intense training schedule began immediately as well as lessons in the French language and culture. They would need to look and act like French girls to avoid the random searches of the paratroopers patrolling the street of Algiers. If found carrying a bomb, they would be arrested immediately and subjected to intensive interrogation to reveal the location and identity of the bombmaker – Saadi.

Saadi planned the first attack down to the last detail. He needed it to go well. The FLN leadership believed in him but had their doubts about how effective he could be with the increase in French paratroopers in the city. The high-explosive clay used in his bombs was not cheap, and the risk to smuggle in the components was high. He needed to reassure the leadership so he would continue to receive their utmost support and give him free rein to carry out his attacks.

March 18, 1957 – Boufarik, Algeria

Amedee Froger was the mayor of Boufarik, a town twenty miles outside of Algiers. He was popular and had won re-election three times. He seemed to have that right mix between complying with French authorities while at the same time supporting a peaceful transition to Algerian independence. He had achieved the impossible. His town and its people were at peace and prospered.

The town's economy was supported by thousands of groves producing the sweet and slightly sour oranges that were exported to Europe. Compared to most of Algeria, the citizens of Boufarik did well, earning almost double the average wage in the country.

Like most days, he purchased two croissants and filled his thermos with the French coffee he enjoyed so much at a local bakery near his home on Rue Michelet. He liked to arrive at his office early, before the other workers. He didn't want his fellow Algerians to see him eating a French breakfast. It was bad for politics. To Froger, politics, like life, was all about balance.

As he left the bakery and climbed into his car, a young woman wearing white gloves crossed the street and walked toward him. Froger was quite used to being approached by the townspeople, but he did not recognize this young lady. She was attractive with her European hairstyle, floral dress, and white pearls. He imagined she was the daughter of one of the wealthy Pied-Noir orchard owners. She tapped on the window with her gloved finger. He rolled it down and said, "How may I be of service, Mademoiselle?"

She pulled a small pistol from her purse and shot him point-blank in the eye. He shrieked in pain as he fell over onto the seat knocking his bag of croissants onto the car floor. She fired three more bullets into his chest just as she had been instructed. Blood flowed, his body went limp, and he died. She tossed the pistol onto the car floor and walked off calmly, snapping her purse shut. Saadi would be proud.

March 21, 1957 – Boufarik, Algeria

Half of the entire town of Boufarik showed up for Mayor Froger's funeral three days later, at the local cemetery. There were dozens of floral arrangements on wooden stands lined up near the coffin holding Froger's corpse. On top of the closed casket was a beautiful bouquet of local flowers that had been donated by one of the town's people.

As the service began, Pied-Noir and Muslim sat side-by-side. The local Imam offered a prayer and a sermon on the need for tolerance. Just as the Imam finished, the bomb inside the bouquet on the coffin exploded, shredding the Imam and the first two rows of mourners. Dozens of others were maimed and seriously injured by the roofing nails and glass marbles that had been packed inside the explosive canister.

Over the next two weeks, the Pieds-Noirs carried out revenge killings of four Muslims that had expressed sympathy for the FLN cause. There was no more peace in the town of Boufarik. No more fence-sitting by the townspeople. Everyone chose a side – the Muslims joining the FLN and the Pieds-Noirs joining the Ultras.

March 23, 1957 – Algiers, Algeria

It was early morning, and the main boulevard in the European quarter was empty. As the sky grew brighter, the street lamps all switched off at the same time.

A utility van pulled to a stop next to a bus stop. An Algerian utility worker exited the van with a bucket of tools. He walked to a nearby street lamp and knelt at its base. He opened the iron access panel revealing the lamp's wiring. He cut one of the wires and stripped the plastic insulation from both ends exposing the copper wiring.

He looked around to ensure that nobody was watching, then reached into the bucket and removed several of the heavy tools. He removed the false bottom of the bucket and carefully removed a bomb with two wires extending from the detonator. He placed the bomb inside the base of the street lamp and attached the lamp's two wires to the detonator's two wires. He closed the access panel, picked up his tools and bucket, walked back to his van and drove off to the next bus stop and street lamp.

The boulevard grew busier as the day progressed. Buses shuttled shoppers and tourists back and forth across the commercial district. Not all the passengers were European. Many Muslims also used the buses to go to and return from work. Children used buses to attend their school classes. It was cheap transportation and almost as fast as a more expensive taxi.

As the sun waned and dove behind the surrounding mountains, the sky darkened, and the workday ended.

The bus stops were crowded with Algerians returning home to prepare their evening meal and tourists returning to their hotels with shopping bags in hand.

An Algerian man in his late forties watched a French woman with her two young children. Their fair skin was pink, turning red from too much sun. The children had sand from a nearby beach all over their bodies, which their mother tried to brush off with her hand. "No. I want my sand. Don't take it away," said the little girl.

"You can't get on the bus like that. The driver will throw you out onto the street for getting the seat dirty," said the mother.

An Algerian woman walked up beside the man and whispered, "Perhaps you would like to take the next bus. I think this one will be too crowded."

The man looked back at the Algerian woman, and she gave him a slight tilt of her head. He knew what it meant and moved away from the bus stop. The woman continued to warn several other Algerians. She glanced at her watch and moved off herself. It was almost time.

The bus approached from down the boulevard, and the remaining passengers crowded together where they thought the folding door would be when the bus stopped. In Paris, it was the tradition to leave the passengers exiting the bus a clear aisle before forming a line, but in Algeria, it was a free-for-all.

At the end of the boulevard, Saadi stood and watched. The street lamp beside him flickered for a brief moment. He turned to watched twelve street lamps on the boulevard explode at the same time. The iron casings at the base of the lamps split apart, sending shrapnel for fifty yards in all directions. The exiting passengers and those waiting at the stop were torn to shreds. The street lamps fell into the street and onto the sidewalk. Forty-two Europeans and Pieds-Noirs died in the blasts, and a hundred more were seriously injured. Many required amputations of broken limbs. Seven Muslims that failed to heed the warnings also died. They would be declared martyrs of the cause and would receive their rewards in heaven. It was glorious.

The bombings had the exact effect Saadi was hoping to achieve. Nobody in Algeria felt safe from the terror attacks unless they pledged their loyalty to the FLN, in which case they would be warned if their lives and the lives of their loved ones were in danger.

Ramdane was impressed by Saadi's planning and flawless execution. Saadi was immediately promoted and put in charge of all further bombing campaigns in Algeria.

Tebessa, Algeria

Tebessa was a small city in the mountains near the Tunisian border. It was considered safe by the leaders of the FLN and a good place to meet. It was far away from the French paratroopers in Algiers. The FLN had learned to fear the paratroopers. They were superior fighters and aggressive even beyond the Mujahideen that the FLN commanded.

Ramdane sat with his two remaining commanders Saadi and Si Larbi on one side of a table in the backroom of a coffee shop. Dahlab, Belkacem, and Benkhedda sat on the opposite side. "We need more recruits for the Mujahideen outside of Algiers, and we need them armed with the latest weapons. You need to stop sending them with World War I surplus rifles. They are fighting a modern army. They need modern weapons."

"And what will you do with these new recruits?" said Dahlab.

"The French have been able to consolidate all their forces on Algiers. They are preventing us from carrying out attacks in the quantity required to win the war. We need more actions outside the capital to force some of the French away from Algiers and the Casbah. We are missing a great opportunity by not attacking other cities while the French are preoccupied."

"This is bullshit. Just admit it. Your plan has failed," said Belkacem. "The French have you and your men penned like sheep ready for slaughter."

"If we are so penned, how are we here?" said Si Larbi, by far the youngest and most impetuous of the group.

"I wasn't talking to you, boy."

"You will excuse my young comrade," said Ramdane. "He is brave and skilled in the ways of war for one so young, but he lacks the patience for FLN politics."

"Then why the hell is he here?"

"You asked to see my commanders and me. I have obeyed your request."

"It was an order given by your commanding council."

"A council of whom we are also members. But we don't seem to remember being involved in the issuing of an order," said Ramdane with a sharp tone.

"This arguing is a waste of time. We are losing the support of the people. That is what is important," said Dahlab.

"We are not losing the support of the people. If anything, they are more determined than ever. But they cannot fight without weapons. That is your responsibility."

"We do not need to be lectured on our responsibility," said Dahlab. "You need to mind your own house, not ours. Your actions have been shameful. You do nothing with the troops we have given you."

"And how would you know? You are in Cairo getting fat off Nasser's hospitality. You know nothing of what is happening on the ground in Algiers."

"How could we? You fail to send even the vaguest report on your actions."

"We don't have time to write your reports. We are too busy fighting for our lives."

"And here we thought you were fighting for Algeria."

"Are you questioning our patriotism?" said Ramdane.

"Just yours," said Belkacem.

Ramdane had had enough and said, "You will send us the recruits we need and the arms we require. If not, my men and I will look elsewhere for support."

"Your men?" said Belkacem.

"Yes, my men. We are the ones fighting the French, not you. It is our blood that will free Algeria, not yours."

"How dare you?" said Belkacem.

"Watch your tongue," said Dahlab. "Or we will be forced to cut it off."

"I do not fear cowards. You will give us what we ask for, or we will no longer obey your commands. This meeting is over," said Ramdane rising and walking out.

Si Larbi and Saadi followed him but not until after giving the three FLN leaders an unsure glance. They wanted the others to recognize that they knew Ramdane had gone too far. The leaders in Cairo had access to the money required to continue the revolution. That made them powerful, even if Ramdane could not see the danger.

SEVEN

March 23, 1957 – Algiers, Algeria

Trinquier and Massu were having lunch at the officer's club at Brigade Headquarters. "We have done a tremendous amount of damage to the Mujahideen forces hidden in Algiers. However, we have been unable to locate the last of the FLN leaders. Our intelligence group has just about exhausted the initial group of collaborators gathered from our random raids," said Trinquier, nibbling at his sautéed fish.

"I see," said Massu, annoyed at the lack of progress. "Well, you will just have to arrest more suspected collaborators."

"Which we will do. But I fear we are trying to squeeze water from a rock. There's not much there that is useful."

"Are you saying Major Aussaresses' interrogation methods are no longer effective?"

"No, not at all. His methods have produced excellent results. I have little doubt that the informants are telling us the truth of what they know. It's just... the FLN keeps moving around. It's difficult to pin them down even with the information derived from the interrogations."

"Perhaps a change in tactics is in order."

"What would you suggest?"

Massu considered for a moment, then said, "Before we arrived in Algiers, the Sûreté was in charge of tracking potential dissidents."

"True. And they turned those addresses over to us. They were the first houses and buildings that we raided."

"Right. What about those that protested peacefully or signed petitions in favor of independence? They have records of those people too."

"I'm sure they have thousands. But they're not really a threat if they were using peaceful means to protest."

"No. But they are sympathetic to the rebel cause."

"Of course."

"Don't you see? The FLN leaders and the remaining Mujahideen are hiding somewhere. The most likely place to look for them is in the homes or businesses of those that are sympathetic."

"If we were to search the home or business of everyone that is known to have sympathies, we would be searching half of Algiers."

"I would suggest creating a master list and rating the sympathizers according to the number and significance of the peaceful actions they have taken in the past."

"Alright. That would prioritize our search efforts. But what is to prevent the FLN leaders from jumping around as they have been doing?"

"They can't jump around if you hit all their potential hiding places at the same time."

"Even narrowed down by priority, the list would be massive. It would take every paratrooper we have in the brigade to search that many places all at once."

"Probably. So, do it."

"What about our patrols and the checkpoints?"

"The police are sitting on their asses since we have taken over. Use them. They may not be good in a firefight, but surely they can check documents and search suspects for weapons."

"I suppose."

"Mix them in with your paras so you can keep an eye on them. Treat them like interns."

"I don't think they'll like that much."

"I would imagine not, but I don't really care what they like. Do you?"

"No. I don't."

"We have a job to do, Roger. Whatever it takes, we must destroy the FLN."

"Alright. I'll see to it. What about Bigeard? We need his men if we are going to hit every location at once."

"Of course. I will see that he is updated on the strategy. You just get those files."

"Yes, General."

Algiers, Algeria

Five military trucks led by a jeep pulled up in front of Sûreté headquarters in Algeria. A platoon of paratroopers led by a lieutenant jumped out of the vehicles and rushed into the building. They were followed by Colonel Trinquier.

The paratroopers filed into the reception area and lined up in three rows. As Trinquier entered, they snapped to attention. Trinquier walked into the police chief's office unannounced. "What in the hell do you think you are doing?" said the police chief.

"You will order your officers and staff to turn over all records concerning the FLN to my men," said Trinquier.

"I will do no such thing. Those records are the property of the Sûreté. We need them to conduct our investigations."

"For now, your investigations are over. The military is taking over."

"By whose authority?"

"Mine."

"I will call the Governor, and we will see what is what," said the chief, picking up the phone.

"Call whoever you wish. We are taking the records. They will be returned when we are finished with them," said Trinquier. "Oh, and I will need your men for about a week."

"How many?"

"All of them. We'll come back to fetch them in a day or two. Have them ready and armed."

Trinquier left the office and walked back to the reception area where his men were waiting. "Lieutenant, you and your men are to seize all FLN records and files. Make sure you leave a receipt for the Police Chief. We don't want to be rude. You have my permission to shoot anyone that stands in your way. Try not to kill them unless absolutely necessary."

Trinquier walked out, and the paratroopers went to work. They used bolt cutters and crowbars on any file cabinets that were locked. They didn't bother asking for a key. The file drawers were removed from their cabinets and loaded into the trucks. The police just stood back and watched.

At battalion headquarters, Trinquier's intelligence unit compiled a massive list of sympathizers along with their last known addresses. Using carbon paper, Heloise Blanc, a civilian office worker, typed copies of the list for distribution. She discretely slipped one of the copies into her purse and continued typing.

Each sympathizer's name, along with a rating, was typed on a color-coded slip of paper and pinned to a map of Algiers showing their location. The Casbah was littered with sympathizers.

When the map was finished, Bruno and his staff were invited to view the results. They were given lists of sympathizers in their area of operation. "You know, as soon as the FLN realizes how we are hunting them down, they will try and make a break for it," said Trinquier.

"Yes. We should coordinate our efforts and prioritize the list so the leaders are arrested first. We can cordon off each area where we believe a leader is located before the search begins," said Bruno.

"Keep the rats in the cage?"

"Exactly. The searches should random with overwhelming force."

"I agree. No warning. No prediction. Anyone that fights is eliminated."

"Of course. Except for the leaders. We should do our best to take them alive and allow our intelligence units to interrogate them."

"I doubt they will give much up."

"Probably not, but the sooner we can end this, the better. I don't like fighting near so many civilians."

"No Algerian is civilian anymore, Bruno. They are all complicit."

"So I have been told. Still, we should end this war as soon as possible."

"Yes. It is a messy affair. On that, we can agree."

March 25, 1957 – Algiers, Algeria

Thousands of French paratroopers snaked through the streets and alleys of Algiers. It was a thrust of overwhelming force against the FLN leaders and their Mujahideen army. French officers referred to the lists and maps they had been given by the intelligence unit. Several blocks were cordoned off using portable barbed wire fencing. Nobody was allowed in or out of the area until the search was complete. Light machinegun posts were set up on the corners of each area to prevent a human wave-type attack on the French soldiers by desperate FLN leaders and their Mujahideen fighters, trying to escape.

A company of paratroopers led by Bruno moved up quietly and surrounded a popular Turkish bath-house in the Casbah. The police files had revealed that the bath-house was where FLN members would often gather to receive instructions from their leaders. The hope was that the paratroopers would catch several FLN leaders inside by surprise assault.

The first two paratroopers breached the locked front doors and rushed inside. They were gunned down by eighty well-armed Mujahideen and FLN leaders that had been hiding and sleeping in the basement of the bath-house.

An all-out gun battle ensued, with the French paratroopers firing and tossing grenades through the windows and doorways. Algerians on the roof of the bath-house tossed grenades and loose roof tiles down on the French positions, driving them back.

The Algerians inside the bath-house used the building's marble columns for cover. They stayed hidden, conserving their ammunition until the French mounted an assault, then unleashed hell on the paratroopers as they entered through the main and back doorways. Anyone inside the building was considered the enemy by the French, although it didn't matter. Nobody was in the mood to surrender. It was a fight to the death on both sides.

Algerian civilians were trapped in their homes as stray bullets shattered their windows and grenade shrapnel splintered their wooden doors. Mothers and fathers turned over the furniture to form protective barriers around their children, cowered in the corners. Escape was too dangerous, with bullets and grenade shrapnel flying in all directions and heavy tiles falling from the rooftops. Their only choice was to wait out the fighting.

Outside the bath-house, Mujahideen that were secretly housed nearby moved in when they heard the gunshots and explosions. They took up positions in the buildings surrounding the bath-house and sniped at the French paratroopers from the windows and rooftops. They forced the French to fight on two fronts, making it more difficult to maintain their assault on the bath-house and reducing the effectiveness of the superior French troops.

Bruno radioed for armored cars to back up his paratroopers. When the armored cars arrived, Bruno pointed out the Mujahideen sniper positions in the surrounding buildings. The armored car gunners strafed the windows and rooftops with their machineguns, killing many of the Mujahideen snipers and forcing the survivors to abandon their firing positions.

With the armored cars protecting the rear, the paratroopers quickly regained the upper hand in the battle. They attacked with their usual aggressiveness, pouring fire on the Algerians inside the bath-house, assaulting again and again until the enemy ran out of ammunition. With their guns empty, the Algerians waited until a large number of paratroopers had entered the building, then attacked them with their knives and scimitars in a last stand counterattack. The hand-to-hand battle lasted just over three minutes when the last Mujahideen fighter was killed by a spray of submachine gun bullets from three paratroopers.

Several FLN leaders were found wounded and taken captive so they could be interrogated. The wounded Mujahideen were not as lucky and were quickly dispatched by the paratroopers. The paratroopers' tradition was to give no quarter and expect none in return. It may not have been legal by international law, but it was the reality of urban warfare. Kill or be killed.

As a warning to others housing the Mujahideen and FLN leaders, the three-hundred-year-old Turkish bath-house was demolished by the French engineers using shaped explosive charges to take out the marble pillars and bring the roof down. A cloud of dust rose up and descended on the Casbah like a veil.

March 26, 1957 – Algiers, Algeria

Heloise met Achiary at a French bakery in the European quarter. They sat inside at a small corner table and ordered two coffees. Heloise handed Achiary a book, "I bought you a copy of that book I told you about. I think you'll find it quite interesting. Especially the last five chapters."

He opened the book and thumbed through the pages until he came to Chapter Twelve, where he found a piece of paper neatly folded in half and wedged in between two pages. The carbon copy had smeared slightly, but the list of FLN sympathizers with addresses was still quite legible. Each chapter heading after that had another folded piece of paper. "Thank you. It looks quite interesting. I'll get right to it," said Achiary with a smile. "Our French friends continue with their visit to Algiers?"

"Yes. I believe they plan to stay much longer."

"Good. I hope they enjoy the city."

"And you and your family?"

"Algiers feels quite crowded at the moment. I think it's time for a visit to the countryside. You will keep me informed if our friends' plans to stay in Algiers change?"

"Of course," she said as their coffees were served.

March 28, 1957 – Mazzer, Algeria

It was early morning and cold in the Atlas Mountains of Western Algeria. Achiary and two dozen of his Ultra fighters armed with rifles and pistols laid flat on a hillside overlooking the small town of Mazzer. The streets were still, apart from the occasional dog wandering.

There were three names circled in pencil on the list Heloise had given him. Achiary pointed out the locations of the three addresses of the FLN members to his unit commanders. The fighters divided into three groups, covered their faces with scarfs and advanced toward the town.

A wooden door crashed open from a boot kick. Ultras rushed into a home and searched the rooms until they found a man still in bed with his wife. His hands were tied, and he was taken outside at gunpoint as his family stood helpless and watched.

In the town square, the three FLN sympathizers were dosed with lamp oil and hung from a tree. As they struggled for breath, Achiary flipped open his lighter and set them on fire. The townspeople gathered and wailed in horror. The Ultras prevented anyone from interfering.

When the last FLN sympathizer stopped writhing in pain and died, Achiary gave the order, and the Ultras began the second phase of their operation. They searched every structure within the town and uncovered several hidden weapon caches. This was the evidence Achiary needed to justify his and his men's actions. As punishment, all the men in the town were hunted down and shot by the Ultras. Wives and children screamed and cried. All of the animals in the town were killed, destroying the town's livelihood. Lastly, all the buildings and houses in the village were set on fire. With the entire town burning, the Ultras withdrew back into the hills.

Achiary had correctly surmised that when the French paratroopers had redeployed to Algiers, the countryside was left mostly undefended. Those FLN sympathizers and Mujahideen fighters that escaped the French siege fled to their homes in the Atlas Mountains. His Ultras would be unmolested as they dealt with the names on the list outside of Algiers. He and his men saw the assassinations as a patriotic service to France. They sent a strong message throughout Algeria that anyone joining the FLN would be hunted down and killed no matter where they hid, and anyone supporting the rebels would suffer the Ultras' harsh justice.

March 30, 1957 – Paris, France

The rumors of the Algerian massacres spread through Paris. Brigitte stood in Damien's office, "I've got to go and investigate firsthand what really happened," she said.

"No," said Damien, firmly.

"What do you mean, no?" she said.

"I think my meaning is pretty clear. It's too dangerous even for you, Brigitte. The very story you want to tell is the same reason you can't go. Outside of the capital, Algeria is lawless at the moment."

"So, you're just going to let the rumors go unverified?"

"We are not a newspaper. We don't have to tell every story that comes to our desks."

"But this one should be told, Damien. If Algeria truly is part of France, then its people must be protected by French law and order. That's not

171

happening anymore outside of Algiers. The Ultras are taking justice into their own hands, and the French authorities are doing nothing to stop them. That's a story worth telling."

"There will be no paratroopers to protect you in the mountains. The Algerians will see your pretty little French face and take their revenge on you. And if they don't, the Ultras could kill you for interfering. I am not going to be part of that."

"That's not your call, Damien."

"As your employer, it is my call."

"Then, I quit."

"God, damn it, Brigitte."

"I'll be writing the story as a freelancer. You can purchase it if you wish when I am done. If not, I am fairly sure there will be other news outlets more open to the truth."

"I am not going to beg you to stay this time, Brigitte. I'm not sending you on a suicide mission."

"Good. I need a change anyway. Things were getting a bit stuffy around here," said Brigitte before she exited.

Coyle sat on the edge of the bed and watched as Brigitte packed. "You know Damien is right on this one. It is lawless outside of Algiers, and Bruno won't be there to protect you," said Coyle.

"I don't need Bruno to protect me. I can handle myself just fine," said Brigitte.

"You shouldn't go, Brig."

"Why do men keep telling me what I can and cannot do?"

"Because we love you and don't want to see you hurt."

"You're preventing me from doing my job."

"I'll do whatever I need to do to protect you."

"Like I said... I can handle myself. I'm a big girl."

Coyle moved to the closet, pulled out his rucksack, and started to pack. "What are you doing?" said Brigitte.

"I'm going with you... to keep you company. It'll be nice to spend time with you."

"What about your job?"

"I'll call in sick. I feel a cold coming on. The Algerian sun will do me good."

"You're such a liar."

"I learned from the best."

Brigitte smiled. She was glad Coyle was going with her. She was stubborn but not oblivious to the danger or without fear. She just didn't let her fear govern her actions. Coyle had proven many times he could handle himself in precarious situations.

Coyle packed his service revolver and shoulder holster along with an extra box of shells. He was uncomfortable with the thought that he might be forced to use it, but he wasn't taking any chances, especially not with Brigitte.

April 2, 1957 – Atlas Mountains, Algeria

It took several days for Brigitte and Coyle to find a driver willing to travel into the Atlas Mountains. The Algerians were frightened of the Ultras as word of more attacks spread through Algiers.

Algiers was not safe either, as bombs continued to explode throughout the city. Algeria seemed more and more as if it was becoming unhinged. Even the French army, with its half a million troops in-country, appeared powerless to stop it. Just as they gained control of one area, terrorist bombings and assassinations would erupt in another.

After bribing an Algerian truck driver working for the Red Cross with an obscene amount of money, Coyle and Brigitte traveled into the mountains. They rode in the back of the truck on top of bundles of food and medical supplies with red cross logos stenciled on the sides. Coyle had rubbed shoe polish on their hands, forearms, and faces to make their skin appear darker. They each wore traditional Algerian clothes with their faces covered and hair wrapped with wool scarves. From a distance, they looked Algerian, but their light-colored eyes gave them away up close. When they rode through a town, they avoided eye contact and kept their heads turned away from anyone watching.

The air cooled the higher the truck climbed the mountain roads. They passed many vehicles that had been burned along the roadside. Some still had the charred remains of the drivers and their passengers inside. Nobody was brave enough to remove the bodies while the Ultras continued their raids. Nobody wanted to be added to the Ultra's death list.

The path of destruction led up the mountain road. Crops burned. Livestock dead and bloated. Homesteads scorched and abandoned. The stench of death was everywhere and strong. It was hard to witness so much destruction.

The truck rolled to a stop at what appeared to be an abandoned checkpoint. A dozen corpses covered in blankets, others with the jackets of the dead, laid along the side of the road waiting for their families to come and pick them up. Brigitte and Coyle climbed down from the truck. The driver spoke French and translated for Brigitte as she questioned a father retrieving the body of his son from the line of dead. "What happened here?" said Brigitte.

The father looked over at Coyle and remained silent. Brigitte could see that he was afraid. "Tom, why don't you go wait by the truck?" said Brigitte.

"Yeah. Call if you need help," said Coyle and moved off.

Brigitte had the driver ask the question again. This time the man responded with tears as he told his story, "He says that the Pieds-Noirs set up a checkpoint late yesterday afternoon when the people working in the city returned to their villages. They separated the men from the group and questioned them. When they didn't hear what they wanted to know, they shot the man they were interrogating. Some of the men tried to fight the Pieds-Noirs, and they were shot too. My son was one of those who fought. He was very brave. He wanted to join the Mujahideen, but I said no. If he had, I think he would still be alive. I killed my son," said the truck driver translating.

"I am so sorry for your loss. Maybe we can help you take your son back to your village?"

"No," said the truck driver. "We cannot do that. If the Pieds-Noirs find out we moved a body they killed, they will hunt us down, then torture and kill us."

"What about the boy's father?"

"They will come for him. But I don't think he cares. He will take his son."

"We can't just leave him here."

"Yes, we can. He will understand."

Brigitte pulled out some money from her pocket and handed it to the father. He pushed it away, not wanting to take charity. She insisted, "Tell him it's to help him bury his son."

The driver told the father. The father nodded and took the money. Brigitte walked back to the truck and climbed on the back with Coyle. They didn't talk. Coyle could see she was deeply affected by the father's story. Some things just couldn't be fixed, and it was best to be quiet. The truck continued up the mountain.

The truck made several stops in small villages. The driver delivered food and medical supplies where they were needed. He talked with the town elders and heard the rumors about the raids. He knew where to go to find the story that Brigitte wanted. He knew it would be risky, but he too wanted the story to be told of what the Pieds-Noirs had done to his people. The killings had gone way beyond the hunt for FLN sympathizers and Mujahideen. Achiary's Ultras were murdering and raping their way across the mountains. The driver wanted the French reporter to see the truth of the French occupation of his country.

As the sun approached the top of the mountains, the truck pulled into a village at the base of a mountain ridgeline. French troops had been posted at a checkpoint after the raid. They were too late to prevent the Ultras from destroying the village but would protect the survivors from further raids and tribal bandits that might take advantage of the situation. The soldiers asked the driver why he had come. He told them he had emergency food and medical supplies that he needed to deliver. They waved him into the village. He drove slowly, not knowing what to expect.

Most of the homes had been badly burned, and the roofs had collapsed. It was cold high up in the mountains, and the temperature would drop as night fell. It would be a struggle for the survivors of the raid to stay warm. Most of their belongings had been destroyed in the fires. Only a tiny mosque at the end of the village was still standing.

All the livestock in the village had been killed, and the carcasses dumped in the well, contaminating the only fresh water for miles. It was against Islamic law to poison wells even during a time of war, but the Pieds-Noirs were mostly Christian and had little regard for the words of Mohamad. The village grain supply had been confiscated by the Pieds-Noirs and carried away. There would be no bread or meat for those still alive in the village.

There were pools of dark liquid along the main street and down the alleys. Brigitte and Coyle knew it was blood leftover from a massacre. They had seen similar scenes in Vietnam after Viet Minh raids on uncooperative villagers. Everyone needed to choose sides in a war if they wanted to survive. "Where are the bodies?" said Brigitte.

"I don't know," said Coyle. "Maybe they've already been buried."

The truck stopped in the square. The smell of death was incredibly strong. The village was silent. No sounds of life. "There must be survivors," said Brigitte.

"Yeah, but where are they?" said Coyle.

They both looked toward the small mosque untouched. "That's strange," said Coyle as he walked toward it. Brigitte followed.

Coyle motioned for Brigitte to hold back as he continued toward the front door. Normally she would argue with him when he failed to treat her as an equal. But not this time. She was grateful for his chivalry and stopped several yards short of the door.

Coyle opened the door slowly. The smell and a flurry of flies making their escape almost knocked him over. It was all he could do not to wretch from the smell. "Coyle?" said Brigitte taking a few tentative steps forward. "Are you okay?"

"Just stay there, Brig. I'll be fine."

He mustered his strength and moved inside, where he found the villagers. Their bodies were all neatly stacked around the inner walls of the mosque like cords of wood. They were stacked in a kind of pyramid – men on the bottom, then women and finally children... dozens of children. It had been two days since the raid, and the faces on the corpses were bloated beyond recognition. He thought he should check if there were any survivors, but the smell was too much. He ran from the building, feeling like a coward and vomited beside the door.

Brigitte knew that Coyle had a strong constitution and was not easily disturbed. She knew what to expect as she moved toward the door, and it frightened her. "Don't go in there, Brig," said Coyle.

"I have to," said Brigitte, her voice quivering. "I have to bear witness. It's why we came."

She steeled herself and walked inside. When she came back out a minute later, something had changed inside of her. It was the same thing that had happened to Coyle a few years before – one human too many having met a violent death with no real purpose beyond hate. She knelt down and wept uncontrollably.

Coyle felt terrible that he had not sheltered her from such savagery. He knew that there was no stopping Brigitte when she set her mind to something, but he felt like he should have at least tried. No person should see that, he thought. It's the stuff of nightmares. "Are you alright?" he said, recovering from his own reaction to the horror he had seen.

"No, I'm not alright. I haven't been alright since this war started," said Brigitte, enraged, wiping the tears from her dirt-stained cheeks. "Those motherfuckers have no right to do this to anyone. It's genocide. They should be tried in The Hauge and hung."

Coyle knew when to keep quiet when Brigitte was in a foul mood. Trying to soothe her would only make it worse. She needed to vent, and he needed to listen.

"We shouldn't be here," she said, deep in thought.

"You want to go back to Paris?" said Coyle, hopeful.

"No. I mean France. We French should not be here in Algeria. It's not our country. Not anymore. We lost Algeria when we started protecting the Pieds-Noirs over the Algerians. Now they feel like they can do anything they want. We just stand by and watch."

"So, what are you going to do?"

"I'm going to tell the fucking world. That's what I'm going to do."

Coyle had seen Brigitte in many dangerous situations over the years, and he had feared for her. But he knew deep down that writing about this damn war could evolve into the most dangerous thing she had ever done.

There were survivors in the village. They had run off during the massacre and hid in the surrounding mountains. They would have to live with the guilt of abandoning their friends and family.

The driver unloaded enough food and supplies for several weeks. Even then, he imagined it would not be enough. This village would not recover anytime soon, probably never. It would be abandoned, and the memory of the massacre left to the wind that whistled down the mountainside.

Paris, France

It took several days for Brigitte and Coyle to wind their way back down the Atlas Mountains to Algiers. They caught the first flight available to Paris.

Brigitte didn't even unpack when she and Coyle arrived back at their apartment. She just went to work. She worked all night, typing and re-typing. It was like she needed to get the story out of her before she forgot any of it, or worse… remembered it more than she needed.

The article was long and scathing. It questioned France's motives for staying in Algeria. It questioned the morals of a country that fought to keep its empire. It condemned the Pieds-Noirs and their raids. It questioned France's complicity. In the past, Brigitte had struggled to stay objective, but not any longer. She couldn't turn away from what she knew was right. Not any longer. She loved her country, but her country was wrong.

Paris, France

Brigitte sat in Damien's office as he read the article she had written. He cringed at times as he poured through the copy. When finished, he said nothing. She watched him rise and walk to his window overlooking Paris. "Well?" she said after a few more moments.

"It's not going to be well received. Not by your readers and not by the government. You should understand that," he said.

"I see."

"I'm not saying it's not good. It's probably some of the best writing you've ever done. It's just…"

"Harsh?"

"Very."

"But it's the truth. I saw it with my own eyes."

"I know it's true. I trust you. That's what is so upsetting. That's why it's so difficult to read. This is France you've written about. Liberty, Equality and Fraternity. They mean nothing anymore."

"Perhaps the prose could use some editing."

"No. I wouldn't change a word."

"But you don't want it?"

"I didn't say that."

"But you didn't say you did either."

"You're not just a journalist anymore, Brigitte. People really listen to you. This will change things."

"Good. It should."

"You need to think about that. Really think about it. Millions of people could be affected by what you've written. France will be disgraced. The world will turn against us. There will be those that hate you for it."

"I know. I've thought about that. But I can't keep silent, not after what I saw. This war is wrong. The days of colonialism are gone. We French need to realize that. We need to understand what is happening."

"Well, this article will certainly open our eyes whether we like it or not."

"It could end my career."

"I doubt that. But it could be a very rough ride for a while... for you and the magazine."

"You're going to publish it?"

"Yes. As long as you've thought it through."

"I have. I want the story published regardless of the consequences."

"Me too. It's the right thing to do. If we don't stand for something, then we don't stand for anything. Right?"

"Yeah," said Brigitte tearing up. "Thanks, Damien."

"You're welcome. Now let's discuss your fee. But be gentle. The magazine could be bankrupt in a few months."

"I don't want anything. I just want it published."

"Alright. I am good with free."

April 10, 1957 – Paris, France

The day after Brigitte's article was published, thousands of protesters gathered in front of the parliament building. Placards and banners revealed the crowd's feelings –

FRANCE OUT OF ALGERIA
SHAME ON COLONS, SHAME ON MOLLET
and
BRING OUR TROOPS HOME

Within days the protests grew in number. Tens of thousands protested every day, and on weekends the crowds grew to over one hundred thousand. Speakers from the opposition parties whipped up the masses. Things turned ugly.

Support for Mollet's government collapsed. Elections were scheduled for early June. The government of France was being made or unmade on the streets of Algiers.

This was good news for the FLN. Their numbers had been decimated, and most of their leaders had been captured or killed. But their original goal was being achieved. All eyes were on France. The politicians could no longer hide behind their beloved paratroopers. The truth was being told.

The members of the United Nations turned on France. More debates were scheduled to discuss the Algerian problem, and more world leaders joined the Algerian point of view that the French should leave and allow the Algerians to rule their own country.

French diplomats continued to remind U.N. members that over one million French citizens lived in Algeria and their safety would surely be in question under an Algerian regime. The diplomats cared less and less for the argument. "France has created this problem. It is up to France to find a way out," was repeated again and again in the halls of the U.N. France was a member of the security council and could use its veto to block any legally binding resolutions, but the pressure of international condemnation was felt nonetheless.

Egyptian President Nasser was particularly vocal in condemning the French. Some thought it revenge for the French invasion of Egypt with the British. Others thought it was a backlash against French imperialism. Middle Eastern countries had already withheld their oil from being shipped to France because of the Suez Crisis. Now their leaders were threatening other nations with embargos if they failed to support an international boycott of French products until the Algerians were set free.

Brigitte's article had shaken France to the core. She was shunned from government circles. Nobody would give her an interview, and everyone avoided her when she appeared at functions. The invitations to foreign embassy parties dried up when it became know that she was persona non grata. French diplomats would decline their invitations or turn on their heels if they discovered she was at any function.

It was almost impossible to do her job as a journalist. Damien had been right – there were many that hated her for revealing the truth. They called her irresponsible and unpatriotic. She never let on that their words hurt her deeply. But Coyle saw it. Mostly at night after she thought he was asleep. She would slip into the living room and close the bedroom door. There in the dark, she wept alone. He wanted to comfort her, but he knew she would only be embarrassed. She was a proud woman. She carried her own water.

Her fellow reporters even avoided her. They, too, were being punished for working at the magazine that published her story. She spent her time working on her memoirs and writing about her experiences in the Indochina War. When she heard the whispers in the hallway, she closed her door. Damien was supportive and reassured her that it would all pass with time. But she knew that the magazine was suffering too. Many newsstands canceled their weekly orders, and subscribers dwindled. It wasn't that Brigitte had gotten the story wrong. Just the opposite. The truth about what was happening was painful, and while the French always loved a good political discussion, this was beyond that. This was a black mark on what it meant to be French.

Even Coyle and Bruno caught flak from the story. But neither cared much for what others thought. They knew Brigitte. She was worth fighting for, and their support was unwavering.

Coyle received veiled threats that his contract might not be renewed. He knew that the Air Force needed him and that the threats were empty. Pilots were in short supply. Many French Air Force officers were retiring so they could accept more lucrative offers to fly for commercial airlines. Coyle hated flying commercial. Cargo was much less troublesome than passengers. Boxes of ammunition didn't complain that their coffee had too much cream or that the cabin was too stuffy. Spools of barbed wire didn't vomit on the deck when the plane hit turbulence.

Bruno was outright scolded by Massu and told to use his influence to get Brigitte to issue a retraction. Bruno refused. Yes, the story was an embarrassment to the paratroopers who were supposed to be protecting Algeria from both the FLN and the Ultras. But the paratroopers had suffered much for France over the years, and their reputation was still held in high regard. Bruno realized that Brigitte's story had brought attention to the fact that the war needed to end one way or another, and quickly. It was tearing France apart.

EIGHT

October 1, 1957 – Algiers, Algeria

Si Larbi walked down a dark street in the Casbah using the alleyways and doorway to cover his movements. Curfew had already begun, and he knew if the French stopped him, he would be arrested. From there, it was only a matter of time until one of his followers, while under duress, identified him as the leader of the Mujahideen. He kept his hand on the pistol tucked into his pants underneath his shirt. He would not be taken alive. He would make sure of it.

He came to the doorway of a small factory, now closed for the evening. The lights were out. He checked both directions of the street before knocking out the code on the door. After a moment, the door opened, and the barrel of a pistol emerged from the darkness. "That's yesterday's code," said Saadi holding the gun.

"Fuck off and let me in before someone sees us," said Si Larbi.

Saadi opened the door and let Si Larbi pass, then checked both sides of the street for anybody watching. He trusted Si Larbi, but it was a force of habit to continually check and recheck for prying eyes. Habit is what had kept him alive all this time, and he wasn't about to change.

The windows in the factory had been blacked out with heavy wool blankets so the dim light from inside could not be seen from the outside of the building. There was just enough light, so the two leaders could see each other's facial expressions. The things they talked about were almost always a matter of life and death for themselves or their followers. It was important not to mislead each other.

Saadi had prepared some tea and poured them each a glass. "Any success with your missions?" he said.

"Missions? We can barely keep our heads on our shoulders between all the searches. At last count, my forces are only one-third of what they were when we first entering Algiers," said Si Larbi. "I spend all my time finding new places to hide my men. How about you?"

"We've had some success, but it's been difficult. Only three bomb actions this week. Hardly a dent in what is needed."

"We need to leave the Casbah."

"That bad?"

"Unfortunately, yes. As much as I hate to admit it, the executive council was right. The French have us trapped. Their methods of interrogation are far more effective than we imagined. They exposed our entire network within the Casbah. If we stay much longer, my entire army will be captured or killed."

"If you leave, the Casbah is lost."

"The Casbah will not survive even if we stay. The French are too effective. Almost all my lieutenants have been captured. I lose dozens of men each day."

"What does Ramdane say?"

"He agrees with me. He's going to stay behind with the rest of the FLN and continue the fight in Algiers."

"And the executive council?"

"I don't think he asked them."

"That's not good."

"No, it's not. But it's the least of our problems at the moment."

"Any ideas on how to achieve a breakout?"

"Yeah, but we need your help."

"How's that?"

"We need a series of diversions."

"Bombs?"

"Yes. Big ones. We need to pull enough paratroopers away from the checkpoints to successfully punch through with an all-out assault."

"How are bombs going to pull the French away?"

"We're going to plant a long list where the bombs will go off. We'll make it look like the largest bomb attack since the beginning of the war. We'll place the list in a house and have one of our double agents tip them off as the whereabouts of an FLN leader. When they search the house, they'll find the list, and the wild rabbit chase begins."

"The French will never believe it."

"They will if the first five or six bombs explode after they find the list. They'll believe the list is legitimate and pull their paratroopers from patrols and checkpoints to search for the remaining bombs before they go off. That's when we'll make our move."

"That's risky. You want to tip them off to the location of the bombs before my operatives plant them. If your timing is off, my people are fucked. They'll be captured and tortured."

"I know. And I wouldn't ask unless it was absolutely necessary. If we don't break out, our part in the revolution could be over by the end of the month. The Mujahideen will be annihilated. The FLN will have to carry on the fight alone."

"I see. And what will you and your men do once you leave Algiers?"

"We'll focus our actions against the Pieds-Noirs. With luck, they'll overreact and call international attention to the war."

"You mean atrocities?"

"Yes. That is what makes headlines these days."

Saadi went silent, deep in thought as he took a few sips of tea, then nodded, "Alright. You've got your bombs. I'll make you a list of the best and most believable targets."

"How long before you are ready?"

"One week. I need time to assemble the bombs and instruct my operatives."

"Thank you, my friend. My men will be ready."

Algiers, Algeria

The bomb attacks and the breakout had been scheduled for a Monday morning when Algerians were on their way to work, and traffic was heaviest. The thinking was that the more people the Mujahideen could mix with after they left the Casbah, the better.

Saadi had decided to place twelve bombs in total – six to explode and another six for the French to find and disarm in order to keep the charade going long enough for the Mujahideen to escape.

One of the Harkis working for the French was, in reality, an FLN spy. He tipped the French off to the whereabouts of an FLN leader. He told his French commander that he had heard a rumor in one of the coffee houses.

The French sent an entire platoon to surround the house. They crashed through the front door to find the house empty of occupants. They tore the place apart. The Harki that had guided them to the house made sure that a backgammon board on a bookshelf was tossed to the floor during the search. The false bottom fell open, but the list was not exposed. He discretely gave it a kick, and the folded piece of paper partially fell out. It was just enough to find but not too obvious. He moved off without pointing it out. A paratrooper spotted it and brought it to his commander. The commander examined the paper and realized it was important. He sent it immediately by courier to the intelligence unit.

Saadi used all three of his personally trained sirens to place the twelve bombs. The timers he used could only be set for a maximum of one hour. Each operative would need to place her four bombs within one hour. It was a very tight schedule. Saadi made them practice setting the bombs and traveling to where the bombs would be placed until their procedures were flawless.

Djamila Bouhired was nineteen with a smile that would light up any room. She was attractive and wore her brown-colored hair in a ponytail. She spoke a little Italian. Her accent was not good, but most French soldiers couldn't tell the difference. It was her fiery attitude that convinced them. A little angel, a little devil. It was a powerful combination.

She had trouble placing her second bomb. The timing switch had malfunctioned. She had to take the entire bomb to a nearby bathroom and disassemble it to find the problem – a tiny piece of cotton stuck between the electrical contacts. She finally got it to work and planted the bomb without being noticed.

She was running eight minutes late when she finally got back to the house to pick up her third bomb. Placing the third bomb went off without a hitch, and she even shaved two minutes off the delivery.

She was only six minutes late when she picked up her fourth bomb. It was the final bomb of the entire mission. The others were already in place and set to go off within the hour. Saadi considered canceling her delivery, but she assured him that she could do it before the other bombs started detonating. He glanced at his watch. It would be very close, but he agreed. She picked up the shopping bag with the bomb inside the tea biscuit tin hidden in the bottom. She trotted away instead of walked.

Something inside Saadi didn't feel right. The timing was too close. Anything that went wrong would put her in danger. He liked Djamila. She was bright, devout, and one of his best pupils. Perhaps he even loved her.

He decided to follow her. He put on the chadaree that he had used in the past to disguise his face. He was tall and had to bend his knees beneath the full-body dress while walking to make the outfit look like it was on a woman. He had practiced walking in the chadaree until he made it look natural. His face was completely covered except for his eyes. He repositioned the face mask to ride low and cover his eyebrows, which were very bushy and might give him away. He rushed to catch up with her. He knew where she was going.

He found her at the bottom of the Casbah near a coffee house frequented by French soldiers. That was where she would have placed the bomb had she not been stopped by a French patrol.

Three paratroopers were standing around her performing a routine check of her documents, which Saadi had ensured were impeccable. One searched her bag and found the tea biscuit tin. He shook the tin to hear the contents. She scolded him for breaking her grandmother's favorite cookies. He placed the tin back in the bag and handed it to her. Her attractiveness was working against her. The soldiers were taking longer than usual to check her documents and using the time to flirt with her. She played their game but tried to rush them along by saying she was late for her guitar lesson. That just made things worse as one of the soldiers also played guitar and started asking questions. She acted annoyed. They finally gave her back her documents and sent her on her way.

She walked twenty yards when the first bomb went off in the distance. She kept walking as if she hadn't noticed the explosion. The paratroopers were suspicious and shouted for her to stop. She didn't. Instead, she ran. One of the paratroopers fired his submachine gun in the air. She stopped cold in her tracks. She was frightened for a good reason. The soldiers ran to her and forced her to kneel while they searched her bag again. This time they opened the biscuit tin and found the bomb.

Saadi stood at the corner of a building watching with sadness as the paratrooper placed handcuffs on her and lifted her. He pulled out his pistol and took aim. He was sure he could kill one, maybe even two of the paratroopers before they returned fire. It might even give her time to escape. But he couldn't risk it. Hundreds of Mujahideen were depending on them. He had to keep the secret. He fired one shot into the back of her head before ducking around the corner of the building. She fell dead. The secret was safe.

Saadi sighed deeply, then ran off before the paratroopers found him. As he was running, he could hear the other bombs going off in the distance. He and his sirens had done their part but at a high cost.

Si Larbi and his Mujahideen heard the explosions. They would need to be patient and wait for their lookouts to report back that the French paratroopers had moved off to find the remaining bombs. Hopefully, enough soldiers would leave to allow his men to break through their lines around the Casbah and escape into Algiers. Once out of the Casbah, they would scatter and rendezvous later outside the city. It was a good plan. It just needed God's help. Si Larbi was not a religious man, but he knelt with his Mujahideen for the first time during the late morning prayer.

The intelligence unit also heard the explosions. Their initial analysis of the list was that it was a fake designed to send them on a wild goose chase. When they heard the first bomb go off at the exact time on the list, their confidence in their conclusions was shaken. The second explosion at the correctly listed time dispelled any doubts they still had as to the list's authenticity, and the race was on to find the remaining bombs listed. They needed help to find all the bombs before they went off. The plan had worked precisely as Si Larbi had hoped.

Within the hour, Si Larbi's lookouts reported back. The French had moved off as he had planned but not enough. The French line around the Casbah was still well manned. He decided that he and his men had to try anyway. Saadi and his operatives had taken a significant risk to help them. Si Larbi could not let that sacrifice go to waste. Besides, God was on their side. He ordered his men to move out.

Si Larbi had spent the week surveying each of the possible exits out of the Casbah. The French were tricky and never posted the same number of men at a checkpoint. Fortunately, there were a few places that the French considered improbable targets for an attack and reduced the number of paratroopers on a continual basis. It was at one of these places that Si Larbi and the Mujahideen gathered. They checked their weapons and readied themselves. Many said extra prayers. Si Larbi knew better than to wait long. They could be discovered by a French patrol at any moment. He gave his men the hand signal to attack.

The Mujahideen broke cover and rushed the checkpoint en masse. A firefight broke out. The French fired their submachine guns, killing several rebels, but the Mujahideen outnumbered the French. They were successful at killing the paratroopers and breaking through the checkpoint.

It was unfortunate for Si Larbi and his men that a French armored car was passing on the street below the checkpoint. The sergeant commanding the patrol ordered his driver to investigate the gunshots. The armored vehicle turned up the street leading to the Casbah just as the Mujahideen rounded the corner at a dead run. Both sides opened fire – the Mujahideen with their antiquated pistols and rifles and the French with a machinegun mounted in a steel turret. It was no match. The Mujahideen fell like dominoes. Si Larbi watched the last of his army being wiped out before his eyes and called for a retreat back into the Casbah. God had not heard their prayers. The breakout had failed.

Algiers, Algeria

Bruno had been ordered to Massu's office at headquarters. "Five bombs went off in the Casbah under your watch, Colonel," said Massu. "I've given you everything you have requested, and you have neglected to bring the FLN to heel."

"You are correct. I will not make excuses," said Bruno.

"I gave you this assignment because of your record of completing the tasks assigned to you. You have failed miserably."

"We have not failed. We just need more time."

"We don't have more time, Colonel. Every day the Ultras are taking more and more things into their own hands. They show little regard for our authority. Soon we will be fighting on two fronts at the same time."

"I realize that. Perhaps they are already part of the problem."

"I have no doubt. But at least they are getting the job done of wiping out the FLN. That is more than I can say for you and your men."

"General Massu, that is not a fair characterization of the situation at hand. We have killed or captured over eighteen thousand FLN and Mujahideen within the Casbah. Their forces have been greatly depleted."

"And yet they still can carry out terrorist bomb attacks like the five today."

"We have determined that the bombs were meant as a diversion to draw off our forces in the Casbah so the Mujahideen could escape. Fortunately, our armored patrol was able to stop the breakout."

"The bombs still killed dozens of civilians and several paratroopers. That is hardly a success I would brag about."

There was a knock at the door, and Major Aussaresses entered and saluted before speaking, "Sorry to interrupt, sir. I have information I thought you should know."

"What is it, Major?"

"We believe we have found the source of the misleading information. It was the Harki that led to the discovery of the list of bombing locations."

"Not really rocket science, is it?"

"No, sir. But he did give us a name before he was executed - Nay Mekhloufi. Mekhloufi is an Imam in the Casbah."

"You're sure Mekhloufi is involved, Major?" said Bruno. "He's very popular with the people."

"And a messenger for the FLN. We crosschecked the information with another interrogation subject, and he confirmed it. We are sure Mekhloufi is at the very least delivering messages for the FLN."

"Well done, Major," said Massu.

"We should act on this right away, General," said Bruno.

"See that you do, Colonel."

Bruno saluted and left the office. "Your results have been impressive, Major Aussaresses. They have not gone unnoticed," said Massu.

"Then you have been reading my reports?"

"With great interest."

"And are they passed on to Paris?"

"Of course."

"Good to know, sir. I was worried that they may contain too much detail about our methods."

"Nonsense. We have the approval of the highest authorities, I assure you. Carry on, Major," said Massu dismissing Aussaresses with a salute.

Massu had lied to Aussaresses. He needed him to continue his interrogations without the burden of worrying about the future. The major was yielding results. But Massu was no fool. He knew that the government officials in Paris would have no stomach for what was required to destroy the rebellion. He could not trust that his commanding officers wouldn't pass on the major's reports to their civilian overseers. After reading each of the major's reports, Massu personally burned them in the HQ incinerator.

Algiers, Algeria

Bruno took charge of the operation to capture Mekhloufi. It was not that he didn't trust the officers under his command. They were fine soldiers but sometimes overly cautious when planning their missions. He needed things to happen fast, and he knew he could make that happen by getting personally involved.

He used a company of paratroopers to surround the Casbah's main mosque during afternoon prayers. He knew that the patrons would be angry when their Imam was taken in for questioning, and he wanted to ensure that he had enough manpower to deter any resistance. The paratroopers kept out of sight until Mekhloufi left the building. The French moved in quickly. "Nay Mekhloufi?" said Bruno.

"Yes?" said Mekhloufi.

"You are to come with us."

"Come with you where?"

"You are to be questioned."

"You mean, interrogated?"

"Come with us now, or you will be arrested."

"Is there a difference?"

A crowd of worshippers gathered around Bruno and Mekhloufi. Bruno had had enough and motioned for two paratroopers to take Mekhloufi by the arms and escort him. As soon as the paratroopers put their hands on the Imam, the crowd interceded by pushing at the paratroopers and demanding the Imam's release. Bruno motioned for more of his men to deal with the angry mob. The French shoved the mob back, using their submachine guns. A man in the crowd grabbed one of the paratroopers' submachine gun and tried to pull it away. Bruno grabbed a weapon from the paratrooper next to him and fired a burst of machinegun rounds in the air. The man let go of the paratrooper's gun, and the crowd recoiled. They could see that the paratroopers meant business. Few thought the French would hesitate to kill them if it came to blows. Bruno and his men moved off with Mekhloufi.

Mekhloufi was turned over to Aussaresses for interrogation. Bruno thought about questioning the Imam himself, but he knew that would take more time. Word of the Imam's detention would have already spread through the Casbah. Bruno didn't want the FLN leaders to go further into hiding before he could find them. Aussaresses was the answer. Bruno didn't like the major's methods, but he had to admit they were effective, especially when time was short.

Mekhloufi sat naked in a chair with his hands tied to the chair's legs so that he had to slump over slightly to keep pressure off his wrists. Aussaresses entered the room with a Harki. The Harkis were not as subtle as the French interrogators, but Aussaresses wasn't looking for subtle. He knew that the Imam would not give up information on the FLN easily. He did not fear death, knowing that he was assured a place in heaven. Aussaresses was interested in having him fear life. "This is outrageous. You cannot treat a man of the cloth as such," said Mekhloufi as they entered.

Aussaresses and the Harki said nothing. The Harki went right to work. He attached two large alligator clips to either side of the Imam's scrotum. "What are you doing?" said Mekhloufi.

The Harki stepped over to the table and connected the wire attached to the alligator clips to a voltage regulator, which in turn was connected to a car battery. He placed a wooden stick in the Aman's mouth to keep him from biting off his tongue. Finished, the Harki turned to Aussaresses and nodded. The major nodded back for the interrogation to begin. The Harki twisted the knob on the regulator, and the Imam went stiff with pain as the electricity pulsed through his genitals. After the second hand on his watch swept past the ten-second mark, the Harki twisted the regulator to zero, the Imam's body went limp, and he urinated on the floor.

After a moment, Mekhloufi looked up and spat out the wooden piece. "You didn't ask me anything," he said, weeping.

"You will tell us what we want to know when you are ready," said Aussaresses and nodded to the Harki to continue.

The Harki picked up the wooden piece now covered in urine and moved to place it back in the Imam's mouth. "No," said Mekhloufi. "You can't do this. It's not humane."

"You will want the wood in your mouth as we increase the voltage. It will keep your teeth from shattering to pieces," said Aussaresses.

Mekhloufi's eyes went wide with fear. The Harki put the wooden piece back in his mouth and continued with the session.

Bruno sat in an office waiting. Aussaresses walked in and handed him a piece of paper with an address on it. "Good hunting, Colonel," he said with a salute. Bruno saluted back and left.

Saadi sat at his table, filled with tools and electronic devices. He was carefully assembling a new bomb. It would be bigger than usual. It was to be used at a nightclub frequented by the Pieds-Noirs of Algiers. He was using a new design of blasting cap as the detonation method. He hoped it would be more reliable, as some of his bombs had not gone off because the detonator had become dislodged during placement. Saadi hated failure.

On returning to Algiers, Saadi had not returned home to his bakery and family. He missed them greatly but did not want to risk their lives by making contact. He never knew when he was being followed or when his end would come. Instead, he had rented a large apartment in the Casbah that could be used by him and his female operatives.

His little workshop had no windows and no doors. It was hidden behind a false wall in the apartment. It was impossible to detect unless someone was smart enough to measure the exterior walls of the apartment against the interior space. He kept the space small so that it was imperceivable at first glance.

He had acquired enough explosive material to make dozens of bombs of a variety of sizes. He wasn't a wasteful person. He always calculated the size of his target and used the right amount of explosive to completely destroy it, but no more than necessary. He saw bombmaking as stewardship. He had been chosen to carry out Allah's will and had performed his calling responsibly. In his mind, this assured him a place in heaven for him, his family, and the young girls he had trained to plant his bombs. They would be his in the afterlife. His reward and theirs.

Smoke rose from the flux when it touched the tip of his hot soldering iron. The flux purified the ends of the wires before joining them with the liquified solder. He always soldered his wires together instead of using the plastic twist-on connectors that were all the rage by electricians. He saw the connectors as unreliable and the electricians that used them as lazy. Once connected, he would carefully wrap his wires with vinyl tape to insulate them and protect his welds. He was a craftsman and took great pride in his work. He knew the French technicians would examine his work as they investigated his bombings. He wanted them to know they were dealing with a seasoned professional.

He heard a secret knock on his false wall. Only his two remaining sirens knew the code. He knew it must be important. They had been instructed not to disturb him during his work. Once inside his workshop, only he could open the wall. He picked up the revolver laying on the table as a precaution and moved to the wall. He pushed the wall forward so that it swung outward. He was startled to see a man's face and pointed his pistol. It was Si Larbi escorted by one of his sirens. "Are you crazy?" said Saadi.

"Perhaps," said Si Larbi pushing past Saadi and letting himself into the tiny room.

Saadi closed the door. "You have been told never to come here. Are you sure you weren't followed?"

"Yes, I'm sure."

"What is it?"

"We have to try again...the breakout."

"Fine. Do what you must. But I will not risk any more of my girls."

"Alright. We can place the bombs ourselves."

"Forget it. There is too much risk of your men being searched."

"We'll have to take that risk. We cannot stay in the Casbah."

"And what makes you think things will be different this time?"

"We need bigger bombs. Something that will really shake up the French."

Saadi laughed and said, "Bigger is always the solution."

"You have a better idea?"

"Yes. Have your men fight better?"

"It's not a matter of fighting better. The French outnumber us, and they have modern weapons."

"A bullet from an Enfield kills just the same as a bullet from a submachine gun."

"Yes, but there are a lot more coming from a submachine gun."

"So, steal yourselves some submachine guns."

"We've tried. It's the ammunition that is the problem. We need more."

"You're very good at coming up with excuses."

"Watch your mouth, Saadi. I lost forty-six men this morning. All patriots fighting for Algeria."

"You're right. I'm sorry for your loss."

Outside the apartment, Bruno and a company of paratroopers quietly surrounded the building. They set up tripod-mounted light machineguns in front of and behind the building. He sent several of his men in through the building's basement windows to cut off any attempt to escape through a secret tunnel they might have dug. The paratroopers moved into the neighboring buildings and used the windows and doorways as firing positions. He had a team of engineers on standby to remove any boobytraps the FLN terrorists might have set. Bruno wasn't taking any chances.

He waited until everyone was in place before giving the signal for the assault team to enter the building.

They went up the iron fire escape in the alley behind the building and in through the front doors. Several men were left in the lobby while twelve paratroopers walked up the stairs trying to keep as silent as possible. Bruno knew there was a very good chance that the rebels had explosives, and he considered evacuating the building before making their assault, but he knew the noise of an evacuation would tip off the suspects. A firefight might kill more civilians trying to escape than a bomb. It was a calculated risk.

Bruno followed his men up the interior stairs. He was unarmed as always, free from giving battle so he could direct his men. It took real courage to enter a building occupied by terrorists intent on killing him without so much as a sidearm. The death of Colonel Bigeard was the biggest prize the FLN could hope for in Algeria. Bruno was a well-known hero, loved by the French people. The FLN would gladly trade even General Massu's death for the death of the great Bruno. It would be a massive blow against French morale and the perceived invulnerability of the paratroopers.

Inside the apartment, Saadi heard another secret knock on the wall. "What now?" he said, opening the wall.

One of his sirens was standing on the opposite side of the wall and said, "The French are here. Paratroopers have surrounded the building."

Saadi and Si Larbi pointed their pistols at each other. "You idiot, they followed you," said Saadi.

"Nobody followed me. You betrayed me," said Si Larbi.

"This is stupid. We've got to get out of here," said Saadi lowering his pistol and moving out past the wall.

Si Larbi followed him. "Follow the girls to the fourth floor. There's a window. You can jump across to the rooftop of the next building. I'll be right behind you," said Saadi.

"What are you going to do?"

"A going-away-present for the French."

Si Larbi followed the two girls out the front door of the apartment. Saadi closed the wall and knelt down. There was a small hidden door the size of a shoebox in the base of the wall. He opened it and reached inside. There was a bomb with a pressure sensor on the detonator. He flipped the activation switch, arming the bomb, and closed the door. He thought for a moment, then pulled a Franc from his pocket and tucked it under the gap between the floor and the bottom of the wall so that half of the coin was exposed. He ran out the front door of the apartment, closing the door behind him.

Si Larbi and the girls had run up the stairway to the fourth floor. It was as Saadi had said. There was a window overlooking the rooftop on the next building. It was a bit of a jump and risky, but Si Larbi didn't hesitate. He jumped and landed in a tumble on the rooftop. The girls followed. They found a good hiding place behind the rooftop access doorway and waited for Saadi.

As Saadi ran from the apartment, he saw the French paratroopers running up the stairway. He was too late. His escape was cut off. He ran back inside the apartment and reached inside a wooden box sitting on a hallway table. Inside the box were two grenades. He grabbed them both. He waited and watched through the crack in the door until he could see the first paratroopers running out the floor landing. He pulled the pin on one of the grenades, opened the door, tossed it toward the paratroopers, and slammed the door shut.

The paratroopers saw the grenade bouncing toward them and scattered. It exploded. Nobody was hurt, but their ears were ringing. They moved again towards the doorway.

Inside, Saadi could hear them coming. He prepared the second grenade putting his finger through the pinhole. He opened the door slightly to look out into the hallway.

The lead paratrooper saw Saadi and opened fire with his submachine gun.

Saadi slammed the door shut. The bullets pierced the door and splintered the wood. One caught Saadi in the shoulder and spun him around. He accidentally pulled the pin on the grenade, and the spoon flipped open, activating the weapon's timer. His revolver and the grenade dropped to the floor as he fell nearby. The live grenade rolled a few feet away. He was stunned, and it took a moment before he realized what had happened. He kicked the grenade with his foot through a doorway into the next room, where it exploded.

The first paratrooper burst through the door and found Saadi on the floor, bleeding from the bullet wound. Saadi reached for his revolver. The paratrooper stepped on his hand. Saadi reached with his other hand. The paratrooper hit him in the head with the butt of his submachine gun. Saadi went limp, unconscious. The paratrooper slapped handcuffs on him as two more paratroopers moved past and continued the search of the apartment. Saadi was dragged out into the hallway and down the stairway, still unconscious.

Outside the building, Saadi was lifted into a jeep where he was placed in back with a guard and driven away for interrogation. He woke and realized he was caught. He thought his life was over. He wondered if Si Larbi and the girls had gotten away.

Si Larbi heard the two grenade explosions and decided he had waited long enough. Saadi wasn't coming. The two girls were in tears. He left them and entered the rooftop doorway leading to a stairwell. He ran down the stairs.

Below, four paratroopers that had taken up firing positions inside the building listened as someone ran down the stairs. They exchanged concerned glances. The largest of the four paratroopers moved to the stairwell doorway and pressed himself flat against the wall. When Si Larbi exited the stairwell, he was facing the barrels of three paratroopers' submachine guns. His eyes went wide. He never even noticed the massive fist of the paratrooper standing by the doorway, smashing him in the side of the head. He collapsed unconscious.

Si Larbi was handcuffed and dragged toward another waiting jeep. He awoke and realized that he was being taken prisoner. He broke free of the grasp of the two paratroopers carrying him. He ran down the street with his hands still cuffed.

Bruno saw the prisoner running and stuck out his boot as he ran past. Si Larbi tripped and fell, landing on his face, breaking his nose and skinning his forehead on the cobblestones. "Ouch," said Bruno as he watched the young rebel struggling to his knees and then feet. He ain't gonna give up. I like this guy, thought Bruno, remembering his own capture at Dien Bien Phu after the fortress fell. He didn't give up either and kept trying to escape his Viet Minh capturers, even when it was beyond all hope and reason.

The two embarrassed paratroopers that were guarding Si Larbi finally caught up and grabbed him by the hair and arms. Still, he squirmed as they hauled him back to the jeep and drove him away.

Inside Saadi's apartment, the French engineers carried out a thorough survey for potential bombs and boobytraps. They were careful to search for tripwires and loose floorboards that may have had plunge-style detonators underneath. Convinced that the apartment was safe, the engineers signaled the paratroopers in the hallway. The paratroopers reentered and went to work ripping the apartment apart in search of evidence and clues to the whereabouts of the remaining FLN members and Mujahideen.

One of the paratroopers saw the coin Saadi had left. He reached down to pick it up, but a nearby engineer stopped him. The engineer knelt down and studied the half-revealed coin, searching for a trigger-wire. There was none. He picked up the coin and flipped it to the paratrooper as a memento.

Scratches on the floor caught the eye of the engineer still on his knees. It wasn't the scratches that were important. It was their shape – an arc. Like something hinged on one end had been dragged across the wooden floor. He examined the wall and found a well-hidden release switch. He pressed the switch and swung the hidden wall open.

The bomb Saadi had set at the base of the wall was triggered. The explosion killed the engineer and the paratrooper holding the coin. The secondary explosions from the already assembled bombs and the remaining explosive material in the hidden workshop were massive. They completely demolished the apartment building and the three buildings directly around it. Over one hundred civilians and twenty-three paratroopers were killed in the explosions. Hundreds of others were seriously wounded. Saadi's two remaining sirens still on the rooftop waiting for him were killed when the building collapsed. It took days to uncover all the survivors from the rubble. Saadi's final bomb was the most deadly of the war.

Algiers, Algeria

Si Larbi's nose healed quickly, even under the harsh conditions of the French interrogation center. Bruno had taken a personal interest in the interrogation of Si Larbi. He refused to allow him to be tortured, believing that Si Larbi would never break or would give misleading information that would lead the French on another wild goose chase. Instead, he talked with Si Larbi as one commander to another, often over supper, in his cell. "How does it feel to allow women to deliver your bombs in baskets?" said Bruno.

"You give me your planes and helicopters, and I'll give you my bombs in baskets," said Si Larbi.

"You know you have lost the war. The last of your men are being rounded up as we speak. It's over for you."

"Another will take my place," said Si Larbi quoting the 'chant des partisans' of the French resistance of which Bruno had been a member.

Bruno tried to keep from smiling, thinking it unprofessional. "Your comrade Saadi has been quite helpful."

"I doubt that."

"You could do yourself some good if you gave us a few names. Perhaps I could get you a blanket or even a book to read."

"I will not stain my honor for trinkets. Besides, I'm not much of a reader."

"Give me something. I do not want to see you guillotined."

"It's a quick death."

"You don't have to die."

"Yes, I do. And the sooner, the better. You will make me a martyr, and I will fight on in the memory of my people. That is enough for me."

"This war will be over soon. You could be released if you cooperate."

"Do you really think it will be over?"

"Of course. You have lost."

"We haven't lost. There are still Algerians. You French learned nothing from Indochina. You cannot beat an insurgency, especially one born of injustice. You can only tamp down the flames for a time. But it will rise up again and again until you French grow weary and leave our country. It is God's will."

"Perhaps. But you will not be around to see it."

"I saw it the moment we started fighting. The end was, and is, inevitable. Algeria will be free."

"Says the man sitting in a prison cell."

"You think I matter. I don't. I am but one. We are nine million. You'll have to kill every last one of us to win your war."

Bruno knew there was truth in what Si Larbi was saying. There was a knock at the door, and a lieutenant entered. "Colonel, the general wishes to see you in his office," said the lieutenant.

"Please inform General Massu I will be right there," said Bruno rising from the box he was sitting on.

The lieutenant left, and Bruno moved to the open cell door. He turned back to Si Larbi and said, "I'll see if I can get you that blanket."

"And a magazine perhaps. I like looking at the pictures," said Si Larbi.

Bruno nodded and walked out, locking the door behind him. Si Larbi liked Bruno and wondered if they would have been friends in another time and a different war.

Algiers, Algeria

It was past midnight when Ali La Pointe entered an alleyway in the Casbah. He had been careful that he was not being followed. The alley looked vacant. He walked cautiously toward the dead-end of the alley, moving past empty shipping crates and trash bins. He had his hand on his pistol tucked into the back of his pants beneath his shirt. He heard the cock of a pistol from behind him. Whoever it was had the drop on him. He released the pistol handle and raised his hands. "Turn around slowly," said a voice.

La Pointe obeyed the voice and turned around. He watched as Ramdane emerged from the shadows holding a pistol. "Are you sure you weren't followed?" said Ramdane.

"Positive," said La Pointe.

Ramdane lowered his gun. "Where are the others?" he said.

"They were caught before I could get to them."

"All twelve?"

"Yes… all twelve. House-to-house picked them up."

"Shit. And they didn't fight?"

"With what? All the weapons have been found. Look, we can still make it out if you wish. I found their map. I know the way."

"I haven't got a choice. I've run out of hiding places."

"Seems like this is a pretty good one," said La Pointe referring to the alley.

"Don't be a smart ass. We should get going. I've got to be out of the Casbah before sun up. Will you be coming with me to Morocco?"

"No. I enjoy killing the French too much. I'm staying."

"Alright. I'll cut you loose as soon as I make it out of the city."

"Sounds good. This way," said La Pointe motioning toward the open end of the alley.

Ramdane turned and started walking. He was almost to the corner at the mouth of the alley when he heard the cock of a pistol. He slid his hand into his jacket pocket. "Don't even think about it," said La Pointe, pointing the gun. "Turn around."

"The French or the FLN?" said Ramdane as he slowly turned.

"Does it matter?

"To me… a great deal."

"I suppose that's true. Now, remove your hand from your jacket pocket… slowly."

Ramdane obeyed. In his hand was a grenade with its safety pin ring already removed. La Pointe's eyes went wide. Ramdane opened his hand, allowing the grenade's safety lever to flip open, activating the timer. "Oh shit," said La Pointe.

Ramdane dropped the grenade to the pavement and pivoted his body around the corner of a stone building at the end of the alley. The grenade rolled toward the La Pointe. He turned to run back deeper into the alley, but it was too late. The grenade exploded, sending shrapnel into La Pointe's back and legs. He screamed and fell to the ground.

Ramdane walked back around the corner and kneeled beside La Pointe. He picked up La Pointe's revolver and examined the wounds in his back and legs. They were extensive, and he was bleeding badly. Ramdane was sure he would be dead before the French arrived. He searched his pockets until he found the map. He rolled La Pointe over on his back. La Pointe moaned. "You picked the wrong side, my friend," said Ramdane.

"God will punish you," said La Pointe writhing in pain.

"Perhaps," said Ramdane rising. "But you won't be around to see it." He walked to the mouth of the alley, checked to see if anyone was coming and disappeared around the corner. La Pointe died.

Algiers, Algeria

Achiary and a large group of his Ultras protested in front of the Governor's mansion. Their banners and signs read:

ALGERIA IS FRANCE, FRANCE IS ALGERIA
PROTECT PROPERTY RIGHTS
HANG THE REBELS

Police armed with long clubs surround the gates of the mansion. One of the Ultras threw a rock that struck a policeman on the head, knocking him to the ground. The police sergeant had had enough and ordered his men forward to disperse the mob.

Fists flew, and clubs swung as the protest evolved into a riot. A platoon of French paratroopers was called in and surrounded the mob. A paratrooper sergeant fired his submachine gun into the air. "Disperse or be fired upon!" said the sergeant and signaled his men.

The paratroopers snapped into a firing stance with their submachine guns leveled at the mob. They meant business. The crowd moved back from the police and the gates of the mansion but didn't disperse. "Who speaks for you?" said the sergeant.

Achiary stepped forward. Two paratroopers grabbed him by the arms and loaded him into a jeep. The Ultras objected by cursing and shaking their fists. Achiary was driven off.

Achiary was escorted into General Massu's office by a paratrooper corporal. Massu sat behind his desk. "Please have a seat, Monsieur Achiary," said Massu.

"I prefer to stand," said Achiary, defiant.

"And I don't care what you prefer."

Massu nodded to the corporal. The paratrooper slammed his boot into the back of Achiary's knees, making them buckle until he sat in the chair offered him. "Algiers is under martial law. Protests are not allowed."

"I am a French citizen. Even under martial law, I have rights."

"Not many, I assure you. You were disturbing the peace. I could have you shot," said Massu.

"You will not shoot me," said Achiary.

"You do not know me well, Monsieur Achiary. I am fond of making examples out of men."

"Perhaps. But you will not shoot me because we want the same thing."

"Really?"

"We both want Algeria to stay French."

"And it will."

"Not if you keep negotiating it away with the FLN. Why do you talk with those murdering bastards? They are terrorists. It is your duty to kill them."

"Monsieur, I do not need a lecture on my duty. I suggest you watch your tongue before I have you imprisoned."

"More threats?"

"What is it you want, Monsieur?"

"End negotiations."

"That is not up to me. Your argument is with the current government in Paris. Why don't you go there and protest?"

"It does not matter where we protest. Our message is being heard. Algeria is French."

"You are correct. But I will tell you what does matter? Calm on the street of Algiers. I will not allow protests. I will not allow violence. Not by you and your Ultras. And not by the FLN and their followers. There will be peace in Algiers, or I will have my men gun down anyone preventing it. Is that clear?"

"Yes, General. I hear you."

"Corporal, take Monsieur Achiary to our detention center and let him spend the night in one of our cells before releasing him."

"Yes, sir," said the corporal snapping to attention and saluting.

The corporal escorted Achiary out of Massu's office.

NINE

Paris, France

It was rare for de Gaulle to attend any government function in his latter years. He preferred to keep to himself, writing his memoirs and spending time with his family. He stayed out of the limelight as much as possible, and that was appreciated by the ministers in Paris. His words carried immense weight with the French people. It seemed the only way to get de Gaulle to show his face in public was to give him a medal. He loved medals. He had over fifty.

The Italians had created a new medal for their highest honor – the Knight Grand Cross decorated with Grand Cordon of the Order of Merit of the Italian Republic. De Gaulle was one of the first to receive it. It was quite an honor and very attractive. The ceremony was held at Il Vittoriano in Piazza Venezia, nicknamed "The Wedding Cake" by the cynical people of Rome for its multi-tiers of white marble.

After the ceremony, a reception was held in the square in front of the Pantheon at de Gaulle's request. De Gaulle was a history buff and had studied the ancient Roman leaders in depth. The cylindrical building with a portico of large granite Corinthian columns was originally a temple commissioned by Marcus Agrippa during the reign of Augustus. De Gaulle loved the feeling of celebrating his accomplishments in the shadow of greatness.

General Massu was among several French generals that attended both the ceremony and the reception. He knew to keep his distance from de Gaulle while he mingled with the leaders of the world. He was surprised when de Gaulle asked to have a word with him in private. He was even more surprised where de Gaulle chose to have their meeting – inside the Pantheon. "Impressive, isn't it?" said De Gaulle looking up at the carved dome.

"Very," said Massu. "You've always loved Roman architecture."

"Among other things, yes. Napoléon recruited many of the most famous Italian architects when he made his mark on Paris. And why not? The histories of Italy and France are intertwined."

"Congratulations on your medal, General."

"Thank you. Pretty little thing. The Italians have such good taste when it comes to design. How goes the war, Massu?"

"We are winning, or hadn't you heard?"

"I heard, but I question whether you are really winning."

"What do you mean? We've almost completely annihilated the FLN leadership. We've got the rebels on the run."

"Yes, you do. And well done. Using the paratroopers in Algiers was quite a masterstroke."

"I wish I could take credit. That decision was made higher up."

"Yes, but you were the instrument that got it done. Too bad it will all be for naught."

"All for naught?"

"The MPs do not recognize when France has won. They continue to negotiate with the FLN leaders in Cairo. Your men bled for Algeria, and now they give it up like it was merely a bargaining chip."

"Yes. It is quite unfortunate."

"Treasonous if you ask me. But nobody asks me these days."

"You sound like you have a plan to remedy the situation."

"Me? No. I merely observe. I told the ministers when we were forming the Fourth Republic that we needed a strong executive branch to govern a country such as France. They sided with the will of the people. And now what do we have? Chaos. No. My time has passed. I had my opportunity."

"You served well, General. The people love you."

"When I keep my mouth shut."

"No. They still listen. You wield a great deal of power. You should be the one leading us."

"No, no. Not me. I have too much history behind me."

"It is your history that makes you great."

"Hmm… perhaps. So what are you going to do?"

"About Algeria? What can I do?"

"You are a commanding general of paratroopers, Massu. You are the one with the power."

"Power I cannot use."

"Really?"

There was a long silence. Massu was unsure what de Gaulle was suggesting. "Are you saying that we should take control?"

"I am merely suggesting someone must save France from itself and its politicians."

"A coup d'état?"

"Don't sound so shocked. Our Republic was built on a coup, or don't you remember?"

"I remember. I wouldn't be honest if I said I hadn't thought about it."

"Of course you have. You are a patriot and a man of action. I know you well, Massu. You are brave beyond measure and would gladly sacrifice yourself for your country."

"I would... and so would you."

"Of course. France is facing a constitutional crisis. Extreme measures may be required."

"If such an extreme measure was required, would you consider leading it?"

"No, no. I cannot be involved in such an event. I am a constitutionalist. I will not go against the laws of the land."

"What if you were not involved in the actual event but came in later... as a peacemaker... a temporary leader to oversee the creation of a new constitution?"

"With a strong executive branch?"

"Of course."

"Massu, you know me. I will always do what is best for France. I will not defy the will of the people. They must demand that I return to power, or I will not do it. One must keep one's honor. I believe it was not far from this very spot that Roman generals would throw themselves on their swords to save their honor after a defeat in the field."

"...Or betrayal?"

"Or betrayal."

Massu thought to himself, You sneaky old bastard. You must have been planning this all along. You just want France to beg you to return without getting your hands dirty. De Gaulle could see that Massu had figured it out and that he had a willing accomplice. The two generals exchanged knowing smiles.

Algiers, Algeria

Trinquier sat in Massu's office, enjoying the cognac his commander had offered him. "Roger, that matter we discussed... concerning the PMs in Paris...?," said Massu.

"Yes, sir," said Trinquier. "I remember it well. Have your plans progressed?"

"Substantially. It has been brought to my attention that we should attempt to recruit Colonel Bigeard."

"Bruno? Why?"

"He is well-known and revered. The people may find what we do more palatable if one of the leaders is a war hero."

"He is an opportunist and a rank-jumper."

"Regardless. We need him."

"Alright."

"I believe you will recognize that it would not be seen as proper for his commanding officer to approach him concerning his participation."

"You want me to do it?"

"You are the same rank."

"He hates me."

"He doesn't hate you, Roger. He just doesn't care for your opinion. But don't let that deter you... He doesn't care for anyone's opinion."

"You think he will listen?"

"I think we must try. His reputation would bolster our cause, especially with the paratroopers. Your participation in his recruitment would not be forgotten, especially if you are successful."

"Alright. I'll do it."

"Good man," said Massu pouring more cognac into Trinquier's glass.

Algiers, Algeria

Trinquier knocked on Bruno's office door. "Bruno, might I have a word with you?" said Trinquier poking his head in.

"Of course," said Bruno. "Please sit, Roger."

"I know we have not always agreed on a strategy. However, I believe we both have France's best interest at heart."

"I have never questioned your patriotism."

"Nor I yours. France owes a great debt to you and your men for your retaking control of the Casbah and capturing the FLN leadership."

"Save your flattery, Roger. It was a team effort. We could not have retaken the Casbah without you and your men managing the rest of Algiers. It is a fact, not a compliment."

"I think we can also agree that the government in Paris fails to recognize what is needed to finish the war. We have abolished the FLN from Algiers, yet they continue to negotiate with the remaining FLN leaders in Cairo. They seek appeasement rather than victory."

"I agree."

"They are abandoning Algeria. We cannot let that stand."

"It is not up to us."

"But it could be."

"Be careful, Roger. We are soldiers. We do not create policy. We implement it. That is our duty."

"They turned Indochina over to the communists, Bruno. They are doing the same with Algeria."

"The Algerians are not communists."

"Yet."

"Roger, why don't you just get to the point? You clearly have something you want to discuss."

"May I have your word as an officer and a gentleman that what we discuss will remain between just us?"

"I am not sure about the gentlemen part, but as an officer... Yes, you have my word."

"Very well. The Fourth Republic has become unstable. One cannot govern a country as powerful as France when ministers are changing seats as if playing a child's game. The constitution is too weak to protect the people and must be replaced."

"I agree."

"I thought you might. If our commanders were to take control of the government, would you support it?"

"A coup d'état?"

"Yes."

"Then, no."

"But you agree that the Constitution is weak."

"I do. It should be replaced... but by referendum, not a Junta."

"There is no time for a referendum."

"There is always time for democracy."

"The ministers would never allow a constitutional referendum. It would remove them from power."

"They will bend to the will of the people. The people must show them the way... not the military."

"And you are quite sure on this matter?"

"You mean treason?"

"That's rather harsh, don't you think?"

"I think we should call it what it is. But be assured... and assure those that send you... I will keep my word as an officer and not discuss our conversation with anyone."

"Yes... We were speaking hypothetically."

"Of course," said Bruno offering his hand to Trinquier.

"As you said... we do not always agree on strategy," said Trinquier shaking Bruno's hand and leaving.

Atlas Mountains, Algeria

It was pre-dawn. As the sky lightened, it outlined the surrounding mountains. Ramdane rode on horseback with his guide and two bodyguards armed with rifles. They were on a roughly hewn goat path used by a local tribe to drive their livestock to market in Morocco. They had chosen to travel at night because the French were patrolling the area with their helicopters. If they were spotted, it wouldn't take much to run them down. Helicopters were faster than horses, and the French had a tendency to shoot first and ask questions later whenever they saw something suspicious in the mountains.

It would be dawn soon, and they needed to find a cave or shelter to hide their mounts. Ramdane was tired, and his ass was sore from riding the horse. He was pretty sure he would get a bad case of hemorrhoids from the saddle and constipation from eating only dried meat for the last three days. He wasn't looking forward to either.

He and his men had been traveling while avoiding French checkpoints and patrols. They had been lucky. They hadn't been forced into combat. They were not afraid of the French, but they did not know the territory well or where they could find good cover in a firefight.

The guide said he knew the area like the back of his hand, but at times Ramdane wondered. He had a bad habit of going up one trail, then reversing back down and taking another. It was not very reassuring. Ramdane planned on looking for a new guide at the next village they came upon.

As they rounded a corner, the guide said, "I need to take a shit. Meet me at the top of the ridge." He kicked his horse in the gut and took off farther up the mountain. One of the bodyguards was about to go after him when Ramdane said, "Let him go. He's useless anyway. The path will lead us to the next village. It's simple enough." The two bodyguards grunted their obedience.

A shot rang out, and a bullet hit the horse of one of the bodyguards. The horse reared then collapsed off the side of the path with the bodyguard still in the saddle. The wounded horse and rider plummeted down the side of the rocky mountain end over end. Two hundred yards lower, they tumbled to a stop. Both were lifeless.

Ramdane and the remaining bodyguard jumped from their saddles and maneuvered their horses between themselves and where they thought the shot might have originated higher up the mountain. The remaining bodyguard fired several shots toward a distant rock grouping. He hadn't seen the sniper in the rocks but figured it as good of a place as any to ambush the riders coming up the trail. "That son of a bastard. I'm going to kill him," said the bodyguard.

"It's not the guide. He's nearsighted. He could barely tell which direction we were heading," said Ramdane.

"Then, who?"

"Someone that wants me dead and knew which way we were going."

"And who would that be?"

"My comrades in arms, I would guess."

"They betrayed you?"

"I gave them little choice. No dissension in the ranks allowed."

"We can't stay here. The sun will be up soon. He'll circle around for a better angle and kill us."

Ramdane chuckled and said, "You're assuming there's just one."

"Why? Did you see more?" said the bodyguard alarmed, looking around.

"No. But I don't need to. Wolves hunt in packs."

"I still don't think we should…" said the bodyguard until he was interrupted by a bullet hitting him in the side of the face. The bodyguard collapsed dead, and his horse bolted up the goat path.

Ramdane was surrounded and alone. Whoever was out there knew what they were doing. They had eliminated the bodyguards first and could now take their time. He wondered if they had been ordered to capture him alive. He wouldn't let that happen. It might buy him a little time but would probably mean that he was killed in some inhumane way as an example to the other members of FLN. He wouldn't let them define him. Not even in death.

He pulled his water bottle and his prayer rug from the back of his saddle. He placed the rug on the ground facing East – the approximate direction of Mecca. He washed his hands and face. As he knelt down and started his morning prayer, the horse wandered off to find its breakfast, exposing Ramdane to the snipers. They waited patiently for him to finish. They didn't hate Ramdane. He was a legend to the FLN and the Mujahideen that were ordered to kill him.

Once finished, he rose and pulled the pistol from his belt. He walked up the goat path, looking for a target. The sun was peeking over the ridgeline. It was a beautiful sunrise, backed by a crystal-clear sky. Two shots rang out, one after the other. The first bullet hit him in the shoulder and spun him around. The second took off the top left side of his head. He fell dead.

Algiers, Algeria

Major Aussaresses and Colonel Trinquier were sitting in Massu's office as Bruno entered and saluted his commander, General Massu. "Sit please, Colonel," said Massu. "How goes the interrogation of Si Larbi?"

"Slow, but I think I am making progress. I think he is beginning to trust me," said Bruno.

"With all due respect, I'm not sure it matters anymore," said Trinquier.

"What do you mean?"

"Anything he might have told is now useless. His comrades have moved to new hiding places at this point, and any operations he might have been involved in have most likely been changed or abandoned."

"The major is right, Bruno," said Massu. "Si Larbi is of little value. He should be executed... as an example."

"I disagree, General. He knows the organizational structure of the FLN and the Mujahideen. That alone could be of immense help to us."

"And do you honestly believe he will divulge such information?" said Trinquier.

"With time, perhaps..."

"Si Larbi is out of time. Execute him. Hanging, I think," said Massu.

"Si Larbi is an officer and deserves to be treated as such under the Geneva Convention," said Bruno

"Si Larbi is a terrorist and shall be executed under Martial Law."

"I will not execute an officer."

"You are refusing a direct order from your superior officer?"

"An unlawful order."

"You are relieved of command, Colonel Bigeard," said Massu. "Colonel Trinquier, you will take command of Colonel Bigeard's para brigade. Colonel Bigeard, you are dismissed."

Bruno was stunned. He was a commander without a command. He would not beg for the return of his command. That was beneath him. He simply stood, saluted, and walked out.

"Major Aussaresses, see that Si Larbi is executed immediately," said Massu.

"Yes, sir," said Aussaresses rising, saluting, and leaving the office.

Trinquier and Massu sat quietly for a long moment. Massu wondered if he had just made a mistake. Bruno was a war hero, and the public loved him. Word would spread quickly of his dismissal. "I suppose a career in politics is now out of the question," said Massu breaking the silence.

"I don't know, General. It's hard to say how the public will regard Colonel Bigeard. Especially if his participation in Si Larbi's interrogation gets out," said Trinquier.

"Perhaps you are right, Roger. One cannot predict the public's temperament."

Aussaresses supervised the removal of Si Larbi from the interrogation center. Si Larbi was placed in handcuffs, and his legs were shackled. A squad of twelve well-armed paratroopers under Aussaresses' command was used to escort Si Larbi as he left. Aussaresses wasn't taking any chances.

Outside the building, a company of paratroopers was lined up in two columns on either side of the path. Bruno stood beside them. He did not order the paratroopers to accompany him. He was no longer their commander. He simply told them what he was doing, and they followed him as they had done so many times before. As Si Larbi appeared, Bruno and the company snapped to attention and saluted.

Aussaresses ordered his men and the prisoner forward. Bruno's paratroopers saluted as Si Larbi walked past. Bruno gave the final salute. Si Larbi gave Bruno a slight nod of respect before he was loaded into the back of the truck and driven away. The company

DAVID LEE CORLEY

commander that followed Bruno was relieved of his command when Colonel Trinquier heard about what had happened. Trinquier had no tolerance for insubordination within his command.

Si Larbi was transported to the edge of Algiers, where he was unceremoniously hung from a tree until dead.

Paris, France

Word of Bruno's dismissal spread like wildfire through Algeria and France. Massu had been correct; the French people did not take well to the hero of Dien Bien Phu being dishonored. The office of the Minister of Defense was flooded with phone calls from irate French men and women.

The Pieds-Noirs in Algeria were especially upset and protested in front of the French Army HQ in Algiers. Bruno and his paratroopers had crushed the FLN and the Mujahideen. To the Pieds-Noirs, it seemed as if Bruno had single-handedly won the war. They wanted him back in command. Massu was livid at all the attention and sympathy that Bruno was garnering.

When Brigitte heard the news, she was shocked and saddened. Yes, Bruno was a close friend, but he was also a brave and well-liked commander of the paratroopers. She wondered what had angered General Massu to the point of firing France's greatest warrior. She thought about how Bruno felt and wondered why he hadn't at least called her. She had to find him. She had to help him.

She attempted to convince Damien that there was a story to be told behind Bruno's dismissal, and she was the one to tell it. "I'll need to go to Algiers," she said.

"That is the last place you should show your face. The Pieds-Noirs want your head after that article you wrote."

"I know. But that's where Bruno will be, and I need to interview him."

"Jesus, Brigitte."

"I'll be careful. Sunglasses and scarf the whole time."

"Let me at least send a bodyguard with you for protection," said Damien.

"That's sweet, but no. I can't do my job with a bodyguard in tow. I'll be okay," said Brigitte.

"Promise me you'll stay out of the European Quarter?"

"I'm going to do my job, Damien. I'm going to follow the story wherever it takes me, as always."

"God, you're a stubborn woman."

"Versus a stubborn man?"

"I didn't mean it like that. Alright. Go."

"Great. I'll grab the next flight out. I need to swing by my apartment to pick up a few things and leave Tom a note. He's on his way back to Paris," she said, moving toward the door. "Are you sure you don't want me to cover that apartment bombing in the Casbah while I'm down there?"

"Not this time, Brigitte. You still need to keep a low profile, and that means staying out of the Casbah. Besides, I've already assigned the story to Joël."

"Joël's a good journalist. But not your best," said Brigitte with a sly smile.

"No. Not my best," said Damien. "But he will have to do. It's his story."

"Right. Of course. I may need to go to Brigade HQ to talk with some of the other officers and confirm Bruno's version of events."

"Fine. Just be smart and don't push the wrong buttons," said Damien.

"Wish me luck," said Brigitte, leaving the office.

Algiers, Algeria

Brigitte's plane landed later that evening. She checked into a hotel along the shore of the Mediterranean, then went out looking for Bruno. She knew the type of place he would hang out, especially when he was angry or lonely. He liked bistros where he could drink and eat if he got hungry. He liked efficiency, and bistros were as efficient as one could get.

There were a lot of bistros in Algiers, especially in the European Quarter, where Damien had warned her not to go. She knew she would be tempting fate if she went there. That was where most of the Pieds-Noirs that lived in Algiers called home. It was enemy territory for her since the publication of her article condemning the war. The magazine had received many threatening letters and phone calls, some against Damien, most against her.

But Bruno needed her. She could feel it. She would not abandon him. She tied a scarf over her hair and put on her oversized sunglasses, even though it was night. She looked in the mirror in her hotel room and imagined herself a star of the cinema. "Darling, you look silly, but it will have to do," she said to herself and left her room.

She went to a dozen bistros just outside the European Quarter along the promenade overlooking the Mediterranean. No Bruno. It was getting late. She decided to try a few bistros in the European Quarter before calling it quits for the night.

It was always possible that Bruno would return to the officer's quarter in Brigade Headquarters and sleep off the drunken bender she was sure he was having. She could check first thing in the morning when it was safe. She didn't dare go near the Casbah at night without an armed escort. The FLN was known for kidnapping Europeans that ventured into their lair. Hostages could be used to negotiate the release of their countrymen.

She entered the first bistro. It was busy and loud, filled with Europeans. She felt like all eyes were staring at her. Stupid sunglasses, she thought. I stick out like a sore thumb. She looked around the room and walked into the back of the restaurant. No Bruno. She walked back toward the entrance, where a group of men was standing. "Bonsoir, Mademoiselle Friang," said a large German-looking man moving to block her path to the door.

Fuck, she thought. The man and his friends had formed a blockade in front of the door. Brigitte was tired and annoyed. "So, are you going to do something or just stand there and hold your cock," said Brigitte defiantly.

The man's expression sharpened, but he didn't touch her, and neither did the other men with him.

"Look. It's been a long day," she said. "Get out of my way, or I'm gonna punch you in the nuts. Your choice."

The men stood their ground for another five seconds, then moved to let her pass. "Yeah, I didn't think so," said Brigitte exiting.

Outside the bistro, she quickly walked to the next street, paralleling the promenade and hailed a cab. She had tempted fate enough for one night. She gave the driver the address of her hotel. He hung a U-turn and headed down the street.

She looked out her window and was surprised to see Bruno passed out with his arms over the shoulders of two French paratrooper officers walking down the sidewalk. All three were clearly drunk. "Pull over, Driver," she said.

The taxi stopped. She stepped from the cab and walked over to face Bruno and the two officers. She knew the officers. She had parachuted with them in Indochina. They had protected her as she reported on the war. Still, she was angry and said, "He was your commander. You are supposed to protect him."

"We did," said one of the officers with a slur, "We drank as much as we could."

"But he's Bruno," said the other officer with a shrug. "What're ya gonna do, ya know?"

"Yeah. I know," she said. "Help me get him into the cab. You two can walk back."

They loaded Bruno into the cab and snapped to attention with a sloppy salute. Brigitte climbed in, closed the door, and the taxi drove off.

She gave the driver instructions to go to the brigade officer's quarters. He turned the cab around.

"Bruno, can you hear me?" she said.

"No," said Bruno.

"Yes, you can. Wake up, Silly. I need to talk to you."

Bruno opened his eyes and smiled, "Brigitte?"

"Yes, Bruno. I'm taking you back to the Officer's Quarters. You can sleep it off, and we'll talk in the morning."

"No. I'm not going back there. I am resigning my commission."

"Boy, you must really be drunk."

"No. I mean it. France has no use for old soldiers like me."

"You're wrong. France needs men like you more than ever."

"I don't care. I'm not going back."

"Okay fine. Do you have a hotel or a place to stay?"

"No. Just drop me off in an alley. I'll be fine. I've slept in much worse places."

"Yes, you have. But I'm not dropping you off in an alley. I'll see if my hotel has an extra room for you."

"I could sleep with you."

"No. You can't. Tom. Remember?"

"Right. Tom Coyle. Good man. American though…"

"Maybe you'd better sleep on the couch in my room. I doubt the hotel manager would appreciate your vomit on his carpet."

"Yes. Yes. Good thinking. I can be a little puke-y when I drink too much."

"Yes, you can. I remember."

"We've had some good times, you and me," said Bruno closing his eyes again and putting his head on her shoulder.

"Yes. We have," she said with a smile, remembering.

Brigitte gave new instructions to the driver. He turned around once again and headed for her hotel.

The bellhop loaded Bruno onto a luggage cart and helped Brigitte get him to her room. They lifted him onto the couch, and Brigitte placed the trashcan on the floor near his head. She tipped the bellhop, and he left. "Nice alley," said Bruno.

"Only the best for my little Bruno," she said. "How are you feeling?"

"Like an idiot that really needs to pee."

"Can you make it to the bathroom?"

"Yes. If you can get the room to stop spinning."

"Maybe I had better help you."

"Good idea."

She helped him stand and walk to the bathroom. He stood at the toilet and did nothing. "I'm not helping take your cock out if that's what you're waiting for."

"You used to like to do that."

"Keep it up, and you'll be sleeping in the janitor's closet."

"I think it would be better if I sat."

"Fine," she said, helping him sit, then pulling his pants and boxer shorts down. She turned around to give him some privacy like he really cared. "That bastard Massu, took away my men," said Bruno.

"Yeah, he did."

"What am I gonna do?"

"I don't know. But we'll figure it out."

"You're gonna help me?"

"We help each other, right?"

"Damn right, we do. We're buddies. Buddies for life. Why are you wearing sunglasses?"

Brigitte realized she had forgotten to take off her sunglasses when she entered the room. "Oh. I was trying to disguise myself."

"As what?"

"A cinema star."

"Really?"

"I could be a cinema star."

"I suppose."

"Are you done? I'd like to get some sleep."

"Fin," said Bruno trying to stand on his own and almost toppling over before Brigette caught him. "I forgot to tap twice."

"You'll survive."

"Yes. I will. I can do that. I'm good at that."

She pulled up his pants and shorts. She helped him back to the couch. He laid down and fell asleep within a minute.

Brigitte woke up the next morning with Bruno lying beside her with his hand on her right breast. Her mind was racing. Did we...? she thought. No. I'm sure you'd remember something like that. He must have crawled in bed in the middle of the night. So, why didn't you kick him out?

She thought for a long moment, then turned over, looked at his unshaven face, and answered her question. Because he's Bruno... and you're in love with him.

It was at that moment, his eyes opened, and she smiled. He smiled back and said, "Why am I in bed with you?"

"Good question," she said.

"Did we...?"

"No. You'd remember."

"Yeah. I guess I would."

"How are you feeling?"

"Hungry."

"Your breath smells like a camel's ass."

"Sounds about right."

She turned to the nightstand, opened her purse, and twisted the top off the small tube of toothpaste she always carried. She placed a dab on her finger, put it in her mouth, then placed a second dab, turned back to Bruno and placed it in his mouth. "Is that better?" he said.

"A little," she said. "Can you wait thirty minutes to eat?"

"Sure. Why?"

She climbed on top of him, kissed him deeply, and they made love. She was through lying to herself.

Algiers, Algeria

Serge Baret, the Préfecture of Algiers, sat in Massu's office. "The war is over. When might my men be allowed to return to their full duties?" said Baret, impatient.

"While it is true that our forces have destroyed the FLN in Algiers, the war is not over until a treaty is signed. The military will stay in control of Algiers until that happens," said Massu firmly. "You and your men will continue to assist us when required.

"Very well. Any word from Paris on the peace negotiations?"

"The peace negotiations with the FLN are going nowhere. The remaining FLN leadership refuses to accept anything but a total withdrawal of France from Algeria."

"France can never allow that. The Algerians would slaughter the Pieds-Noirs and the Harkis."

"Regardless, it puts us in a bad position. We have won the war by capturing the FLN leaders in Algiers and by destroying their Mujahideen fighters throughout Algeria. We have cut off their reinforcements and supplies with the Morice Line. And yet, we cannot end the war without the surrender of the FLN leaders in Cairo. They simply refuse all of our proposals, no matter how reasonable. They won't settle for anything less than complete Algerian Independence."

"Why don't you send in your paratroopers to capture the remaining FLN leaders?"

"The politicians in Paris have no desire to return to Egypt, where the FLN leaders are being protected by Nasser. They do not want to widen the war any more than necessary."

"So, what do they plan on doing to end the war?"

"I don't know. But my fear is that they will eventually capitulate to the FLN leaders."

"You mean declare Algeria independent?"

"Yes, I believe they might. Sweep the whole bloody mess under the carpet as they did in Indochina and the Suez Canal."

"My God. That cannot be. We have sacrificed so much."

"Yes. And those sacrifices will be for nothing if France loses Algeria. It is a disgrace."

"So what do you purpose to do?"

"It seems to me the military has little choice. We cannot allow the FLN to win, not after Dien Bien Phu.

It would tarnish France's reputation as a world power beyond repair. And there is, of course, the other problem…"

"What is the other problem?"

"Our paratroopers and your police officers were forced to take extreme measures to find the FLN in Algiers. If France wins the war, then it is France that writes the history of what happened. If the Algerians win… well… I doubt their version will be very flattering toward us. Some of our commanders and leaders might even be accused of war crimes."

"War crimes?" said Baret, concerned. "The FLN has done much worse to their prisoners than we did to ours."

"Yes. But a new Algerian government would offer them amnesty and deny any charges of their illicit conduct. The FLN will be protected. I believe that is why they will not negotiate for anything less than Algerian Independence."

"But surely France will protect us?"

"Perhaps… in the beginning. But international pressure can do strange things over time."

"We did what was necessary."

"Yes, but will the people understand? Their memories are short. They will forget the atrocities of the FLN, but the international community will not let them forget our own. The resolve of our politicians will sway with the electorate."

"So what do we to do?"

"We defend ourselves against the politicians in Paris."

"How?"

"We take over Algeria, then France itself if we must."

"A coup d'état?" said Baret, shocked.

"Honestly, I don't see any other way."

"Is a coup even possible?"

"Yes. I believe it is… if it has the right leaders. Men of integrity and honor. We have had three Prime Ministers in less than a year, and the recently formed coalition is hanging on by a thread. The people are growing weary of the disorganization of our government. Nothing is getting done. They want a final solution for the war, and we can give it to them. The question for you, Monsieur, is will the police in Algiers side with the Junta or against it?"

"You are talking about treason."

"I am talking about survival."

"Then we are damned if we do and damned if we don't."

"Not quite. If we are successful, we can ensure that the new government offers amnesty to both the military and the police for past indiscretions."

"I see. And if you fail?"

"Then we hang."

Baret took a long moment to consider before he said, "Then my men and I will hang with you."

Baret and Massu shook hands.

TEN

Algiers, Algeria

In the early morning, a long caravan of cars and trucks pulled up in front of the Governor General's building in Algiers. Achiary and two hundred of his Ultras exited the vehicles. They were armed with rifles and pistols. They advanced on the building. Achiary motioned for some of his men to enter through side entrances.

Seven French soldiers under the command of a lieutenant stood inside the building with their rifles raised. Achiary and his Ultras entered through the main doors. "You will leave the premises immediately," said the lieutenant.

"We will not," said Achiary.

"Then you will be shot."

"Are you sure about that?" said Achiary as his men raised their weapons and more men streamed in from the side entrances to surround the French soldiers. "There is no need for you or your men to die here today. We are all Frenchmen and patriots."

The lieutenant could see his men shuffling and mumbling. They were completely outgunned and outnumbered. It would be a very short battle. "Hold," said the lieutenant to his men.

"Don't be a fool," said Achiary, slowly raising his hand to signal his men to fire.

"Aim for the leader," said the lieutenant to his men.

His men shifted their rifles toward Achiary. "It would be an honor to die for my country," said Achiary.

One by one, the French soldiers laid down their weapons until only the lieutenant was left holding his pistol. Achiary walked forward and presses his chest against the end of the barrel of the Lieutenant's pistol. "Well?" said Achiary.

The lieutenant lowered his pistol and offered it to Achiary. "Keep it, son," said Achiary. "I think you're gonna need it."

The lieutenant holstered his pistol. "You are free to leave on your honor that you will not return," said Achiary.

The soldiers and the lieutenant walked out the front door. "Let's go," said Achiary.

The Ultras ran up the grand staircase and occupied the building. The Governor General was absent, conveniently away from Algeria at hastily-called meetings in Paris. Achiary and his men took over the Governor General's office and hung a banner outside on the balcony that read:

DE GAULLE TO POWER

Throughout Algiers, Achiary's men took over government and media buildings, including the radio station, the power station, and the waterworks. They only needed to hold the buildings until other forces could weigh in on their revolt.

Informed of the takeover, René Coty, the new Prime Minister of France, called General Massu and ordered him to immediately restore order and retake the occupied buildings. Coty requested that force only be used if absolutely necessary. Massu laughed to himself and thought, Even with his government in jeopardy, the Prime Minister shows his lack of courage. But Massu played his part in the charade and told the Prime Minister that he would do his best not to kill anyone and that things would soon be in hand.

Escorted by a company of paratroopers, Massu arrived at the Governor General's building. He ordered his men to take up offensive positions but to hold their fire as he went in alone to talk with Achiary.

He walked in through the front doors and was met by four armed Ultras. They removed his pistol from his holster and escorted him upstairs.

Massu entered what was now Achiary's office, and the doors were closed to give them privacy. "Welcome, General," said Achiary.
"Let's get this over with. What do you want?" said Massu.
"De Gaulle back in charge," said Achiary.
"That may take some doing."
"Of course. The wheels of government are slow to turn… or in this government's case, they don't turn at all. De Gaulle is a man of action. He will do what is required to protect France's reputation and honor. In

the meantime, we want a Committee of Public Safety formed to take control of Algeria."

"And if such a committee were formed, would your men withdraw from the buildings they have occupied, including this one?"

"Yes… as long as the primary objectives of the committee are to keep Algeria part of France, to protect French citizens and to end this damn war once and for all."

"Naturally."

"And who do you propose to head this committee?"

"You, of course," said Achiary with a smile.

Massu nodded in agreement. The deal had been struck long before the meeting, but appearances had to be maintained.

Massu left the Governor General's office and returned to Brigade Headquarters. He gathered the officers under his command and explained the situation. The officers agreed with Massu's assessment – Algeria must stay under France's control, and the current government in Paris was not supporting the war effort as they should. Something had to be done, and Massu was going to do it with the help of his paratroopers.

Prime Minister Coty called for a report on the results of the meeting with Achiary. Massu refused the call. He was not ready to speak to the Prime Minister. He needed more support. Instead, he phoned Admiral Philippe Auboyneau, the commander of France's Mediterranean fleet.

Auboyneau had previously commiserated with Massu over the lack of military support from Paris. They had discussed the idea of de Gaulle returning to power until the Algerian War was over. The leaders of the military were well aware that a weak government was an invitation for France's enemies to take advantage of the situation and even attack her. France could not sustain another military defeat after Dien Bien Phu and still hold on to its predominance as a world power.

"Admiral, thank you for taking my call. I would have preferred to discuss the matter in person, but time is short," said Massu.

"Of course. How are things proceeding in Algiers?" said Auboyneau.

"Not well, I am afraid. Achiary, the leader of the Ultras, refuses to give up the government and media buildings he and his men have occupied until a Committee for Public Safety is put in temporary control of Algeria."

"I see. And I suppose he wants to be the head of such a committee?"

"I fact, no. He asked that I take the position but under the condition that I guarantee that Algeria will remain under the control of France."

"Interesting tactic. Smart, I think. And what are your thoughts?"

"Something must be done before the government surrenders Algeria to the FLN. I see this as an opportunity to keep Algeria part of France, but only if you join me on the committee."

"You want me to join the coup?"

"Yes. Phillippe, we cannot let this government continue to negotiate away France's honor. It must be stopped."

"Who else have you recruited?"

"I would like to know that you are on board before revealing the others' names."

"And I would like my wife to be thirty years younger, but that is not going to happen."

"Alright. Generals Salan, Jouhaud, and Gracieux. We also have control of the garrison at Rambouillet should we need to take direct action against the government in Paris."

"Impressive. You would put yourself as the new head of government?"

"Of course not. The people would never support me, and without the people, we would have a civil war. No, I purpose de Gaulle as the new president."

There was a long silence as Auboyneau considered. "Will de Gaulle accept?" he said.

"He will if the people demand it."

"And will the people demand it?"

"I believe they will, and I believe Parliament will follow the will of the people and elect de Gaulle as an interim president. Once de Gaulle is in power, a new constitution can be drafted, and a referendum can put the Fifth Republic in place."

"You've thought this through."

"I have... but I had help."

"By whom?"

"De Gaulle himself."

"De Gaulle planned all of this?"

"No. But he did suggest a path that might be taken for his return."

"Alright. I have heard enough. I agree to support your coup and become a member of the Committee of Public Safety."

"Thank you, Admiral. I look forward to working with you," said Massu and hung up.

With the fleet in control of the Mediterranean, France would be cut off from oil and trade if the leaders in government did not capitulate to the coup leaders' demands. Massu had what he needed for success as long as everyone that had agreed stayed loyal to the Junta.

Colombey-les-Deux-Eglises, France

De Gaulle had agreed to Brigitte's request for an interview after his name was so prominently displayed on the Ultras' banner hung from the Governor General's balcony. "This is becoming a habit, Brigitte. My wife will be jealous," said De Gaulle.

"Thank you for agreeing to the interview, General. Were you surprised when the Pieds-Noirs posted your name on their banner?" said Brigitte.

"Surprised? No. I hear the Pieds-Noirs, and I understand the predicament they face. They have invested their lives into their farms and businesses. They feel the native Algerians will take away everything they have struggled to build if Algeria gains its independence. I cannot say that I blame them for searching for a solution."

"And are you that solution?"

"I doubt I could do any worse than the current government. They see-saw back and forth on their policies like a weather vane in a hurricane. That is no way to run a government. Our leaders must be driven by principals, not the ballot box."

"So, you don't believe that our leaders should listen to the people?"

"Of course they should listen, and they should do what is right for France as a whole. One that chooses to always please everyone ends up pleasing no one. Our leaders must be guided by their intellect and experience."

"There are few with a stronger intellect and more experience than you, General."

"You flatter me, Mademoiselle."

"Do you support the coup?"

"How could I? A coup is against our constitution. I will never go against the rule of law. But while I cannot support the actions of General Massu, I do support the intent behind those actions. Like me, he wishes for a strong and stable republic. Clearly, France is far from that under the current administration."

"Then you will accept the presidency if offered by the leaders of the Committee of Public Safety?"

"No. Under the current constitution, only parliament can place me in power... even if it is only temporary, until a new Constitution is drafted and new elections can be held. It is parliament that must act."

"And if parliament elects you as an interim president until a new constitution can be drafted, would you accept?"

De Gaulle considered the question for a long moment and then said, "I was not expecting to return to power. I enjoy my peaceful life with my family and my books. But I could not refuse France in her hour of need if she calls. Of course, I would serve if that is the will of the people, and my office abides by the laws of the country."

"General, there is some that worry that you might need to infringe on civil liberties to restore order. Should they be worried?"

"Have I ever done that? Quite the opposite, I have re-established civil liberties when they had disappeared. Who honestly believes that, at age 67, I would start a career as a dictator?" said de Gaulle indignantly.

Brigitte smiled. She had what she came for.

Paris, France

Prime Minister Coty sat in his office waiting to talk with Massu about the meeting with Achiary. His secretary walked in and handed him a telegram from General Massu which read:

Given the serious disorder which threatens the national unity in Algeria, which cannot be stopped without the likelihood of bloodshed, the responsible military authorities believe there is a pressing need to call upon a national arbiter to form a Government of Public Safety... An appeal for calm from this high authority is the only means of restoring order.

"What in the hell does he think he is doing? Get me General Massu on the phone immediately," said Coty.

"I'm sorry, sir, but all the phone lines are down as well as the telegraph. This was the last message to get through," said the secretary.

"What about radio?"

"The Ministry of Defense has tried to get through to Headquarters in Algiers, but all signals are being jammed."

"Algeria is completely cut off from all communications?"

"It appears so, sir."

Coty was stunned. "Send a messenger. I don't care how. Parachute him into Algiers if you must. Inform General Massu he is ordered to contact me immediately by whatever means available or he will face the severest of consequences."

"Yes, sir," said the secretary, and left the office.

Paris, France

Massu waited ten days to contact Prime Minister Coty. Coty was seething when he picked up the phone handset and said, "What the hell is going on, General Massu?"

"You got my wire?" said Massu.

"Of course I got your damn wire."

"Very well. Before I begin, I should inform you that my paratroopers have taken over Corsica. There was no bloodshed during our operation, but the military base and port are firmly in our control."

"This is treason."

"Only if we lose."

Coty wanted to bite Massu's head off. Instead, he took a moment to regain his composure and said, "What is it that you want?"

"De Gaulle as president and a new Constitution."

"You really are insane."

"You don't have much choice in the matter, Rene."

"Prime Minister Coty to you, General."

"As you wish, but it still does not change the reality of the situation. We control the Mediterranean fleet and all of the paratrooper brigades. You have no way to retake Algeria. We, on the other hand, can assault Paris and take over parliament anytime we wish."

"You would not dare attack the mainland."

"We don't need to attack the mainland. We already have forces in place."

"You will be starting a civil war."

"Yes, and thousands could die needlessly. Your situation is untenable, Prime Minister Coty. If you do not agree to our demands, we will cut off all trade through the Mediterranean, including oil. How long do you think your government will last once the French people are denied gasoline to fill their cars and heating oil to warm their homes? How long before the machines of industry grind to a halt because of lack of fuel? Unemployment will be rampant, inflation will skyrocket, and the Franc will be crushed."

"You would do that to your own country?"

"I will do whatever is necessary to save my country. You've been PM for less than a month, and unless I am mistaken, your coalition is already falling apart. Five months from now, you will be voted out of power, and we will have our fourth Prime Minister in a little over a year. There is no continuity from one government to the next. That is no way to run a country and certainly no way to run a war."

"The war is over. We won. You said it yourself."

"If we won, then why do you insist on giving Algeria away?"

"You know why. The FLN leaders in Cairo will not accept our terms."

"Then kill them, damn it."

"That is not an acceptable option."

"For you, maybe not. But for de Gaulle?"

"Has he even agreed to your plan? Last I heard, he was happily writing his memoirs."

"He will accept if parliament puts him in the presidency and gives him a free hand."

"Wait... Are you suggesting that I, as Prime Minister, back your coup and put de Gaulle in charge?"

"Yes."

"No fucking way will I do that."

"Sir, with all due respect... you must. France is falling apart. We need a strong voice that the people trust to pull our country back together."

"The people elected me."

"Because there was no other. Now there is. The Algerians fought for De Gaulle in World War II. They trust him. The Pieds-Noirs trust him to keep Algeria part of France. The French people trust him because he has always had their interests at heart. He is the one man that can pull the people together and heal our nation. Prime Minister, I have known you for a long time. We may not always agree, but I know you are a patriot. I know you, like me, would sacrifice your life for your country. I know what I am asking is not easy."

"Not easy?!"

"Of course, it isn't. But it is the right thing to do. Deep down inside, you know that what I say is true. We need Charles de Gaulle... or French blood will flow."

May 29, 1958 - Paris, France

President René Coty stood before parliament and spoke words he never thought would come from his mouth. "France is on the brink of civil war," he said. "So I am turning towards the most illustrious of Frenchmen, towards the man who, in the darkest years of our history, was our chief for the reconquest of freedom and who refused dictatorship in order to re-establish the Republic. I ask General de Gaulle to confer with the head of state and to examine with him what, in the framework of Republican legality, is necessary for the immediate formation of a Government of National Safety and what can be done, in a fairly short time, for a deep reform of our institutions."

The chamber erupted into applause and cheers. Ministers from all sides shook each other's hands and slapped each other on the back. De Gaulle would surely save the day and bring peace back to France.

Paris, France

The French parliament voted de Gaulle into power with sweeping authority. For six months, he was like an emperor, able to command by decree with no vote required by the ministers.

On leaving his estate in Colombey-les-Deux-Eglises, the people of the town came out to wish him well. They were his neighbors, and it warmed his heart to see them. They threw freshly picked flowers wrapped with silk ribbons on the hood and roof of his limousine as it drove past. He did not wave back or even smile. That was not his style. Instead, he was stoic, weighed down by the tremendous responsibility he faced.

But nothing had prepared De Gaulle for his entry into the capital where over one million Parisians lined the streets and cheered as his motorcade, escorted by thirty-two policemen on motorcycles, drove past. The French had great faith in De Gaulle. He had led them through the war with the Nazis. Surely he could lead them to the end of this war in Algeria. The Parisians were confident that De Gaulle would bring peace to their city once again. No more bombings in their cafes and shops. No more assassinations on their streets and in their parks. The people would soon be able to enjoy their beautiful city without fear. De Gaulle would see to it.

The crowd in front of the main gates of the Palais de l'Élysée was massive. An entire company of soldiers was required to keep a path open for de Gaulle's motorcade. The crowd roared as his limousine slowed and the gates opened to welcome the return of the former president of France.

Once the pomp and circumstance of swearing him in were over, de Gaulle wasted no time organizing his government. While six months of untethered power seemed like an entirety to some, de Gaulle knew time would fly by like the blink of the eye. There was much to do.

As expected, General Massu was one of the first called to Paris by de Gaulle. He was, after all, the man most responsible for ushering de Gaulle back into power.

Upon arriving at the Palais de l'Élysée, he entered through the Vestibule d'Honneur, where the president of France had greeted world leaders and dignitaries for centuries. The fact that he was walking on the very marble floor where Napoleon had once stepped was not lost on Massu. He was greeted by de Gaulle's personal secretary and escorted through the halls to the

Salon Pompadour. "The president will be with you shortly," said the secretary and left Massu alone with his thoughts.

Massu thought it slightly strange that de Gaulle had chosen to meet him in a salon on the ground floor rather than in his office, the Salon Doré, on the first floor. The Salon Pompadour certainly was one of the more impressive salons in the palace – a grand room with its intricate tapestries and a full-length portrait of the Marquise de Pompadour, the owner of the mansion before it was acquired by the government of France for its president. But it wasn't the President's office. In fact, it was about as far away from De Gaulle's office as one could get and still be in the palace.

Massu was sure that de Gaulle had a story that he wanted to tell concerning the history of the room and how it tied in with their historic meeting. De Gaulle is such a showman when it comes to knowing his history, thought Massu shaking his head. And why not? He has spent a lifetime of study and can rattle off the most mundane historical date and fact from memory. Impressive for a man his age.

De Gaulle entered and greeted Massu with a customary kiss on each cheek. "Where is your coffee?" said de Gaulle looking around the room.

"Your secretary offered, but I had just finished breakfast and couldn't drink another drop," said Massu.

"Ah, well… Please sit. We have much to discuss."

"So, how does it feel to be back?" said Massu sitting on a sofa next to de Gaulle.

"Like I never left. They even had my old desk."

"You would have thought they would have burned it after you left last time."

"They would not be so bold. How is the handover of the buildings to civil authorities going?"

"Fine. It should be completed on my return to Algiers."

"Ah, about that... So, Jacques, I am sure you understand that I must ask for your resignation as commander 10th Para."

"Ah, well... of course. I expected as much. I assumed you would have a cabinet position for me in your new government?"

"I'm afraid not. That would never do."

"What? Why?" said Massu, dumbfounded.

"You were the leader of a coup."

"A coup that was designed to put you in power."

"But a coup nonetheless. Do not worry. The ministers will be satisfied with your resignation. There will be no court-martial. I have seen to it."

"Court-martial?!"

"You did not think your actions would ensue without consequences?"

"If we lost... yes."

"You did lose. You are no longer in power."

"This is outrageous. It was your plan."

"Come now. I had no plan. Just suggestions. It was you and your men that took action against the legitimate government of France."

"I will not stand for this."

"Well, I suppose you could retire. You have a nice pension coming and memoirs to write. Or perhaps you could take a teaching position at the academy or a university. Your experiences as a soldier and a commander would be most appreciated by the students."

"You can't be serious."

"France owes you a great debt, General. You are a true patriot and friend. It was good seeing you. I wish you the best of luck, and please come back to visit me when you have time," said de Gaulle, standing and offering his hand to Massu.

Massu stood slowly and shook de Gaulle's hand. What else could he do? De Gaulle excused himself and left. Massu sat back down, too stunned to move.

Algiers, Algeria

Achiary and six of his Ultras were walking down the main boulevard in the European Quarter of Algiers when they passed a newsstand. The afternoon newspapers had just arrived, and the owner of the kiosk was cutting open the bundles. The photo of Massu and the headline 'GENERAL MASSU RESIGNS' immediately caught Achiary's attention. He picked up a newspaper and read of de Gaulle's dismissal of Massu. "My God. They sacked him."

"Good riddance," said one of his men.

"Don't be a fool. We may not have always agreed with him, but Massu is a hero. He defeated the FLN and brought peace to Algiers. His dismissal shows a shift in national policy. De Gaulle is siding with the Algerians. He has betrayed us."

"This cannot be."

"France will pull out of Algeria and give the Arabs their independence unless we can stop it. We need to get every Pied-Noir in Algiers to protest."

The next morning, tens of thousands of Pieds-Noirs marched through the streets of Algiers demanding the reinstatement of General Massu. Their banners and signs read:

DE GAULLE TO THE GALLOWS
and
RETURN MASSU TO COMMAND

Abraham Toledano's second son, Petros, was in Algiers that morning delivering a shipment of oak planks to the harbor when he heard the news of Massu's dismissal. He joined the protest and marched with a group of young Pieds-Noirs near the front of the procession. He hoped his father did not find out, knowing that he would not approve. He loved his father but did not agree with his neutrality in the war, especially after the death of his older brother. He felt it was cowardly and dishonored Victor's memory.

When the crowd approached the Governor General's palace, they came face to face with a line of paratroopers and seven armored cars with turret-mounted machineguns. Most of the paratroopers agreed with the Pieds-Noirs that Massu's dismissal was unjust and he should be reinstated. But they were ordered to keep the peace in Algiers, and for a paratrooper, duty superseded their personal political views. They stood like an invincible wall between the palace and the protestors.

Achiary and his men had lost the element of surprise that they had when they first occupied the Governor General's office. He knew from experience that the paratroopers were a mean bunch. Even with superior numbers, he had little hope of breaking through the line of paratroopers and retaking the palace. However, he had no intention of giving up. Achiary knew that De Gaulle's plans would be the death of the Pied-Noir's way of life. If there was ever any hope of saving Algeria, it was held at this moment. They must win the day.

He motioned to one of his lieutenants, who he had given tactical orders before the protest. The lieutenant, in turn, walked over to the leader of the young protestors and whispered instructions in his ear. It was hard to hear over the shouts from the crowd, but the young leader understood what was expected of his group.

The young leader removed a Molotov Cocktail from his satchel and lit it. He hurled the homemade firebomb at a nearby car parked along the street. The car burst into flames. Five protestors ran to another car and rocked it until it flipped onto its side. The leader threw another firebomb that hit the toppled car's undercarriage and set it aflame. A few minutes later, the fire reached the gas tank, and the vehicle blew up, sending flames in all directions.

The major in charge of the paratroopers ordered the armored cars to advance and disperse the crowd. As they rolled slowly forward into the mob, the protestors became more agitated and determined. They threw rocks and broken bricks at the armored vehicles. The machineguns twisted around on their turrets, threatening to fire but remaining silent.

Petros pulled off his shirt. He ran up to the front of one of the armored cars and stuffed his shirt in the driver's view portal, preventing him from seeing out.

The armored vehicle continued forward at a crawl as the driver tried to clear the shirt from the portal.

One of the other young protestors threw a Molotov Cocktail. It shattered against the front of the vehicle setting it afire. Petros moved to get out of the way and tripped over the bottom of the broken bottle. He fell directly in front of the advancing vehicle. The driver cleared his viewing portal of Petros' shirt, but the flames still prevented him from seeing clearly. The wheels of the eight-ton vehicle rolled over Petros, crushing him to death. Another Toledano had died in the struggle for independence.

After watching the death of one of their protestors, the crowd became furious. Bricks and rocks were no longer reserved for the armored cars. The paratroopers were pelted with the projectiles. They kept their formation but were forced to pull back. They used spring-loaded grenade launchers to hurl tear gas canister into the mob. The young protestors covered their faces with wet Bandanas to help them breathe. They picked up the canisters spewing the painful gas, ran forward, and threw the canisters back at the paratroopers.

The street battle continued. The paratroopers had orders not to shoot the protestors unless fired upon. They were disciplined and obeyed the order. That didn't prevent them from rushing the mob, surrounding several demonstrators, beating them with wooden batons and kicking them with their jump boots.

The young protestors tried the same tactic – rushing forward, trying to break the paratroopers' line. It didn't work. The paratroopers held their line and beat the young protestors, cracking them on their heads with their batons. The overly ambitious demonstrators quickly retreated back to the safety of the mob.

In the Casbah, the news of the Pied-Noir protest spread quickly among the residents. The FLN was all but gone. But the people of the Casbah were determined not to let the fight for independence die out.

Many of the paratrooper units had been repositioned to the countryside to hunt down the remaining Mujahideen fighters. The checkpoints in the Casbah were undermanned, and the perimeter was lightly patrolled. The Algerians flooded out of their houses and ran down the streets. They used street vendor carts to ram the barbed wire barricades around the perimeter and threw woolen blankets over the loops of sharp barbs. The crowd was in the tens of thousands and quickly overpowered the French soldiers who had been ordered not to fire except if fired upon. The Algerians burst out of the Casbah and ran down the streets to the European Quarter.

The Algerians were out of their prison and rampaging through the streets. Dozens of vehicles parked on the streets were overturned and set ablaze. Windows and doors to restaurants and shops were smashed with homemade clubs and rocks. Buildings were set on fire, and crews with firetrucks were prevented from putting them out even if there were people trapped inside. Dozens of Europeans were burned alive in the chaos.

The Algerian mob advanced down the boulevard and approached the Governor General's palace.

The Pied-Noir mob saw them coming and turned away from the paratroopers to face the approaching threat.

The armored cars stopped as the Pieds-Noirs moved away in the opposite direction to confront the native Algerians. "What should we do?" said an armored car driver.

"We pull back," said the vehicle commander.

"They'll kill each other."

"Works for me."

Under Achiary's commands, the Pieds-Noirs united in one big group. They formed a line from one side of the boulevard to the other.

The Algerians could not move past them. They could only move through them. And that they did. The Algerians ran forward like a tidal wave and hit the Pied-Noir line. The two sides unleashed all the hatred they had been holding inside for all the years. Anything that could be used as a weapon was used. Bricks were torn from the sidewalks and the fronts of buildings and hurled into a crowd only to be picked up with blood on them and hurled back to the opposite side. Heavy iron mailboxes and sidewalk benches were torn from their bolt anchors and used as battering rams or thrown by several men, crushing their enemies. Long glass shards from broken doors and windows were wrapped with cloth on one end and used as knives to slash the arms of anyone reaching across the line.

Once the two sides had clashed, there was no stopping them. Blood flowed. Bones were crushed. Dozens died. Fires consumed cars, trees, and buildings. More died from the smoke and heat. The paratroopers stood back and watched. Their commanders were waiting for the right moment when their soldiers could enter the fight and divide the two sides. But the street brawl was far from over, and the paratroopers were outnumbered. Without the authorization to use their weapons, there was little the paratroopers could do. Algiers burned, and a dense plume of black smoke rose over the city. It was total mayhem.

Algiers, Algeria

De Gaulle's plane landed in Algiers Airport. Security was tight. Achiary, battered and bruised from the riots, waited outside for him to emerge. Achiary had little hope that he, or anyone else, could change de Gaulle's mind. He was a stubborn man, like Achiary. That's what made him great; de Gaulle followed his own counsel and was confident in his decisions. Achiary would use other means besides persuasion to solve his problem.

There was an Algerian man also waiting outside. He had a pistol under his shirt given to him by Achiary. It was meant for de Gaulle. He was a Harki and had a great deal to lose if de Gaulle went through with his plan to free Algeria. He had fought for the French, and most Algerians saw that as a betrayal. Without the French to protect him, he would be hunted down by the kin of the families he had killed in a gruesome manner. He had little hope that the French authorities would allow him and his family to migrate to France. Once independence was granted, the French would want to forget that the war ever happened like they did with Indochina. He and his family would be a reminder of the Algerian war, and therefore not welcome. Achiary had reminded him of this when he gave him the gun and explained how he would escape after the assassination of the new president.

Achiary knew that even with the Ultras' help, the Harki would most likely be captured and tortured by the French. He would reveal Achiary as the mastermind behind the assassination of de Gaulle, and Achiary would be guillotined. Achiary could not let that happen.

He had arranged that two French police officers would be in the path of the Harki's escape route. The policemen would gun down the Harki and ensure he was dead. The police officers would both be made heroes and receive medals. It was a good plan. Achiary waited and watch. Nothing happened.

De Gaulle's security team had made preparations to avoid the crowd at the airport. They knew very well of the unrest in Algiers and weren't taking any chances. A motorcade including twelve officers on motorcycles emerged from a nearby hanger. They sped across the tarmac as the plane rolled to a stop, and the ground crew rolled the stairs up to the door. Four very tall police officers ran up the stairs, surveyed the surrounding area for threats, then knocked on the aircraft door. De Gaulle emerged, and the four officers surrounded him as he descended the stairs. De Gaulle was angry and objected that he could not greet the crowd outside. The captain that had organized the motorcade knew very well that he might lose his job, but he persisted. De Gaulle climbed into the limousine.

The motorcade sped off. They exited the airport through an access gate leading to a road that paralleled the runway. It was nowhere near the terminal where Achiary and his assassin were waiting. When Achiary caught a glimpse of the motorcade heading in the opposite direction, he was furious. He motioned to the Harki to follow him. They ran to Achiary's car and climbed in. Achiary drove in the direction of the motorcade, but it was too late. De Gaulle was gone.

Achiary and his Ultras waited in Algiers for news of de Gaulle's appearance, but it never came. Instead, Achiary discovered that de Gaulle had bypassed Algiers and most of the large cities. He would travel through the countryside and visit the small villages that were mostly occupied by native Algerians. He would take his campaign for the constitutional referendum directly to the people.

De Gaulle had gained widespread support among the French citizens on the mainland of France for the referendum on the new Constitution. But he felt he needed the support of the Algerians too. It was their country that would be affected the most by the new Constitution. The new Constitution gave de Gaulle broad powers as president of the 5th Republic. He wanted the Algerian people to trust him and stop fighting. He wanted to show France that the Algerians were ready to govern themselves and there would be no reprisals against the Pieds-Noirs and Harkis. He would declare amnesty for all – Algerian, Pied-Noir and French. His offer to all sides was no retribution or trials in exchange for peace and an independent Algeria.

De Gaulle was greeted by cheering crowds in the villages that he visited. He refused to listen to his security team. He climbed out of his limousine and shook hands with thousands. He had to show them that he was not afraid. The native Algerians saw him as their savior. They trusted him and wanted to help however they could. At his request, the native Algerians unilaterally stopped fighting. Even the bombings in Algiers slowed to a trickle and then stopped altogether.

Algiers, Algeria

Achiary could feel Algeria slipping from his fingers no matter how hard he held on. He needed to stir up the war again. The best way to do that was to anger the French, especially the paratroopers. Once the fighting began again, all sides would enter the fray, and the war would widen. He had no long-term plan beyond war. He would figure out his next move later. Right now, he needed kerosene poured on the smoldering fire. He considered the problem for several days and finally came up with a plan. "We are going to kidnap Brigitte Friang," said Achiary to his captains.

"How is kidnapping a journalist going to help us?" said one of the leaders.

"She is the paratroopers' most important advocate. She wrote stories about their valiant defense of Dien Bien Phu. She makes them look like heroes. We take her captive and bring her to Algeria. The paratroopers will leave no stone unturned trying to find her. They will be aggressive. People will die. The war will begin again."

"And if she dies in the attempt?"

"Then, the paratroopers' revenge will be swift, and we still get our war."

Paris, France

Coyle felt bad that he had been working so much lately. He and Brigitte had not had a lot of time together in the last few weeks. It seemed like when they missed each other, they actually fought more rather than less.

Returning to Paris after a series of cargo runs to Algiers, Coyle went straight to Brigitte's office and waited outside until she emerged at the end of the workday. "Tom, what are you doing here?" said Brigitte, surprised.

"What? A guy can't pick his girl up from work without receiving the third degree?" said Coyle.

"The third degree?"

"Nevermind. Bad choice of idioms. I thought we could go for a walk before dinner."

"Of course. I've been cramped up in my office all day. A walk would be lovely."

Coyle hailed a taxi, and they climbed in.

Coyle and Brigitte walked along the stone path next to the Seine River near Pont Alexandre III with its gilded statues and empire architecture. The sun was setting, and the glass-blown street lamps flickered on with a yellow glow. "This is why I love Paris," said Brigitte looking out over the river.

"Yeah. I gotta admit… it's a jaw-dropper," said Coyle.

"You have such a funny way of saying things. You make me laugh."

"It's been a while."

"What do you mean?"

"Things have gotten so serious lately. I mean… I understand why. The war and all the bombings.

Sometimes I wonder how you write about all that stuff and stay sane."

"So do I. It's difficult not to let it overwhelm one's life. I suppose that is why journalists are so aloof."

"Yeah, well... that just makes you more desirable... your aloofness."

"I prefer smoldering."

"Okay. Smoldering. Still, I miss your smile. You can light up a room with that smile."

"Oh, come on... I still smile."

"Sure. Just not as much as you used to."

"Perhaps."

"I worry that you're not happy... with me."

"No. That's not it. You're fine," she said, considering, then lied. "It's just work, Tom."

"Good. Because there is something I've been meaning to ask you about."

"What's that?"

"We've been together for almost five years now."

"God, has it been that long? It seems like it has gone by so fast."

"Yeah, it's been five years. And it's been great. And I want it to continue... forever. So, I think we should make it official."

"Official?"

"Yeah, official. I think I should make an honest woman out of you."

"You do not think I am honest?"

"No. I think you are honest. I just think that... well..."

Coyle stopped walking in the world's most romantic city, next to the most romantic bridge and said, "Brigitte Friang,..."

Brigitte slowed and stopped a few feet in front of him as she realized what was happening. She was afraid to turn around. Coyle waited. She turned to see him on one knee with a ring box in hand. "You're the most beautiful, intelligent, and exciting woman I have ever met. Every day I feel lucky and honored to be by your side. Will you marry me?" he said with hopeful eyes, opening the box to reveal a gold ring with a small diamond.

She teared up. It was just so damn romantic... and wrong. "I slept with Bruno," she blurted out. "I'm sorry."

Coyle was crushed. He felt like a fool. He stood up, closed the ring box, and put it back in his pocket. Brigitte cried. "So, was it an accident? Were you both drunk or something?" said Coyle.

"No," said Brigitte.

"When?"

"In Egypt... and again in Algiers..."

"Twice?"

"Yes."

"When in Algiers?"

"Does it matter?"

"Yeah. It matters to me."

"Six months ago."

"And you waited to tell me?"

"I couldn't. I didn't know how."

"Well... you certainly figured it out."

"I never meant to hurt you. I love you, Tom."

"But you love him more?"

"I don't know. It's so confusing."

"Well... let me make it more clear for you," said Coyle as he removed the ring box from his pocket and pitched it into the river. She gasped as the little velvet box skipped across the water and sank. He walked away, leaving her in tears.

Paris, France

Coyle was in the flight operations building, clearing out his locker. Bruno walked in. "You can hit me if you wish," said Bruno.

"That would just make you feel better," said Coyle.

"I never meant to hurt you, Coyle."

"You know people keep saying that to me, but somehow I don't feel any better."

"You were my friend. It was a shitty thing to do."

"I'll say."

"You'll say what?"

"I'll say. It's an expression. I am agreeing with you."

"That you were my friend?"

"No. That it was a shitty thing to do."

"Ah. Well... In my defense... What could I do? It was Brigitte."

"Yeah, well... She's all yours now."

"She still loves you, you know?"

"She has a lousy way of showing it."

"You do not think a woman can be in love with two men at the same time?"

"I don't know. It doesn't matter. I've had enough. I'm through. Congrats."

"Congrats?"

"Congratulations. You win."

"Ah. Thank you. So, are we still friends?"

"I suppose."

"That is good. I would hate to think you are still mad at me."

"I didn't say I wasn't still mad at you."

"Ah. Is that why you are leaving the Air Force. So you don't need to fly with me... because you are still mad?"

"No. It's just time for a change."

"Yes. For me too."

"I'm sorry to hear you lost your command."

"Me too. They were good men. It was an honor to fight beside them."

"What will you do now?"

"Ah, well... They have promoted me to Full Colonel."

"Really?"

"Yes. The generals in Paris must 'save face' as you say."

"I don't say that."

"But you understand?"

"Yeah, sure."

"They have offered me a teaching position at the military academy or a staff position with the Minister of Defense."

"So, which are you going to take?"

"I suppose I will teach. I don't think I could do much good sitting at a desk arguing about what should be done rather than actually doing it."

"Yeah. You don't play well with others."

"Why would I want to play with others?"

"Nevermind. I think teaching is the better choice."

"Yes. Yes. I must pass on what I have learned. Where will you go?"

"Back to Vietnam."

"Why go back there? The war is over."

"I have unfinished business."

"I see. When do you leave?"

"Tomorrow morning."

"Time for a drink or two?"

"As long as it's not that nasty paratrooper wine."

"Vinogel? No. No. That is only for real men."

Coyle laughed.

ELEVEN

Paris, France

Brigitte was getting ready for work when she heard a knock at her front door. It was Bruno. She smiled. She liked seeing him. "If this is an intimate rendezvous, your timing is lousy. I'm late for work," said Brigitte.

"No. No. Just a kiss good morning," said Bruno.

"That I can do," she said, pulling him close and kissing him.

When finished, Bruno said, "Coyle's leaving this morning. I thought you might want to know."

"Leaving? Where is he going?"

"Vietnam. Something about unfinished business."

"Did he say when he would be back?"

"I don't think he's coming back."

"I've got to see him. I don't want our last words to be in anger."

"I know. That's why I told you."

"Where is he?"

"At the airport. I just dropped him off. I can take you there if you wish."

"I don't think you should be with me, Bruno."

"Yes, I suppose you are right."

"Stay here. I'll call into work and take a vacation day. We can spend the day together after I talk to Tom."

"Alright."

Brigitte kissed Bruno again and headed out the door. Bruno thought for a moment, then walked to the apartment window and looked out. He saw Brigitte run outside and hail a taxi. As a taxi approached, a blue van pulled up in front of it, cutting it off. The back doors opened, and two men with pistols climbed out. They grabbed Brigitte and shoved her into the van.

There was nothing Bruno could do. He had no weapon to shoot at the van, and it was too far anyway. He might have accidentally hit Brigitte. He ran out of the apartment, down the stairs and out the front door.

The van was already gone. He ran into the street and flagged down a car. He ran around to the passenger side and jumped in beside the driver – a woman. "You're Bruno… the paratrooper, aren't you?" said the woman, surprised.

"Yes. Yes. Drive that way very fast, if you don't mind." said Bruno pointing down the street in the direction he supposed the van went.

The woman nodded and hit the accelerator. "This is quite are an honor," said the woman. "I've read so much about you. But I never thought I would actually meet you in person."

"Lucky day for you then. Could you please drive faster?" said Bruno looking for signs of the van.

She accelerated and said, "Are we chasing bad guys?"

"Yes, very bad, I think."

"Are you going to kill them?"

"Yes, I suppose I must."

"You have no gun."

"Yes. Thank you for pointing that out. A little faster, please."

She weaved her car through traffic and drove down the wrong way on the street to go around slower vehicles. She drove through intersections with red lights, swerving to avoid cross traffic. "How am I doing?" she said.

"Very good. Very good. There," said Bruno spotting the van and pointing. "That blue van. That's the one."

"What are you going to do when we catch up?"

"I don't know. You wouldn't happen to have a weapon in the car?"

"I have an umbrella."

"I don't think that will be much help."

"So, what shall we do?"

"Follow it, I suppose. Find out where it's going."

"I can do that. Why are you following the van?"

"They kidnapped Brigitte Friang," said Bruno, distracted.

"The journalist?"

"Yes. Yes. The journalist."

"Wow. Brigitte Friang. This really is my lucky day. Maybe we should keep our distance. Like the police detectives do?"

"I don't know. I'm a paratrooper."

"I think we should. That way, they won't be suspicious that they are being followed and try and lose us."

"That sounds good. Do that."

They followed the van to the airport and drove along an access road paralleling the runway. The van pulled up to a guard gate, where it was waved through onto the tarmac. "What should I do? The guards won't let us pass."

Bruno's mind was racing as he watched the van through the fence. The van pulled up to a DHC-2 Beaver – a single-engine passenger plane – the engine already running with the propeller turning. The men pulled Brigitte from the back of the van. She was bound and gagged. Bruno could see her struggling. Time was up. He had to do something. He leaped from the woman's car and said, "Merci. Au Revoir."

"Au Revoir. Bonne chance," said the woman with a wave goodbye.

Bruno took off, running in the direction of the plane. He scaled the fence and leaped down onto the tarmac as the plane pulled away. He ran after the plane cutting across the grass between the taxiway leading to the runway. The aircraft turned off the taxiway onto the runway. Bruno kept running after it.

The men inside the plane saw Bruno running toward the plane. One of the men jumped out of the plane and fired his pistol at Bruno. Bruno kept running toward the plane and the man shooting at him. Bruno prayed that he was a lousy shot. He could hear the bullets zipping past his head. Bruno didn't flinch.

It was unnerving having a man like Bruno running straight at oneself, and it didn't help the shooter's aim. The man's pistol clicked empty. He climbed back into the plane and yelled, "Go, go, go."

The plane sped down the runway. Bruno ran after it. After two hundred yards, he caught up with the plane. Another man opened the door and fired his pistol at Bruno. Bruno dodged for a moment to prevent from being hit. The plane picked up speed.

Bruno was running as fast as he could, but it wasn't enough. He was losing it. He grabbed the horizontal stabilizer as it passed him and gave it shove, thinking it might have some kind of effect on the aircraft. It didn't. It threw him off balance, and he fell hard on the tarmac. Bruno rolled to a stop and looked up as the plane continued down the runway and took off. Brigitte was gone.

Coyle was sitting in the airport lounge when Bruno entered, his knee bleeding through the hole in his trousers. "Bruno, what the hell…" said Coyle.

"Brigitte. Kidnapped. Airplane," said Bruno, out of breath.

"When? Where?"

Bruno pointed in the direction the plane had headed after taking off. It suddenly occurred to Coyle that this was no longer his problem. He had risked his life for Brigitte many times, but that was when he was in love with her. She had rejected him for Bruno. There was a part of Coyle that wanted to tell Bruno that Brigitte and her mishaps were now his problem and that he would need to deal with them. But that wasn't who Coyle was, and he knew it. Brigitte needed him, and he couldn't refuse. "Alright. Okay. What kind of plane was it?" said Coyle.

"I don't know. It was white. One engine," said Bruno.

"Do you know what direction it was heading?"

"South."

"Good. We might be able to catch it. We need a fast plane," said Coyle. "Something with two engines, maybe four."

"Yes. Plane. That's good. With machineguns."

"We're in a public airport, Bruno. I doubt we're gone find a plane with machineguns."

"Okay. Okay."

"Let's go."

They ran out of the terminal onto the tarmac. "How about that?" said Bruno pointing to a passenger jet.

"I can't fly that. It's a jet," said Coyle. "There…"

Coyle pointed to Vickers 700 - a four-engine passenger plane. A fueling truck had just finished filling its wing tanks and was pulling away. They ran down the tarmac and up the stairs.

Entering the aircraft, Bruno said, "Everybody out."

"You can't take this plane," said a stewardess. "You don't even have a gun."

"He's a paratrooper. Trust me. He doesn't need one," said Coyle.

"Everyone out, or I will throw you out," said Bruno with the meanest tone he could muster. "And take the stairs with you."

The crew left and pulled the stairs away. Bruno shut and secured the outer door. He ran into the cockpit where Coyle was already firing up the engines. Bruno sat in the co-pilot's chair. "You need any help?" said Bruno.

"Do you know how to fly a plane?" said Coyle.

"No idea."

"I don't need a co-pilot to fly this beast. But I do need an engineer to watch the gauges. I'll tell you what to look for."

"Copy that."

"And if I were you, I'd start figuring out what we are going to do once we find their plane."

"Right. I'm working on it," said Bruno.

The aircraft took off, banked hard and flew in the direction of the smaller plane – South.

Inside the cockpit, Coyle spoke to the control tower over his headset and explained their rapid takeoff without permission. "Okay, Bruno. They're about twenty miles ahead of us. We should be able to catch up with no problem. The pilot filed a flight plan for Algiers, but I doubt they will land there."

"Why is that?"

"Because they'd get arrested as soon as they land. My guess is that they will land on a private airstrip or maybe a road someplace in Algeria. But before that, they're gonna need to refuel, probably someplace on the other side of the Spanish border."

"Okay, so we follow them and see where they land, then call in the Spanish police."

"Not quite that easy. The control tower called civil defense. They've scrambled two Mirage fighter jets to intercept the aircraft before it leaves French air space."

"That's good, yes?"

"No. If the plane looks like it will leave France, they have orders to shoot it down."

"What?"

"Yeah. They think they are terrorists and have bombs on board. They think they may crash the plane into a government building."

"Did you tell them Brigitte is onboard?"

"Yes. But I don't think that's gonna stop them. We've got to stop that plane before it reaches Spain."

"How are we gonna do that?"

"I've got a few tricks up my sleeve. But just in case, you need to work on a plan B."

"I am."

"Yeah? Any ideas?"

"No. Not one."

"Well... at least you're honest."

"Of course."

After another thirty minutes, Coyle spotted the small aircraft flying low to the ground. "Is that it?" said Coyle pointing.

"I think so," said Bruno.

"You think so?"

"I was running after it. I didn't make a note of every detail."

"Look real close. We're only gonna get one shot at this. I'd hate to be wrong."

Bruno studied the plane as they drew closer. "Yes. That's it. I am sure of it."

"How sure is sure?"

"Ninety-five percent. Maybe eight-five."

"Great," said Coyle, unenthusiastically.

Coyle caught up with the smaller plane and matched its speed by pulling back on the engine throttles. He flew above the smaller aircraft.

The pilot of the little plane looked up through his windshield as the bottom of Coyle's aircraft crept forward. It was close. Real close. He dove down toward the ground to give himself some breathing room.

Coyle followed him down, staying above him. They continued to dive together until there was no more room to maneuver. "Now what?" said Bruno watching.

"Now we give 'em a little tap and show 'em who's boss," said Coyle.

"But you could crash their plane and kill Brigitte."

"I am open to other ideas."

"I haven't got any."

"I don't think they will crash. I'm just going to get their attention."

Coyle lowered the landing gear while increasing the aircraft's throttles to compensate for the additional drag. He lowered his altitude until his front wheel hit the top of the smaller plane's cockpit, jostling the kidnappers' aircraft. The pilot had no more room to go lower and was forced to veer off course to escape the larger aircraft.

Bruno howled, "Get 'em, Coyle."

Once out from underneath the larger aircraft, the smaller plane gained altitude and corrected its course.

Coyle repeated the process with the same result. "Shit," said Coyle as two French Mirage jets roared past the two prop-driven planes. "We're coming up on the border."

"Alright. I'll jump," said Bruno.

"Jump where?"

"On top of the cockpit."

Coyle laughed, "That plane's propeller will chew you up like an egg beater. And if that doesn't kill ya, the fall will. We ain't got any parachutes, dummy."

"I don't need one."

"You're insane."

"I can do it... for Brigitte."

"You ain't gonna be alive for Brigitte."

"Perhaps. But I must try."

"Don't be a fool, Bruno."

"Too late. I'm in love. I'll use the back door."

"I can't even see where you are to line up the two aircraft. At best, it's gonna be a wild guess."

"Get me as close as you can," said Bruno leaving the cockpit.

"You don't even have a damn gun!"

Too late. Bruno was gone. "Damn it," said Coyle as he maneuvered his aircraft into position.

The two jets flew up next to his cockpit and motioned him to break off. He got on the radio and called the jet pilots, "Ah, hang on a minute, boys. We're gonna try something here."

Bruno moved down the passenger aisle to the back of the aircraft and released the handle on the back door. Nothing happened. The external pressure was pushing against the door, preventing it from opening. Bruno pushed with the full weight of his body, but the door didn't budge. He kicked the door again and again. Finally, it slammed open as the air caught the edge of the door. The aircraft jolted from the additional drag of the open door. The wind was loud. He could see the smaller aircraft below. Coyle had done a good job of ballparking the distance. It was still a long jump without a parachute. Bruno looked at the single engine's propeller. Coyle was right. If he missed and fell short into the propeller, he would be a red splat of the plane's windshield. If he fell long, he would miss the plane's wing and fall to his death. And if he did land correctly, there was a good chance the kidnappers would just shoot him through the aircraft's thin aluminum skin.

Bruno appeared in the cabin doorway. "What happened?" said Coyle.

"That was a really dumb idea," said Bruno.

"Yeah… it was."

"You got any other ideas?"

"Just one… but it's risky for Brigitte and us."

"Riskier than jumping without a parachute?"

"Nothing is riskier than that."

"Okay. Let's try your idea."

Coyle increased the throttles to full and sped ahead of the smaller plane. Several miles ahead, he banked hard in one direction then banked hard in the other direction performing a sharp U-turn. He flew back in the opposite direction, straight at the smaller plane. He slowed his engines.

The pilot's eye went wide as he watched the approaching plane and said, "What in the hell is he doing?"

The pilot banked hard to get out of Coyle's way, but Coyle corrected his course and kept aiming for the smaller plane. The pilot tried again, this time flying in the opposite direction. Coyle altered his course and flew straight at the smaller aircraft. At the last second, the pilot dove down and missed one of the larger plane's props by just a foot or two. The smaller plane shook violently in the turbulence of the larger plane.

"The real key to a good game of chicken is the appearance of true insanity," said Coyle to Bruno as he banked his aircraft for round two.

"Appearance?" said Bruno, wide-eyed.

The larger aircraft roared past the smaller aircraft with one of its wheels scraping the smaller aircraft's left wing. The impact and the turbulence shook the smaller plane even more violently. "He's fucking crazy, "said the pilot.

Coyle flew ahead and performed his sharp U-turn maneuver. He came about and aimed for the smaller plane once again. This time he increased his speed to full power.

The pilot in the small aircraft had had enough. He spotted a dirt road in a valley below and dove for it. "What the hell are you doing?" said one of the kidnappers.

"I'm setting it down before he kills us."

"He's not going to kill us. He's just messing with your mind."

"Well, he's doing a good job. I'm setting it down."

The other kidnapper put his pistol to the pilot's head and cocked the trigger. "Go ahead. It's better than falling from the sky when he hits us," said the pilot as he continued downward.

Coyle did not let up. He dove the big beast of the plane downward, chasing after the smaller aircraft like a mad dog chasing a cat. "You know what you are doing, right, Coyle?" said Bruno.

"Sort of," said Coyle. "But it's kinda hard to predict which direction the other guy is going to fly."

The smaller plane landed on the dirt road, kicking up a long plume of dust. The larger plane zoomed overhead, its props just a foot from the smaller plane's overhead wing. The smaller plane was again caught in the bigger plane's turbulence and wiggled from side to side as it landed.

"One more time for good measure," said Coyle banking the beast at the end of the valley and coming back in the opposite direction.

The kidnappers leaped from the plane, and ran for cover as the larger plane approached once again, its props were so low to the ground they clipped the tops of the bushes and small trees. It roared over their heads at full throttle.

Inside the cockpit of the larger plane, Bruno turned to Coyle. "Now what?" said Bruno.

"I kinda thought that was your department," said Coyle.

"Can you put her down?"

"Sure. But they've got guns."

"Right. Well… I'll just have to deal with that, now won't I?"

"Putting her down."

Coyle banked the aircraft at the opposite end of the valley, then slowed the engines. The plane dropped down. The dirt road was not wide enough for the wing's landing gear, but Coyle did his best to keep the aircraft's front wheel on the road. It was a very bumpy landing as the wing wheels hit boulders. He reversed the pitch on the propellers to slow the plane's speed. Dust and dirt flew in all directions. Tiny vortexes whooshed upward like mini tornadoes of dirt. "I'll deal with the kidnappers. You get Brigitte," said Bruno.

"Deal," said Coyle.

As the plane slowed to a stop. Bruno jumped out the back. He used the natural cover of the valley floor and the dust cloud from the plane's landing to mask his movements as he advanced on the three kidnappers and the pilot. As he moved through the low brush and

286

grass, he picked up fist-sized rocks and slipped them into his pockets. He found a baseball-bat-sized branch broken from the larger plane's propellers strikes and picked it up. It wasn't much. But Bruno didn't need much.

One of the kidnappers peeked from behind a rock grouping and shot at Coyle, still in the cockpit. The front windshield spider-webbed from the bullet holes. Coyle ducked down and moved to the back of the aircraft. He jumped out the back door and made his way toward the smaller aircraft, using the natural cover as Bruno had done.

Bruno approached the area where the kidnappers and pilot were hiding. He had maneuvered so that the low sun was at his back. He was a fast, deadly silhouette. As Bruno came upon a boulder, the weaponless pilot stepped out, clenching his fist at Bruno. It was almost laughable as Bruno slammed him in the side with the tree branch then cracked it in half over his head. The pilot went down with a severe concussion. Bruno didn't even slow down. He was hunting more deadly prey.

He pulled two rocks from his pockets, one for each hand. A kidnapper emerged from behind a boulder and shot at Bruno with his pistol. Bruno pitched to the side, and the first two bullets missed. Bruno hurled a rock at him. He ducked. Bruno kept running towards him, closing the distance between them. The kidnapper popped his head up again, and Bruno caught him with a well-placed stone in the middle of the forehead. There was a loud crack as his skull fractured. He went down, more dead than alive. Bruno kept moving, picking up the fallen man's pistol, opening the chamber, counting the unfired bullets, snapping the gun shut. Armed with the pistol, Bruno was more deadly than ever.

He moved to where he had seen the kidnapper shooting at Coyle. He was gone. Bruno kept moving, knowing that a moving target was harder to hit, and that surprise was an advantage he needed. He stopped and listened for a moment. He heard footsteps nearby, moving toward him. He moved sideways, circling around, changing his position. A kidnapper moved around a tree. He was behind Bruno. But Bruno was moving, and it was hard to get a good angle. The kidnapper stepped sideways as he took aim. His boot stepped on a dry leaf. It crackled.

Bruno heard the noise behind him and dropped instantly. He twisted as he turned and fired his pistol twice. His aim was deadly, and his bullets struck the man in the chest. Bruno knew how that felt. He had been shot in the chest on two different occasions and survived both, but not without a lot of pain. Unlike the assassin that tried to kill him, both of Bruno's bullet entered the kidnapper's heart, killing him. He picked up a second pistol and checked it for unfired rounds. He kept moving.

Coyle reached the small plane without being detected. He quietly opened the door and took a quick peek inside. It looked empty. He climbed inside and moved toward the back of the passenger compartment, where he found Brigitte. She was unconscious. He looked at her arm and saw the small bloody mark where they had stuck her with a syringe. She had struggled, making the mark bigger than expected. "Brigitte," he said softly.

She didn't move. He untied her hands and feet. He called her name again. This time she moved, and her heavy eyes opened a crack. "Tom?" she said.

"Hey. You can't seem to keep out of trouble, can you?" he said with a gentle smile.

"I'm so sorry, Tom."

"Don't be. I'm a survivor. I can live through Brigitte Friang."

"I never wanted to hurt you. I love you, Tom."

"I know… just not enough. Let's get you out of here."

"Where's Bruno?"

"Hunting, I would imagine."

Coyle helped her get up and moved toward the aircraft door. They stepped out and turned to see the final kidnapper pointing his pistol at them, squeezing the trigger. A shot rang out. Blood poured from a wound in his neck. He dropped his pistol and grasped the wound with both hands in hopes of stopping the bleeding. There was no stopping it. Bruno knew where the artery was located. He would have shot him in the head, but the airplane's wing strut was in the way. No matter. Dead was dead. The man collapsed and bled out. "Is that the last of them?" said Coyle.

"By my count," said Bruno hugging Brigitte. "Are you hurt, Brigitte?"

"No, just a bit dizzy," she said.

"I saw a town to the North on the way in. How are we gonna get out of here?" said Coyle.

"We can't fly out?" said Bruno.

"I'll never be able to get that beast in the air. It's too big. We'll run out of road."

"I see. Well, we walk then," said Bruno.

"It's gotta be ten to fifteen miles, and the sun's going down," said Coyle.

"You're right. We should run," said Bruno.

"Why don't you go ahead, Darling? I don't have the right shoes for it. We'll just wait here," said Brigitte. "Tom can build a nice fire. We'll be fine."

"Suit yourself," said Bruno taking off at a brisk pace. He disappeared over the top of a hill.

"Why can't we just take the small plane?" said Brigitte as her mind slowly cleared.

"Oh, we can, and we will... in a few minutes," said Coyle.

"Aren't you going to run after Bruno and stop him?"

"Nah. He likes to run. It's good for him."

Paris, France

Brigitte and Bruno walked through the airport with Coyle. Nobody spoke. Brigitte was doing all she could to keep from bursting into tears.

They arrived at the gate for Coyle's flight. Passengers were already boarding. "Not much time," said Coyle.

"Good. I was hoping to get a café soon," said Bruno chiding him.

Brigitte hit Bruno as hard as she could. It hurt her hand. "Stop it," she said.

"Yes. Yes. Let's all cry. That will make him stay."

Coyle smiled and said, "Nah. A rolling stone gathers no moss."

"Of course not. But what does that have to do with anything?" said Bruno, confused.

"It's a saying, Bruno. It means it's time for one to move on."

"So, why don't you just say that?"

"Because it's funny."

"I do not think it is funny."

"That's because you have a lousy sense of humor."

"Are you two seriously going to argue at a time like this?" said Brigitte angrily.

"It's what we do, Brig," said Coyle.

"Well, stop it."

"Do you have a better idea?" said Bruno.

"Yeah. Say nice things. We don't know when we'll see Tom again… if ever," she said, breaking down and crying.

Coyle and Bruno exchanged shrugs. "You're gonna write, aren't you, Tom?" said Brigitte.

"If I must."

"You must. I need to know you're safe."

"I ain't the one that keeps jumping out of planes."

"No. You just crash them," said Bruno.

"Yeah, but I'm good at it," said Coyle.

"God, I'm really gonna miss this," said Brigitte crying even more.

She grabbed Coyle, hugged him tightly, and said, "I'm so sorry I hurt you, Tom."

"I'll be okay, Brig. I'm a lot tougher than you think."

"No, you're really not… and neither am I."

She let him go, pulled a compact mirror from her purse, and looked at her raccoon eyes. "Well, you have succeeded in messing up my makeup," she said, pulling out a handkerchief and dabbing the mascara running under her eyes. "There is nothing to be done."

"You look beautiful," said Coyle.

"Damn right I do, and don't forget it."

"How could I?" said Coyle trying not to tear up.

The airline gate attendant announced the last call for the flight. "I gotta go," said Coyle.

"Come here, ya big bastard," said Bruno to Coyle, hugging him and slapping him hard on the back. "Americans."

"French," said Coyle slapping Bruno even harder where he knew he had been shot.

Bruno yelped quietly. They finished their embrace, and Coyle headed for the door. Brigitte wept. Bruno put his arm around her. Coyle stopped at the door, turned with a tear rolled down his cheek and said. "I'm really gonna miss you guys."

Brigitte wept even harder, and Bruno said, "You're not helping things, Coyle. Get on the damn plane."

Coyle laughed and walked through the doorway. He was gone.

After the airliner took off from the runway, it banked hard. Coyle looked down at Paris. It was a beautiful city. He wondered if he should have fought harder to keep Brigitte. He still loved her, even after what she had done. He hated the idea of losing her, even to Bruno. He considered it for a moment and then realized it wasn't really his decision. She had chosen Bruno, and he had to respect her choice. He wasn't sure of his future, but he knew it would be without Brigitte Friang. He ordered a double scotch from the stewardess. It was going to be a long flight.

July 5, 1962 - Algiers, Algeria

The French voted on the Algerian Independence referendum. Those that voted in Algeria were mostly Pieds-Noirs and voted almost unanimously to reject the referendum, while those on the mainland voted almost unanimously for the referendum. In the end, seventy-nine percent of the people voted yes, and the referendum was passed. Algeria was to become independent. After eight years of war, the paratroopers were going home.

The native Algerians poured into the streets and formed huge cheering crowds. They waved the flags of the FLN. Arabs would lead Arabs. There was no violence. The future and Algeria were finally theirs to do as they saw fit.

The Pieds-Noirs commiserated in bars and coffee houses. They had finally lost, and their future was unsure. Most agreed that staying in Algeria would be paramount to suicide. They were French citizens, and as much as they hated what their fellow Frenchmen had done to them, France was the safest place for them. They would abandon their homes and businesses in Algeria and start again across the Mediterranean.

For the Harkis that had sided with the French and Pieds-Noirs during the war, it wasn't that easy. They were native Algerians by birth, and few would be allowed to emigrate to France. They were trapped in a country that many felt they had betrayed. Many crossed the borders into Tunisia and Morocco to start new lives. Others went into hiding within Algeria. They changed their names and their stories. Some stood proud and refused to deny their past. After all, the French had required amnesty be declared for all sides as part of the deal for independence. They would be

the first assassinated in the revenge killings. The
majority of the Harkis had little faith that their fellow
Algerians would accept their innocence. They knew
what was coming and did their best to prepare for it.

Over thirty thousand Harkis and their families were
massacred as the Algerians took over the reins of
government from the French. Algerian police turned a
blind-eye to revenge killings. In their eyes, the Harkis
were traitors and deserved what happened to them.
Some police officers even helped by revealing
information about a suspect's true identity and
location. Kill lists were created in each province. One
by one, the Harkis were hunted down and killed by the
grisliest methods – the Algerian necktie being one of
the favorites.

The new Algerian army was given the task of
clearing the minefields that the French had created on
the borders of Tunisia and Morocco. The Harkis were
conscripted for the job because many of them had built
the minefields in the first place. In many cases, the
soldiers forced the Harkis to form tight lines and walk
over recently cleared minefields to ensure all the mines
had been removed. There were always some mines that
had failed to be detected, and these blew the traitors to
bits. Thousands of Harkis died during the operation.
Nobody bothered to pick up the pieces. They were left
for the crows.

Ahmed Ben Bella, one of the founders of the FLN,
who had been captured and jailed for many years by
the French, became the first president of Algeria. As
president, he nationalized all European-owned land
and businesses. He began a program of redistribution
to the people of Algeria. His biggest hurdle was
administering a county of nine million without any

trained government officials. Under France's rule, all the officials had been French. Algeria had to start governing from scratch. It was a very bumpy beginning with a harsh learning curve.

Saadi Yacef, the bombing mastermind and FLN leader, survived French captivity. Many accused him of betraying several other FLN leaders by revealing their hiding places while under torture from the French paratroopers. Saadi denied it ever happened. He went on to become a Senator in Algeria's new parliament. He wrote his memoirs while in prison and went on to help produce the motion picture "The Battle of Algiers," which won critical acclaim. He played himself as the lead character in the movie.

Northern Algeria

The men of the Toledano family loaded boxes and furniture considered family heirlooms into several of their sawmill trucks. They were leaving Algeria for good. The men worked quickly but quietly.

Inside the house, the women in the family wept and comforted each other as they loaded boxes with vases, framed photos, and dishes wrapped in newspaper.

Abraham, too old to help with the heavy items, packed his precious books from the library. He was unsure what the future held in store with his family. It felt like too much of a step back to return to Spain, where his ancestors had lived. Like most of the Pieds-Noir, they would go to France and start again. There were promises of jobs for his sons, but he had little faith in the politicians that offered them. His family would do as the Jews had always done. They would survive however they had to, then find a niche business that suited them.

Like Algeria, France had sawmills, but most of the forests that fed them were already owned by wealthy families. There was little chance they would make room for outcast Algerian Jews. He considered furniture manufacturing. His boys knew wood. Unlike him, his sons had boundless energy and were fast learners. That was a start.

He took a brief break from loading the books and stood at the window looking out at the mountains surrounding the valley in which they lived. Even with the forest burnt by the French, the view was glorious as the sun hung on the horizon giving everything a golden hue. He doubted that he would ever live in a home such as this one. It had taken decades to construct. He was too old, and the thought of building again made him feel tired.

The trucks were packed, and the families were loaded up in their vehicles. Abraham stood alone in front of the sawmill. His sons had dosed the lumber and machinery with kerosene. Even though they could have sold the estate and business, he and his family had decided to leave nothing for the Algerians. He pulled a box of matches from his pocket, struck one and tossed it to the wet ground. A line of fire raced into the sawmill and another to the lumber yard, with a third going to the villa.

He waited until there was no doubt the fire would consume everything – his home, his business, his memories. He walked to his Mercedes Benz, climbed behind the wheel, and started the engine.

With the estate burning in the background, the Toledano family drove off in a caravan as Abraham imagined his ancestors had arrived hundreds of years before. They were done with Algeria, and Algeria was done with them.

LETTER TO READER

Dear Reader,

Thank you for reading *Battle of the Casbah*. Our heroes have survived yet another war.

The Airmen Series will continue with Tom Coyle heading back to Vietnam as the American War begins. For Coyle, this war will be different. It is his country and his fellow Americans that will sacrifice their lives to preserve freedom and democracy. It will also be confusing for him, as it was for most Americans. For my part, it will also be personal. I grew up during the Vietnam War and it's the first war I remember. I hope you will join me on a journey that changed the world as we once knew it. Here is the link to the next book in the Airmen series:

Momentum of War
https://www.amazon.com/dp/B08MVBRT33

Sign-up for my never-boring newsletter and you will receive a free book – Prophecies of Chaos (one of my favorites) in addition to new release updates, special offers, and my thoughts on history. Here's the sign-up link:

Newsletter Sign-Up
https://dl.bookfunnel.com/5tl2favuec

Reviews and recommendations to friends and family are always welcome. And again, thanks for reading my stories.

Sincerely,
David Lee Corley

LIST OF TITLES WITH READING ORDER

The Airmen Series
1. A War Too Far
2. The War Before The War
3. We Stand Alone
4. Café Wars
5. Sèvres Protocol
6. Operation Musketeer
7. Battle of The Casbah
8. Momentum of War
9. The Willful Slaughter of Hope
10. Kennedy's War
11. The Uncivil War
12. Cry Havoc
13. When War Dawns

The Nomad Series
1. Monsoon Rising
2. Prophecies of Chaos
3. Stealing Thunder

Facebook Page:
https://www.facebook.com/historicalwarnovels
Shopify Store: https://david-lee-corley.myshopify.com/
Amazon Author's Page:
https://www.amazon.com/David-Lee-Corley/e/B073S1ZMWQ
Amazon Airmen Series Page:
https://www.amazon.com/dp/B07JVRXRGG
Amazon Nomad Series Page:
https://www.amazon.com/dp/B07CKFGQ95
Author's Website: http://davidleecorley.com/

DEDICATION

I dedicate this book to my brother, Stephen Corley. He is one of the funniest people on the planet, loves his family deeply, and makes excellent chicken and waffles.

NOTE FROM AUTHOR

Many of the characters in this story are based on real people. In some cases, I use their real names so the reader can look up more information on the individual. This is especially true when I think the character has historical significance. While I always try to be historically accurate, this is a fictional story. Some events and characters are changed or compiled to make the story flow better.

AUTHOR'S BIOGRAPHY

 Born in 1958, David grew up on a horse ranch in Northern California, breeding and training appaloosas. He has had all his toes broken at least once and survived numerous falls and kicks from ornery colts and fillies. David started writing professionally as a copywriter in his early 20's. At 32, he packed up his family and moved to Malibu, California to live his dream of writing and directing motion pictures. He has four motion picture screenwriting credits and two directing credits. His movies have been viewed by over 50 million moviegoers worldwide and won a multitude of awards, including the Malibu, Palm Springs, and San Jose Film Festivals. In addition to his 23 screenplays, he has written three novels. He developed his simplistic writing style after rereading his two favorite books, Ernest Hemingway's "The Old Man and The Sea" and Cormac McCarthy's "No Country For Old Men." An avid student of world culture, David lived as an expat in both Thailand and Mexico. At 56, he sold all his possessions and became a nomad for four years. He circumnavigated the globe three times and visited 56 countries. Known for his detailed descriptions, his stories often include actual experiences and characters from his journeys.

CPSIA information can be obtained
at www.ICGtesting.com
Printed in the USA
BVHW031548060323
659797BV00001B/97